MY
DAUGHTER
IS MISSING

BOOKS BY JD KIRK

ROBERT HOON THRILLERS

Northwind

Southpaw

Westward

Eastgate

Stateside

DI HEATHER FILSON SERIES

The One That Got Away

This Little Piggy

JD KIRK

MY
DAUGHTER
IS MISSING

bookouture

Published by Bookouture in 2025

An imprint of Storyfire Ltd.
Carmelite House
50 Victoria Embankment
London EC4Y 0DZ

www.bookouture.com

The authorised representative in the EEA is Hachette Ireland
8 Castlecourt Centre
Dublin 15 D15 XTP3
Ireland
(email: info@hbgi.ie)

ISBN: 978-1-83525-613-8
eBook ISBN: 978-1-83525-612-1

For Quinn.
Running free, beyond the Rainbow Bridge.

PROLOGUE

I can feel her pain in my chest, like it's my own.

Is she crying, I wonder?

I don't want to think about it. I don't want to picture her calling my name. Crying out for me. Begging for me to come find her, come get her, come take her back home.

Or maybe she's too exhausted now. Maybe she's all cried out, too hoarse and raw to do anything but sit there. Silent. Mute. Struck dumb with terror.

I don't want to think about any of it, but I don't have a choice. I can't stop the images flooding my head. Her face. Her voice.

Nine years old, all alone, and so very, very afraid.

I feel sick. I feel helpless. I feel like my whole world is collapsing around me, like every good thing in my life has been torn away. Torn apart.

My daughter is missing.

My daughter has been taken.

It's all my fault.

But I'm going to get her back. I'm going to bring her home.

No matter what it takes.

PART 1
FRIDAY

ONE

ELIZABETH

Tonight may be the night that I finally kill her.

Mabel Walker. My arch enemy. The bane of my life. The Uberbitch of Edinburgh's West End. Possibly of the whole of Scotland, in fact.

She's the head of the school's parent council – a position she both busybodied and bought her way into, using her own supe-riority complex and her husband's money. Rich, glamorous, and with a daughter who is top of the class in everything, she's the apex predator of the PTA, and everything I'm not.

And wow, does she like to remind me of that.

I have this fantasy where I grab Mabel by the ears and twist her head off like it's the lid of a jam jar. Or a jar of mayonnaise. Or any sort of jar, really, the contents aren't all that important. What's important is the look on her face when I do it, and the fact that – for once – she stops complaining.

It's not a regular thing. I don't dream about it daily, or anything like that. In fact, I only ever think about it at very specific times.

Specifically, any time when I'm in her company.

Of course, the reality of it wouldn't be as satisfying as the fantasy. In the real world, as I was wrenching her head from her shoulders, Mabel would be criticising my technique. 'Elizabeth,' she'd say, 'you're making a mess of this. You're doing it all wrong!'

She'd then explain in oh-so-condescending tones how she'd do it differently. By which she'd mean 'better'.

Like I need someone else reminding me of my faults.

It's a fun fantasy, but a pointless one. I doubt even decapitation would be enough to prevent Mabel Walker from ruining my life.

Tonight, we just might find out.

The Halloween disco is a big event in the school social calendar, and Mabel insisted that the PTA – which she strong-armed me into joining the first day I met her – needed to bring 'our A-game'.

Mabel brought her A-game to taking the money and stamping hands at the door, meaning she was finished in the first ten minutes and could head into the hall to watch the parade, help judge the best costume prize, and all the other fun stuff.

I, meanwhile, was assigned snack duty, meaning I've been stuck out here all night, peddling my wares to screaming nine-year-olds in fancy dress.

The things we do for our children.

Thankfully, I was able to nip into the hall for the costume parade, just in time to see my Hollie striding along in her butterfly outfit – nine years old, hair in bunches, looking proud as punch. There may have been a few tears shed. Me, not her.

I did try and point out earlier in the week that butterflies aren't particularly scary creatures, but she told me that *actually* the Milkweed butterfly is not only highly toxic but has even been known to 'display cannibalistic tendencies'.

Her words, not mine. I think she'd been rehearsing them, because she grinned and did a little fist pump when she managed to say them correctly.

She hasn't come as a Milkweed butterfly, though. She's come as some luminous pink monstrosity with symmetrical love heart patterns on the wings that took me the best part of two days to paint, while she slouched on the couch and scrolled through her iPad with her headphones on.

Although, that said, I have absolutely no idea what a Milkweed butterfly looks like, so maybe she has come as one of those.

I gave her a wee wave from the door as she strutted past to 'Monster Mash', and her face lit up. I wish I could say the same for Mabel. When she clocked me watching, she nodded back in the direction of the snack table, rubbed her thumb and forefinger together like she was a drug dealer demanding payment, then returned to waving at her daughter, Jessica.

Jessica Walker. A more unpleasant child you would not wish to meet. Ignorant, arrogant... abhorrent? Is that too strong? Maybe. But I'm pretty sure she's been bullying Hollie, even though they both deny it. There's something going on. I can feel it.

It's lucky for Jessica and her mother that my sister isn't around. Sasha would get to the bottom of it. And Sasha does not take kindly to bullies.

Or, for that matter, to children. Hollie being the exception, of course. With Hollie, it was different. Even Sasha wasn't immune to her brown curls and freckles, or the giggle that seemed to start from somewhere near her toes. With Hollie, it was love at first sight.

I stood my ground until the parade ended, then slunk back out front to the snack table, where I've been perched ever since, with mostly just tiny Dracula for company.

He's been back four times now with a shrinking handful of

warm coins that he dumps on the desk in front of me so I can count out the exact change for him.

I wouldn't mind if he was one of the younger kids, or even one of the less able ones, but he's a bright lad on a collision course with secondary school.

Of course, it can't be easy seeing through that plastic mask, and he's bound to be buzzing on those three Fruit Shoots and the big bag of Skittles he's already had off me. His eyes, or what I can see of them, are two big black circles, like he's tripping off his face.

A few moochers popped round, too – poor souls whose parents had either been unwilling or unable to give them money. I snuck them a few sweets here and there, on the understanding that it stayed between us. They're good kids. I reckon my secret is safe.

And if it isn't? If someone spills the beans and Mabel Walker comes storming out of the hall demanding to do a stock check?

Well, maybe today *will* be the day for that head twisting, after all.

* * *

The snack table is packed up, the parents have arrived for collection, and *Darren's Cheesy Tunes* is blasting out some particularly turgid Barry Manilow track in an attempt to clear the hall. It's working, too. No surprise there.

Jessica Walker won the best costume prize, of course. No real shock there, either. I wouldn't have minded so much if she hadn't come dressed as Belle from *Beauty and the Beast*. I mean, no, a butterfly's not exactly much better, but Belle? Seriously?

The only thing remotely scary about the costume is that, with her hair and make-up done, she looks like she might well get served at some of the sketchier local pubs, despite being literally half the legal drinking age.

I just hope Hollie isn't too disappointed. She's wanted to win that prize since her very first Halloween school disco, back at her old school, and has now fallen short six times out of a possible seven. Next year will be her last chance before she goes to secondary school. We'll have to go all out.

Or sabotage Jessica Walker.

Hollie is really taking her time coming out of the hall. Most of the other kids have already come racing out to be met by smiling mums and dads, or older siblings, then run off to get their jackets from the hooks outside their classrooms. Harry Potter goes past waving his wand at me. Over by the main door, the red Power Ranger waits patiently for his mum.

I feel a pang of guilt when Dracula almost runs straight through his granny, who's apparently looking after him while his mum's in hospital. The poor old woman looks like she's pushing ninety, and it'll be hours before all that high-fructose corn syrup has been burned out of his system. He's going to be rattling off the walls all night.

Still, I'm sure the PTA will put the one pound eighty he spent to good use.

Speaking of which...

'You got the takings there, Elizabeth?'

I turn from the door of the hall to find Mabel standing less than a foot in front of me, Jessica hovering impatiently beside her like my very existence is a major inconvenience to her.

'The takings,' Mabel says again, her gaze flitting to the dented little lockbox I'm clutching in my hands. Something about the look and her tone suggests she's just caught me walking out the door with it. 'Do you have them?'

I don't think I'd despise Mabel quite so much if all that poison simmering around inside her showed itself on the outside. Sadly, it doesn't. She's almost ten years older than me, but we look around the same age. It's amazing what a little bit of care, a few basic moisturising products, and seventy-odd grand of cosmetic surgery can do.

I don't bother answering her, and just hand over the box I've been collecting the night's earnings in. Mabel lifts it to her ear, rattles it, then shows her disappointment with a heavy sigh.

'Sounds like that climbing frame is going to have to wait a bit longer,' she mutters, then she nods at me.

It's a curt, sharp, up-and-down. Assuming it's just her idea of a polite farewell, I nod back, earning myself a tut of annoyance.

'Well?' she demands, and I realise my nod-reading skills were way off the mark. 'Don't you have something you want to say?'

I stare blankly back at her for a moment, then finally figure out what she's pushing for.

'Oh. Yes. Congratulations, Jessica,' I say, pulling together the friendliest smile I can muster for the girl. 'You look very...'

I look her up and down, searching for the right word. She holds her trophy loosely at her side, like she's already forgotten about it.

'Yellow,' I conclude.

'*Mum!*' Jessica whines, dragging the word out so it ends in about six M's and a rising inflection.

'Alright, alright, yes,' Mabel replies, then they turn and swan off without so much as a parting glance in my direction, no doubt to Jessica's father waiting in his Bentley outside.

I'm still watching them leave when I realise I can no longer hear Barry Manilow. Any other time, this would be welcome news, but Hollie still hasn't appeared. I have a sudden vision of her huddled behind a stack of chairs, wrapped in her paper wings, sobbing her heart out about the best costume prize.

Oh, no.

I'm such an idiot.

She'd had her heart set on that plastic trophy. She'd been convinced this was her year. She's going to be devastated.

I'm already workshopping a pep talk when I shove open the hall doors. The music has stopped, but the lights on the DJ decks are still flashing, painting the monkey bars and scuffed wooden flooring with swooshing circles of red, green and blue.

The DJ himself is too busy unplugging his audio equipment to pay me any attention as I come rushing in. Paper pumpkins and skeletons leer at me from the walls, their eyes empty and dark.

Donnie, the school's janitor, glances up at me, then returns to sweeping the floor with a ludicrously wide brush that scissors together in the middle. He's already gathered up an impressive haul of half-chewed sweets and discarded crisp bags and is visibly seething with rage at having to be here at this time of night.

Then again, visibly seething with rage is pretty much his default state.

Mr Wilkinson, the school's only male member of teaching staff – and, not by coincidence, I suspect, the acting head teacher – is standing on a chair, unpinning a crepe paper Frankenstein's monster from above the fire exit door. He's in his mid-forties, but in the shape of a man ten years younger, and is the unknowing subject of many a lustful school gate conversation between the other mums.

Miss Goodall, Hollie's teacher, stands close by, offering supportive giggles and eyelash flutters. Clearly she's not immune to Mr Wilkinson's charms, either.

But Hollie herself is nowhere to be seen.

The stack of chairs I visualised her hiding behind doesn't exist. There's some gym equipment that's been pushed into a corner, though, so I hurry over, rehearsing my 'we'll get them next time' speech in anticipation of the mess of snot and tears I'm going to find tucked back there.

But I don't. I don't find anything.

She isn't there.

The disco lights sweep across the hall like searchlights, reaching into all the corners. Hollie isn't in any of them.

Hollie isn't here.

TWO

ELIZABETH

Some trapdoor in my chest swings open, sending my heart tumbling down into my stomach. I hear the change in my breathing before I feel it. It rasps in and out through the narrowing gap of my throat.

Hollie isn't here.

My daughter isn't here.

I've been out front the whole time. She hasn't passed me. I'd have seen her. Aside from the fire exit, which would have triggered the alarm, there is no way out of the hall other than right past where I was sitting.

She has to be here. She has to be.

But she isn't.

Goosebumps prickle my skin, telling me that something has happened.

Something is wrong.

Donnie, the janitor, sweeps on past, making me jump. He mutters something – or growls, maybe – as he passes. The smell of his sweat sears my nostrils and snags at the back of my throat.

And the dazzling spotlights continue to dance their colours across the walls.

I don't hear the voice talking to me at first. I'm too preoccupied with trying to think, trying to reason, trying to breathe.

It's only when the DJ flicks on the overhead lights that the rest of the world snaps back into focus.

'Uh, hi! Um, Elizabeth?'

'What?' The word is a yelp. A sob. I spin round to find Miss Goodall smiling at me. She's young – barely in her twenties – with a sort of chirpy children's TV presenter vibe that makes all the kids love her.

She's wearing a woolly cardigan, and has her hands clasped in front of her like she's a librarian about to introduce me to the wonders of the Dewey Decimal System.

'Everything OK?' she asks in her perky, upbeat trill.

'Hollie,' is all I manage to say.

The young teacher's eyebrows dip momentarily, but she doubles down on the smiling front.

'Aw, she looked brilliant tonight! What's the matter? Did she forget something?'

The words stick in my throat. I don't want to say them out loud.

Saying them out loud makes them real.

Saying them out loud makes them true.

I shake my head. I swallow. I try to force the words into existence, but they won't come.

Instead, I take off at a run. I'm across the hall in seconds, grabbing for the door handles, headed for the corridor. Maybe she's there. Maybe she's waiting.

She's bound to be. I'm overreacting, panicking about nothing. She's probably waiting for me out there. Probably wondering where I am. I'm being silly.

But the corridor is empty. The entrance hallway, where the snack table was set up, is deserted, too.

Miss Goodall hurries out of the hall, calling after me.

'Elizabeth? Are you OK?'

The words bubble up. There's no swallowing them back down this time. No denying them. I give voice to my worst, most awful fear.

'Hollie. I don't know where she is.'

'What do you mean?'

I'm striding through the corridors now, even though most of them are in darkness. The teacher has to jog to keep up.

'I mean I can't find her!' I cry, and my desperation bounces back at me off the gloss-painted walls. 'She's not in the hall. She didn't come out. I don't know where she is!'

'I'm sure she just nipped to the toilet or something,' Miss Goodall says.

She could be right. Of course she could. But it feels patronising, like I'm one of her sobbing eight-year-olds who needs reassuring that a lost toy will turn up.

We round the corner onto the corridor by her classroom. Sensing movement, the automatic lights clunk on, driving back the dark.

'I was sitting right out front all night,' I say, then I call Hollie's name. My voice is shrill and sharp. It races ahead of me, searching through the corridors and passageways, before echoing back empty-handed.

'You probably just didn't notice her passing.'

I know she doesn't mean anything by it. I know that she's just trying to keep me calm. But the note of amusement in the teacher's reply stops me dead in my tracks and spins me round.

'She's dressed as a giant butterfly!' I all but scream at her. 'She's got a three-foot wingspan. How could I not have noticed her?'

Miss Goodall shrinks back a step in shock. I have to fight the urge to apologise, and instead I turn and press on towards the classroom.

I only make it a few steps, though, before I see something that brings me to a stumbling halt all over again.

Hollie's jacket is still there. Still hanging on its peg. The only one left.

It looks out of place. And it looks so very, very small.

Her outdoor shoes are there, too, right where we left them after I helped her change into her ballet pumps. They're tucked under the bench, nice and neat, side by side.

Hollie's clothes are here.

But though we'll check bathrooms, and classrooms, and everywhere in between, the knot in my stomach already knows the truth.

My daughter's clothes are here.

But my daughter is not.

And, like that, the bottom falls out of my world.

THREE

ELIZABETH

Miss Goodall is once again reassuring me that everything is going to be fine, but I'm not listening. She has no idea what she's talking about.

But then, how could she? How could she know that I've been living in fear of this moment? How could she know that I've structured the last eight years of my life specifically to avoid this happening?

Nobody does. Nobody knows.

Well, almost nobody.

She's offering some more platitudes when her male counterpart comes jogging along the corridor behind her.

'Hey, ladies, you lost?' Mr Wilkinson asks, hitting us with both barrels of a winning smile.

Rather than immediately pulling him up on his patronising greeting, Miss Goodall sweeps a strand of hair back over her ear and tries very hard not to blush.

I wheel round, ignoring them both, and try the handle of the classroom door. The whole thing *clunks* against the frame. Locked. It was open earlier when we arrived. Some of the kids got changed in there.

'Can you open this?' It's a demand, not a question. 'She could be in there.'

'Who?' Mr Wilkinson asks.

'Who do you think?' I spit back at him. 'Hollie!'

'Hollie?' He looks from me, to the door, to Miss Goodall. 'Why would Hollie be in there?'

'She thinks she's lost,' Miss Goodall says, and I can't help but wonder if primary school teachers are given lessons on how to sound condescending, or if it comes naturally.

'I don't *think* she's lost!' I cry, and I can hear the anguish in my voice as it goes rolling off along the corridor. 'I can't find her, so she's lost.'

'Hey, it's OK. I'm sure she's fine. I'm sure she'll turn up,' Mr Wilkinson assures me.

He's smiling as he says it, and some part of me, deep down, wants to hit him. Instead, I direct the aggression towards the door, shaking it violently in its frame.

'Can somebody *please* open this?'

The teachers swap looks. I can feel them judging me. The hysterical mother, losing her mind over nothing.

'Sorry, I don't have my key,' Miss Goodall finally offers. She tries to soften it with a little wince and a shrug, like the fact my child might be locked in there alone and terrified is just a funny little faux pas on her part.

Mr Wilkinson jabs a thumb back over his shoulder. 'Don-nie'll have the master key.' He looks over at me, his head tilted in affected sympathy. 'Do you want me to get it?'

I don't trust myself to answer out loud, so I just give the door another shake and glare at him.

'I'll go get the master,' he says.

Just briefly, blink and you'd miss it, his hand brushes against Miss Goodall's lower back. She tries not to let on, but I can see the flicker of excitement in her eyes. They're either in the early days of a relationship, or building up to one, despite the fact he must be at least fifteen years her senior.

'Well, hurry up, then,' I bark, taking affront at their affection, now of all times.

He scuttles off, and I knock on the door, cupping my hands against the frosted glass like I might be able to see through it, and through the darkness beyond.

'It's OK, baby. I'm here. Mum's here.'

I don't know why I've pinned all my hopes on her being in the classroom. There's nothing to suggest that she is, and every reason to believe she isn't. But I need to focus on something. Somewhere. She's either in there, or she's *anywhere else that isn't there*.

The thought of that second one is too big, too overwhelming. I can't entertain it. She has to be in the classroom. She has to be.

If she isn't, it almost certainly means only one thing. My deepest, darkest fear has come true.

'Could Sasha have come to collect her?'

The casual dropping of my sister's name hits me like a sledgehammer. It feels like all the air leaves my lungs in one sudden strike.

'What did you say?' I whisper.

'Sasha. Hollie's aunt? She mentioned her a few times recently.'

'What? Why? When?'

It's been years since Hollie and I have spoken about Sasha. Even longer since she saw her.

'Just...' The teacher shrugs. Smiles. 'I don't know. A couple of times recently. We were talking about different types of families, relatives, that sort of thing, and Hollie mentioned she has an aunt—'

'Sasha's not around any more,' I say. 'She's not part of our lives.'

'Oh. I'm sorry to hear that.'

'Don't be.'

I turn away from her and try the door again, and do my best not to show how badly my hands are shaking.

She lurks there, saying nothing. I can feel her eyes on me, watching me, studying me, judging me.

'Can you please do something?' I cry. 'Standing there staring isn't helping us find Hollie.'

The sharpness of my voice rattles the teacher, but it doesn't last. She's soon smiling again, like this is all a lot of fuss about nothing.

'Right. Yes. Tell you what, I'll go and check the hall again, just in case she's gone back in there,' she says.

'Fine,' I say, and she hurries off, leaving me alone with my daughter's clothes and the locked classroom door.

Now that both teachers are gone, there's nowhere for me to direct my anger but inward. I can feel it, scorching hot, blistering my insides.

How could I have let this happen?

How, after everything, could I just lose Hollie like this?

She didn't come past me. I'm sure of it. I'd have seen her, even in the mad crush at the end of the night, I'd have seen her. I was watching for her. The only time I looked away was when Mabel Walker spoke to me, and that was only for a minute, if that.

We were right in the middle of the corridor. Hollie would have seen me.

Unless...

Could she have snuck past then? Is it possible she crept by me while my attention was on Mabel and her horrible daughter?

Theoretically, yes. But why would she? Hollie has no reason not to trust me.

She doesn't know.

Bubbles of nausea burble up in my gut.
She doesn't know my secret.
She can't know.
Can she?

FOUR

ELIZABETH

The return of Mr Wilkinson snaps me back to the here and now. He's fiddling with a giant bunch of keys, sifting through them, trying to find the right one.

'Hurry up!' I urge, and he flashes me an apologetic look, then settles on what he thinks is the right key.

A quick check in the lock reveals that it isn't. I clench my fists and grit my teeth and shuffle from foot to foot as he tries another two, before finally finding the right one.

As soon as the key turns, I push past him, throwing the door open and feeling for the light switch. They click on, driving back the dark, and revealing the clutter of the classroom. Colourful artwork covers almost every square inch of the walls, along with times tables posters, quotes about kindness, and the spelling words they've been working on this week.

The last time I was in this room was on the day before half-term, when parents were invited along to see what the kids had been working on. Hollie had taken me by the hand and guided me around on a whistle-stop tour of her various artworks and accomplishments.

She'd eked out every moment of my visit, making me kneel by her desk as she went through page upon page of spelling and sums, showing me all the ones she'd got right, and casually explaining away the very few 'silly mistakes'.

She had held onto me for as long as she could, long after all the other parents had left. I didn't mind. Quite the opposite.

My gaze goes instinctively to Hollie's desk now, and to the half-sized chair pushed in beneath it.

Empty. Like the rest of the room. My legs shake. I grab for a bookcase, holding myself up, just as a commotion in the corridor behind me signals the return of Hollie's teacher.

'She's definitely not in the hall, and she's not in the toilets, either,' Miss Goodall says. This time, for the first time, I detect a note of concern in her voice.

I listen to the conversation taking place behind me. My heart becomes a drumbeat in my chest.

Ba-dum. Ba-dum. Ba-dum.

'Donnie hasn't seen her,' Mr Wilkinson says. 'He's going to take another look, and then check the security camera footage.'

'I asked, and none of the other teachers saw her after the disco,' Miss Goodall adds.

Ba-dum. Ba-dum. Ba-dum.

I haven't turned yet. I'm still staring at Hollie's desk, the empty silence of the classroom taunting me.

Can they hear the thudding of my heart? How could they not?

My mind races ahead, like it's fast-forwarding through their conversation, spooling past all their prattling, hurtling towards its awful, inevitable conclusion.

The only possible conclusion they can make.

A conclusion that will tear my world apart.

It's Miss Goodall who reaches it first.

'Maybe we should think about calling the police?'

There's silence from the corridor. Heavy. Pressing. It wasn't a statement, it was a question, and they're waiting for my answer.

I close my eyes. Take a breath. Try to steady my heartbeat.

Even with my eyes shut, I can see Hollie's empty desk. Her little chair. All those drawings and paintings she so proudly showed off.

We can't get the police involved. If we do, it's over. Hollie will be in even more danger than she is already. They'll look into everything. They'll dig into every element of my past, and rifle through all my dirty laundry.

Just like last time.

I let out a groan and turn to the teachers standing in the doorway, Miss Goodall just a step in front of Mr Wilkinson. Their smiles are gone, replaced by expressions of concern.

Their frowns deepen when they see the embarrassed smile on my face. 'Oh, God. I'm so sorry.'

Another look passes between them. This time, it's mostly confusion. 'Sorry? What do you mean?' Miss Goodall asks.

'You've nothing to be sorry about, Mrs Jones,' Mr Wilkinson assures me.

'She's at home,' I say. I bury my face in my hands, trying to both buy myself more time, and to really sell the thing. 'God. I'm such an idiot.'

'What do you mean, she's at home?' Mr Wilkinson asks. He looks around the classroom. 'I thought...'

'Ugh! I'm so stupid. I forgot my partner was picking her up. I wasn't sure if I'd be stuck here helping tidy up, so I asked him to come collect her for me. She's probably already in her jammies.'

The lies tumble easily out of my mouth. But then, they always did.

I hoped this explanation was going to be enough to

convince the teachers, but they both stare back at me, their expressions unchanged.

'Oh.' Mr Wilkinson blinks a couple of times, like he's struggling to process this new information. 'Are you sure?'

'You said you were out front all night. And she's dressed as a giant butterfly,' Miss Goodall says, using my own argument from earlier against me. 'You really seemed quite insistent about—'

'I know what I said,' I say, cutting her off. 'And I'm sorry. But Mabel cornered me. You know Mabel? From the PTA.'

Mr Wilkinson shudders. It's barely noticeable, but it's just enough to make me warm to him a little. It also gives me an opening.

'You know what she's like when she gets started. Clive – my partner – he can't stand her, and probably just bundled Hollie past us under his arm. He'll have been in too much of a hurry to escape to worry about Hollie's jacket and shoes.'

I laugh. It sounds hollow and fake to my ears. Every part of me feels like it's a betrayal, but I have to convince them. They have to believe me.

'God. I'm so embarrassed. You must think I'm insane.'

The smile, which has been notable by its absence from Miss Goodall's face, twitches back into life. Mr Wilkinson looks less convinced, though. It makes sense. The head teacher is off on maternity leave at the moment, and he's filling in. The responsibility of a missing child ultimately rests on him.

I head off his objections before he has a chance to make them.

'Hang on, let me text him to make sure,' I suggest, taking out my phone. I rattle off a quick message to Clive. My fingers tremble. Only autocorrect makes the message legible.

Heading home soon. Want anything picked up?

The message is read almost immediately. I feel the gazes of the teachers on me as he types out his response.

I'm fine ta x

I let my body sag, pretending all my tension has left me.

'Yep. Yep. She's there,' I announce.

'Oh, thank God for that,' Miss Goodall says. 'You had us worried there.'

'I know. I know, I'm sorry,' I say, edging past her. I need to get out. I have to find Hollie.

She shifts out of the way, but Mr Wilkinson still blocks my path. He's smiling at me, but there's something slightly quizzical about it, like he can sense he's missing something, but can't put his finger on what it is.

'Sorry for the drama,' I say, and he just shakes his head, dismissing the apology.

'Don't worry about it,' he says. He chews down on his bottom lip for a moment. 'You're sure everything's OK? You seemed really distressed.'

'Well, I was,' I say, almost choking on another burst of laughter. 'But it's fine. All good.'

He's still staring at me. His eyes are such a deep, dark brown that they're almost black. You could drown in them, if you weren't careful.

'So... we'll see Hollie on Monday morning,' he says, and his tone makes it clear – he's not asking me, he's telling me. If Hollie isn't in school after the weekend, he's going to have questions.

And he won't be the only one.

'Of course. First thing Monday,' I say.

I have no idea where my daughter is. I have no idea where to start looking.

But I have around sixty hours in which to find her.

And if I don't? If I don't have her safely back in school by then?

Then all hell is going to break loose.

And everything I've done to protect us will have been for nothing.

FIVE
ELIZABETH

I want to run, but I daren't. The teachers could be watching – anyone could be watching – and I can't risk them seeing me panic.

I can panic in a minute, when I'm safely in the car, but for now, I keep it together.

My breath forms clouds in the cold night air as I walk, as slowly and calmly as I can, to my car. Mine is the last one parked on the narrow one-way street that runs behind the school.

We were too late to get into the car park, and almost too late to squeeze in at the far end of the line of cars on this road.

Everyone has driven off now. Everyone but me.

I'm carrying Hollie's jacket. It feels so light. So small. There's not a trace of her warmth in it, not even when I clutch it to my chest.

I keep walking. Eyes darting back and forth, searching the darkness around the school building.

I think I see movement by the car, and almost call out Hollie's name. But it's my shadow blurring across the paint-work. It isn't my daughter. It isn't anyone.

The car unlocks with a press of a button and a flash of its lights, dazzling me. I slip inside and pull the door closed. Even as it's swinging shut, the echo of my breathing becomes raw. Ragged.

My chest swells, expands, like my lungs are growing too big for it. I hold it together long enough for the overhead lights to dull back down into darkness, then I bury my face in my hands to muffle the scream I can no longer contain.

It erupts from inside me, from somewhere ancient and primal. Somewhere long buried. I stifle it, try to force it back, but there's nothing I can do to stop it, and my whole body heaves with the strain of it.

I don't know how long I stay like that, alternating between sobbing and screaming. Thirty seconds? Five minutes? More? Time means nothing.

Eventually, my anguish burns itself out enough for me to take back control. I sit up straighter, hands gripping the steering wheel, eyes scanning the darkness outside.

I need to think. I need to logic this out. Where might Hollie be?

We argued tonight, just before we left the house. The memory of it makes the tears return, but this time I'm able to swallow them back down. I can't waste any more time.

She was complaining her costume didn't fit properly, telling me it was uncomfortable, that it was all wrong.

We were already twenty minutes behind schedule. I knew Mabel Walker was going to be raging. I snapped. I told Hollie that maybe if she'd bothered to help or tried the costume on last night, when I told her to, we wouldn't be in this situation.

She bit back at me. It was her anxiety about the costume prize. I knew that, even then, but it didn't stop me from retaliating and raising my voice. I'm not proud of it.

My partner, Clive, had tried to act as peacekeeper, but neither Hollie nor I were in any mood to entertain him, so we'd gone storming out of the house, then spent the short drive here in silence.

But she'd waved at me during the parade. She'd smiled and seemed happy to see me. I felt sure things were OK.

But what if they weren't? What if Hollie was still upset? What if she saw the chance to sneak past me in the corridor, and ran away? Would she do that?

It's a horrible thought that chills me to the bone. Right now, though, it almost feels like wishful thinking.

It's early November – Halloween was actually two days ago – and there's only so long a nine-year-old will hold a grudge on a cold, dark Scottish night before the lure of hot chocolate and fluffy pyjamas becomes too tempting.

If she ran away, she won't have gone far. She can't have. She'll be nearby. We're less than half a mile from home, and it's a good area of the city, even at this time of night on a Friday.

I turn the key in the ignition. The rumble of the engine firing up and the lights on the dashboard feel oddly reassuring.

She'll be in the huff, that's all, blaming the fact she didn't win the contest on me. She'll have run away to make a point, to teach me a lesson.

But the mercury is plummeting, and she's afraid of the dark. She'll have realised her mistake by now. If she isn't home already, she'll almost certainly beat me there.

I feel a little surge of hope. Of elation, even. I laugh, and this time it doesn't feel fake or forced.

She'll be fine. I'm worrying about nothing. She's just stormed back to the flat. Hollie is going to be OK.

Hollie is going to be OK. I repeat the words like a mantra in my head, as I pull away from the kerb.

And the flickering streetlights cast long, finger-like shadows behind me that seem determined to follow me home.

SIX

ELIZABETH

The drive home is fast and frantic. I scour the streets as I drive, searching for any sign of pink butterfly wings making their way home.

I don't find them.

Opposing rows of sandstone Georgian buildings on India Street tower over the car on either side as I pull around the corner. I've never noticed how tall they were before, and suddenly feel as if I'm driving along the bottom of a high canyon.

Lights wink down at me from a dozen sash windows, most of the curtains drawn against the darkness.

There's no light from Hollie's bedroom window, though. Her curtains are open, just as we left them. Miraculously, for this time of evening, I'm able to pull up more or less directly outside our block's front door.

I lock the car and hurry up the steps. The two terrier-sized stone lions that stand either side of the door – hangovers from much grander days, long before the conversion of the building from single house to three flats – watch on in silence as I fumble my keys from my bag.

With some effort, I get the door unlocked, then take the stairs two at a time until I am standing at the front door of our top-floor apartment.

Technically, Clive's top-floor apartment, but it's our home, too, he insists. Mine and Hollie's.

I waste a few seconds catching my breath and smoothing down my hair, then I fix on a smile and push on inside.

The next few moments will determine everything.

From the hallway, I can see directly into the kitchen at the far end. The light is on, and I can hear Clive talking away to one of his podcasts, as if they can hear what he's saying to them. Rather he talks back to them than to me. If I have to hear one more summary of whichever tedious political show he's obsessed with this week, I'll...

Well, I won't do anything, obviously. But I'll think about it.

With Clive busy in the kitchen, I'm able to check the other rooms. Hollie isn't in the living room. She's not in her bedroom. I try the handle of the bathroom door and it swings open. Pulling back the shower curtain, I confirm she's not in there, then return to the hall to find Clive with a kitchen knife in his hand.

'Jesus!' I hiss, and he steps back, the flat of a hand pressing against his chest.

'Bloody hell. You nearly gave me a heart attack,' he cheeps. His voice is raised, although that might be because of the podcast. He still has his earphones in, and I can hear the *tsst-tsst-tsst* of scathing political commentary from here. 'I thought you were a bloody burglar.'

'Well, I'm not,' I say, then I shoot a very deliberate glance at the knife he's still pointing in my direction. There are smears of milk chocolate along the sides of the blade, and I'm suddenly aware of the smell of cookies baking.

Clive follows my gaze to the knife, stares at it like he's not sure what he's doing with it, then hurriedly lowers it.

'Whoops! Sorry.' He runs a hand back through his thinning grey hair. He's seven years older than me but looks double that. His thin lips twist into something that's midway between a smile and a grimace. 'I really did think you were a burglar, though. Didn't hear you come in.'

He points to his ear, then rolls his eyes, like he's letting me in on some corny joke he's heard.

'Alastair Campbell's asking why Venezuela isn't the Saudi Arabia of Latin America!'

The question is out of me before I can stop it. 'What the hell does that mean?'

I don't care. Even at the best of times, I wouldn't give a damn. But I've asked now. I've engaged, and his face lights up at my apparent sudden interest.

'Well,' he begins, but – mercifully – another thought distracts him. He looks past me along the hallway, and at the open doors on either side. 'Wait. Where's Hollie?'

There's a jolt in my chest, like my heart has stopped. I'd rapidly started losing hope that she was here as soon as I stepped inside. But I was holding on to the thought that she might be in the kitchen, telling Clive all about the night, and how she'd been robbed at the best costume competition, and how she'd walked home all by herself, and how she had the worst mother in all the world.

But she's not in there. He hasn't seen her. My baby girl is still out there.

Alone.

The lies take shape before I can even think about them. I hear them at the same time Clive does.

'She's staying at a friend's house tonight,' I say.

'A friend? Like a sleepover?' He pulls a funny little frown, like the very suggestion is absurd. 'What friend?'

'Just a friend from her class,' I say. 'Suzie. I told her I'd drop off some pyjamas and clothes for the morning.'

I'm amazed by my own quick thinking. Hopefully, it doesn't show on my face.

'Suzie?' He scrubs his tongue across the front of his teeth. They're veneers. Done on the cheap in Turkey. You can tell, though I always assure him that you can't. 'Don't think I've ever heard her mention a Suzie before.'

Nor have I. I drew a blank trying to remember any of the kids in Hollie's class who weren't Jessica Walker. She lives about five houses away, so is no good for me. Besides, Clive would never buy the idea of Hollie going to stay there. Suzie's just a name I plucked out of thin air.

He raises an inquisitive eyebrow at me. 'You sure you haven't killed her?' he asks.

'What?'

'Just teasing,' he says, smirking at me. 'That was quite a barney you two had before you left. You sort it out? You friends again?'

'Yeah. It's fine,' I say, itching to get moving.

'Good. I couldn't have my two favourite girls at each other's throats,' Clive says. I think that's him done, but then he continues. 'Whereabouts does she live, this Suzie?'

This time I hesitate, just for a second or two, my brain whirring wildly as I try to recall the extent of the school's catchment area. I need time to look for Hollie, but if I give an address that's too far away from the school, Clive might get suspicious.

'Rose Street,' I blurt. It's right by the boundary. Far enough away to buy me some searching time.

'Oof,' he says. His lips draw together, puckering up the lines of his face. 'Going to be a nightmare getting parked at this time. Unless...'

He taps the flat of the knife against the side of his leg, deep in thought. For a moment, the tinny voices in his ears are the only sound in the hallway.

Finally, he nods. 'Yep. So. George Street. That's your best

bet. Park there, walk down. Be careful, though. Friday night? Lot of idiots about round there. It's going to be a nightmare for her trying to get to sleep. You sure she doesn't want to bring Suzie round here?' He proudly puffs himself up. 'I'm making her favourite cookies.'

Of course he is. He's always doing thoughtful little things like that for her. For both of us, really. He's good like that.

'It's fine. She's excited about it,' I say, glancing deliberately at the door to Hollie's room.

Clive leans against the wall, his eyebrows waggling suggestively. 'Oh well, some grown-up time alone, then,' he purrs. 'Whatever shall we do to occupy ourselves?'

'Haha, yeah,' I say, scratching at a sudden itch on my neck. 'I'd better get a move on, or I'll never hear the end of it.'

I sense him leaning in to give me a kiss on the cheek, but I'm already turning, already moving, already headed for the exit.

'Hold on a minute.'

The command is sharp and sudden. I stop just a few steps from the front door and look back at him over my shoulder.

'Aren't you forgetting something?' Clive asks.

He points with the knife at Hollie's room.

'The clothes?'

'Oh.' I fake a laugh and stop just short of slapping myself on the forehead. 'Duh. Idiot.'

He watches me as I back up a few paces, then enter Hollie's room. Her school uniform is strewn across the bed. Half a dozen teddies lie scattered on the floor. Only Mr Floppsity remains upright beside her pillow, his long, tatty ears hanging down either side of his flocked, glassy-eyed face.

Hollie has had him almost her entire life. He's watched over her from day one, her constant companion. Her comfort. I grab him by the head and stuff him under my arm. I'm not sure why, exactly – he's just a stuffed animal – and yet I know I'll feel better having him with me.

I grab a random mishmash of clothes, stuff them in Hollie's schoolbag, then sling it over my shoulder.

I make it all the way to the front door this time, and out into the stairwell, before Clive's shout can chase me down.

'Elizabeth, wait!'

I almost don't stop, keep running, but I can't alert him to the fact that something is wrong, and so I play the dutiful partner, and wait until he catches up.

He's swapped the knife for a plastic tub. I feel the warmth in the bottom and smell the aroma wafting through the vented lid as he thrusts it into my hands.

'Cookies,' he tells me. 'Fresh from the oven. They're her favourites.'

I look down at the box. Even through the scuffed plastic, the chocolate chips shine as they cool.

'There's half a dozen of those bad boys there. Make sure she shares them with Suzie!'

'I will,' I tell him. Then I make my way down the stairs, out past the concrete lions guarding the front door of the building, and off in search of my daughter.

I just pray that I'm not too late.

SEVEN

ELIZABETH

I drive back towards the school at a crawl, scouring the pavements, oblivious to the taxis tooting impatiently behind me. I expect to see Hollie around every corner and bend, but if she's making her way home, then she's gone a different route.

I swing by the playground we sometimes visit on the days we walk home in case she's gone there. All I find are a few broken bottles and a gaggle of drunken teenagers, though, so I don't hang around. Hollie would have turned around the moment she heard them and run all the way home.

She's anxious around older kids. Fragile. The thought of that makes my throat tighten, and hot tears stream down my cheeks. I waste a few seconds sobbing when I'm back in the car, before I pull myself together enough to carry on to the school.

There are no vehicles left in the car park when I arrive. Even so, I creep slowly past the building, then pull up and kill the engine a little way along the road.

Some part of me reasons that I should phone around the parents of the other kids in her class. Maybe she did go with one of them – not the fictional Suzie, of course, but someone.

I can't remember any of the kids' names right now, but I

should have the telephone numbers of a handful of parents from my PTA duties. I daren't call them, though. If I call them, I'll have to tell them why.

And I can't have anyone knowing. Not yet.

Besides, I doubt they'll be able to help me.

If there are answers to be had, they'll be in the school.

My eyes meet those of Mr Floppsity, sitting on the dashboard in front of me, and I swear that the floppy-eared bastard is judging me as I grab a cookie from the box, stuff it in my mouth, and clamber out of the car.

Oakbridge Primary is a small, yet impressive, B-listed building from the Victorian era, built in sandstone that shimmers golden-grey in the sun. Now, though, set back from the streetlights, it lurks in the shadows, its spires and high windows shrouded by the dark.

The front gate of the playground is locked, but the side fence is barely four feet high. When I'm sure the coast is clear, I hop over it and, keeping low, jog round to the back door.

Along the way, I check in every little alcove, in case Hollie is hiding in there, shivering and sheltering from the cold.

Every empty nook brings only more heartache and disappointment.

The building is alarmed, but my position on the parent council means I'm privy to the security code. What I don't have, however, is a key.

I hunt around the playground for a rock to break the frosted glass in the door, but I'm out of luck. Instead, my gaze settles on the frog-shaped bin standing near the bike shed, mouth wide open to wolf down any offered rubbish.

It isn't fastened down, but it's not light, either. Dragging it over to the back door, I brace myself against it, ready to hoist it up to shoulder height, when a little nagging voice tells me to try the door handle.

It turns. The door swings inward. The warm air generated

by the industrial heating system makes it feel like the building exhales, its breath hitting me in the face. A dark corridor looms ahead of me, and I suddenly get the sense that I'm standing in the jaws of some terrible giant beast, about to be swallowed whole.

The door being unlocked is both good news and bad. It means I don't have to smash through a window with a big metal frog.

But it also means that I'm not alone. Somebody else is still in the building.

I step inside. The floorboards beneath me groan out a warning. I ignore it and press onwards into the belly of the beast.

EIGHT

ELIZABETH

Someone stares at me from the shadows as soon as I step inside. Eyes peer from the dark, studying me, scrutinising me, demanding to know what I'm doing here.

I gasp and start to blurt out an explanation before I realise it's my own reflection staring back at me from the glass of an inner door.

It takes a few seconds for my heart rate to slow down enough for me to continue, and I push onwards into the school.

The building is spread over two floors, with most of the classrooms, the hall, and canteen downstairs. Upstairs, there are two other classrooms, the staff room, and the head teacher's and janitor's offices. There's also a dedicated music room, and a little recording studio the PTA raised the funds to pay for a few years back, but which very rarely sees any use.

The PTA also paid for the school's security cameras, after some random nutter wandered into a Primary 5 classroom one day, sat down, and refused to move. He was eventually dragged off the premises by the police and charged, but the incident triggered a full security review that led to the installation of cameras inside and outside the building.

Cameras that I had, until now, completely forgotten about, and which I'm suddenly aware would have watched me dragging the bin across the playground.

And are watching me now, as I creep through the corridors leading to the main hall.

The foyer rings with silence, like the echoes of ten thousand children past and present still vibrate its very fabric. The snack table has been cleared away. The chair I spent the evening sitting on is stacked with a pile of others in the corner. All the spilled Wotsits and Skittles have been swept away.

If I hadn't been here to see it for myself, I'd never be able to tell that the disco had ever happened.

The big swing doors of the hall, unlike the classrooms', don't lock. I inch one of them open enough to peer inside. Then, when I'm sure the coast is clear, I sneak in and ease it shut behind me.

The only windows are high up near the ceiling, and there's very little light outside, anyway. The beam of my phone's torch paints an elongated oval on the floor. I sweep it left and right as I walk along the outside edges of the hall, searching for...

What? What am I even looking for? What do I possibly hope to find? It's not like Hollie's going to jump out at me from the shadows. I'd probably immediately die of fright if she did.

But I'd take it, if it meant she was safe.

I stop when I reach the fire exit. It's on the back wall, near a corner. A lump of the Blu Tack that stuck the Halloween decorations to the wall above the door sprouts from the gloss-white paintwork like a tumour. It draws my eye, and I stare at it, like it holds some hidden significance.

If it does, then I have no idea what it is.

I turn my attention to the fire exit itself. It has a wide bar across the middle and is only supposed to be used in case of emergency. On warmer days, though, teachers sometimes open it to let fresh air into the hall, and so it has been disconnected from the fire alarm system.

Even with everyone running around and dancing in here tonight, it would be too cold outside for them to have opened the door, wouldn't it? I try to think back to the costume parade. Was it open then?

There's no handle or latch on the outside, so nobody could have come in that way, but could Hollie have opened it herself and snuck out? Or, worse, could she have opened it on the instructions of someone outside and gone with them?

Or been taken by them?

I can't remember if there's a camera in here, so I aim my torch up at the walls and sweep it along them. There's a glint from the opposite end, right above the main door. A reflection of light on polished glass.

As I move closer, the shape of the camera comes into view. It's staring directly at me, a beady electronic eye, gazing down.

If it's on – and I have no reason to suspect it isn't – then someone could be watching me right now. The thought of it makes me angle the torch to the floor, then tap frantically at the screen until the beam shuts off.

The acoustics of the hall seem to amplify the sound of my breathing. I listen, expecting to hear footsteps, or raised voices, or approaching sirens.

Nothing.

Just my breathing. Just my heartbeat. Just my terror pounding in my head.

If anyone spotted me, they've made no move to do anything about it.

But, the camera. The camera saw me. The camera saw everything that happened here tonight.

Which means I know exactly what I have to do.

NINE

ELIZABETH

The school's staircase is almost as old as the building's Victorian foundations, and it creaks and groans under my weight as I creep upwards. I pause on every other step, straining my ears for any sound that might warn me of someone approaching.

The silence is oppressive, broken only by the pounding of my heart and the occasional settling of ancient timber.

As I reach the top, I'm met with a maze of shadowy corridors. The layout of the upper floor has always confused me, even in broad daylight. Now, in the dark, and in my panic, it's full-on disorienting. I consider clicking on my phone torch again, but the risk of detection is too great. Instead, I let my eyes adjust to the gloom and inch forwards.

The floorboards beneath my feet are traitorous, each step threatening to announce my presence. I hug the wall, testing each board before committing my full weight. The smell of old damp timbers and floor polish is both familiar and alien. I've smelled those odours a dozen times before, at PTA meetings and school plays. Tonight, though, they snag at the back of my throat, more pungent and pronounced than ever.

The door to the staff room is slightly ajar as I pass it. For a heart-stopping moment, I think I see movement within, but it's just my imagination playing tricks on me in the half-light.

Still, I can't shake the feeling of being watched.

The janitor's office is at the far end of the corridor, past the head teacher's room and the music studio. Each door I pass is a potential hiding place for whoever else might be in the building. I expect them to swing open at my approach, to reveal some terrifying hooded figure lurking within.

They don't, but my nerves are stretched to breaking point, every shadow a threat, every sound – real or otherwise – a warning.

I'm only a few paces away when a sudden clatter from downstairs freezes me in my tracks. I press myself against the wall, hardly daring to breathe. Is it the wind? A falling object? Or something – someone – else?

Could it be Hollie? The thought makes my heart surge, and I almost call out to her, before stopping myself. I daren't. I can't utter a sound. If it isn't her, then whoever is down there will know I'm here, and it'll all be over.

There's a wooden cabinet next to the door to the janitor's office, filled with cleaning supplies and paper towels. I duck down, taking refuge in the darkness beside it, listening for any more movement from down below.

Nothing.

It takes several seconds for my heart rate to settle down again, and several more before I can work up the courage to move. I stay low, and slide my hand up the door, feeling for the handle. It's an old brass knob, cold and smooth against my fingertips.

Slowly, ever so slowly, I turn it. I'm prepared for the door to be locked, although I have no idea what I'll do if it is. To my surprise, though, the catch disengages, and the door swings inward an inch or two.

There's no shout from within. No urgent warnings or

panicky demands. Still squatting, I waddle into the office, close the door, and waste a few seconds resting my forehead against the cool timbers of the wood.

The room is small and cluttered. It's as much a broom closet as it is an office, even though most of the bulkier cleaning equipment is kept in a cupboard downstairs. Brushes and mops stand lined up against one wall, like they're waiting to be executed by firing squad.

A pair of old boots stands just to the side of the door and helps explain the rancid smell that seems to permeate everything in the place. Three empty mugs stand on various surfaces. The bin – somewhat ironically – is overflowing and should have been emptied days ago.

For a man tasked with keeping the school in good repair, there's a general state of neglect to the janitor's office.

The security camera monitor is mounted on the wall at the far end of the room. I creep over to have a prod around at it. Despite everything, the sight of the keys turns my stomach. The gaps between them are full of dust and crumbs.

There's a pen on the table. I use it to poke at the keyboard until the darkened monitor wakes up. The light from the screen is near blinding in the darkness, and I hurriedly angle the whole thing down a little, terrified it'll attract attention.

There are twelve boxes on the screen, each showing the feed from a different camera. Most of them are in darkness, and I can only tell where they are thanks to the text displayed at the bottom of each.

Hall, Dining Room, Corridors One to Six, Office, and then three external feeds from the cameras outside. There's just enough light in one to see that it shows a very clear view of a frog-shaped bin standing by the back door.

I'll have to find a way of deleting the footage. The hall and the corridors, too.

There's no camera in the staff room, I note. Clearly, the teachers value their privacy.

These live feeds are all very well and good, but they don't help me. If I want to cover my tracks and search the footage for Hollie, then I need to find a way of accessing the recordings from earlier, and I have no idea how the system works.

I'm looking around the room for some sort of user guide or manual when I find them.

They're tucked in the bottom drawer of a rusted and battered old filing cabinet. Jammed at the bottom. Hidden away, out of sight. Scrunched up.

A pair of paper butterfly wings, pink love hearts painted on. They've been torn off, their edges jagged and uneven.

There's a whoosh of blood through my veins. A cacophony of noise inside my head.

I don't fully notice the footsteps out on the landing, or the sound of the door being opened.

I don't really register any of it until a hand grabs me by the back of the neck, and a blast of warm, fetid breath hits me on the side of my face.

'And just what *the hell* do you think you're doing?'

TEN

ELIZABETH

I twist, bringing up my arm and tearing myself free of the grip. Donnie, the janitor, scowls back at me, his gnarled fingers curled into claws, his thin lips drawn up to reveal his scum-coated teeth.

The kids call him 'Janny', which always seemed like far too affectionate a name for this wretched old monster, with his fixed scowl and wild eyebrows, who always seemed just a wrong word away from flying off the handle.

He's a cantankerous, spiteful man, who never bothers to hide his dislike for his job, the other staff, or people in general.

And he has part of Hollie's costume hidden in his bottom drawer.

'Wait a minute.' His voice has the gravel of old Glasgow to it as he looks me up and down. 'I know you.'

Of course he knows me. He's seen me almost every school day for the past two years.

Then again, I'm generally careful not to leave too much of a lasting impression on anyone.

'You're that lassie's mum,' he concludes, which seems to be about as much narrowing down as he's prepared to do.

He still looks angry, but his hands no longer look ready to make a grab for me.

'What the hell do you think you're doing in here?' he demands. 'You shouldn't be here. I thought you were one of them bloody teenagers up to no good. I could've caved your skull in.'

He says it like it's an offhand comment, but given what I've just found, it feels like a gut punch. I'm still holding one of Hollie's butterfly wings. My voice is a croak as I hold the crumpled paper out for him to see.

'Where did you get this?'

He doesn't look at it, just holds my gaze.

'None of your business.'

'It's my daughter's. They were part of her costume.' I thrust it towards him, more urgently, my fear bubbling over into desperation. 'Where did you get it? Where is she? What have you done to her?'

His weathered brow furrows, the deep crags of his forehead lines drawing downwards, his wild eyebrows knotting together into a single grey caterpillar.

'What the hell are you talking about? They were on the floor. I swept them up. Alright?'

I realise that the paper wings are sticking to the tips of my fingers. There's something on them. Something tacky. Something red.

'Blood. There's blood!' My voice cracks as I blurt the words out. I didn't want to admit it to myself, but what else could it be? 'Why's there blood on them? Where's Hollie? What have you done to her?'

'They were on the floor!' He roars the words at me, the cords of his neck standing out like ropes, flecks of foamy spittle flying from his mouth. 'I saw them, I thought whoever they belonged to might be looking for them, so I kept them here.'

He's lying. I'm sure of it. He knows something.

He's done something.

'Now, I'm going to be nice to you,' he tells me, though his tone doesn't back that up. 'I'm going to allow you to piss off out of here, and we won't say a word about this to anyone.' The pointed purple tip of his tongue flicks across his lips. 'It'll be our little secret. No harm done.'

My head is shaking. So is the rest of me. 'No. No, I'm not going anywhere. Tell me where she is!'

He draws himself up to his full height. I can practically hear the bones in his back creaking into place.

'Don't tell me you're going to make me do this the hard way,' he says. His voice is a hiss. A whisper. A *sneer*.

I hear the crinkling of the paper butterfly wing and look down to see it crumpling in my hand. I watch, detached, as my fingers bunch into a ball, and my feet launch me forwards, and I hurl myself at him, fists flying, screaming at him.

'Where is my daughter? What have you done?'

He's slow to react. His eyes have barely had a chance to widen when I start hitting at him, scratching at him, pushing and shoving him with all my strength, and a little more to boot.

He lets out a cry of shock and brings his arms up to defend himself, but I've caught him off guard, off balance. He grabs for me, trying to stop himself falling, but goes stumbling backwards out of the office, already past the point of no return.

There is a sound. It's impossible to describe it. It's solid, yet wet. Sharp, but blunt.

It's not a good sound. It upends something in my gut, and suddenly I'm no longer just an outside observer, but back in my body, back in the room, back in control.

I can hear the wet rattle of my breathing. Only mine. From out on the landing, there is silence. Heavy, ominous, life-changing silence.

My feet, so willing just a moment ago to launch me into action, now seem determined to keep me rooted to the spot. I force them onwards, though, creeping step by step towards the door.

The smear of blood is the first thing I notice. It's right on the corner of the cabinet I hid behind just a few minutes ago, and oozes in rivulets down the grain of the wood.

Donnie lies on his back, one leg folded beneath him, his head twisted at an awkward angle. The fixed grimace that always seemed like a permanent arrangement he'd made with his face, is now gone. He looks peaceful, if you ignore the streak of red on his temple, and the slowly expanding pool of the stuff on the floor beneath him.

My head swims. The floor beneath me feels soft, like warm toffee, pulling me down, threatening to suffocate me.

It's not the blood – not *just* the blood, anyway. It's the fact that I caused this.

'Oh, God,' I whisper. I clamp a shaking hand over my mouth to stop myself saying anything more, but the words find their way out, all the same. 'Oh, God, what have I done?'

It's a stupid, pointless question. I know exactly what I've done. There's no escaping it.

I've killed him.

The real question is, what am I going to do about it? Maybe it's time to bring in the police. If Donnie hurt Hollie, they'll understand what I've done. If he stashed her away somewhere, they'll help find her. They'll tear this place apart, if they have to.

She might be alive. It might not be too late to save her.

Even if that means I never get to see her again.

I'll call them. This has gone too far.

I take out my phone before I can change my mind. There's a message notification on the screen. It's from a number I don't recognise. Sent three minutes ago.

I tap it and have to choke back a sob when a picture expands to fill the screen.

It's Hollie, bound and blindfolded, shivering on a tatty leather couch in the leggings and top she wore for her butterfly costume. There's a sheet of paper propped up beside her, two words written in blocky marker pen.

I KNOW.

I don't think about what that means. I daren't. Instead, I focus on my daughter. Though I can't see her eyes, the streaks in her pink face paint tell me she's been crying.

I drop to my haunches, unable to keep standing, and rock back and forth. Images of her calling for me, screaming for me, begging me to come and get her fill my head until they spill out as snot and tears.

My stomach twists. I fall forwards on my hands and knees, unable to hold back the spray of vomit that burns its way up my throat. It splatters across the floor and the dead man.

It wasn't him. Donnie was with me in the room when that message arrived. I've killed him, and it wasn't him, and now my DNA is all over him, like my face is all over those cameras.

Someone has my baby. Someone has Hollie. If I go to the police now, I'm done. It's over. If I knew the police would bring Hollie home safely, then I'd do it in a heartbeat, but I know, first hand, how useless they can be.

If I want my daughter back, I can't rely on them. I need to find her myself.

But I need to clean up this mess, too. I can't do it all alone. It kills me to admit it, but I'm going to need help.

And that means I'm going to have to break a promise I made to myself a very long time ago. I have no other choice.

I'm going to have to speak to my sister.

ELEVEN

ELIZABETH

I try calling the number that sent the photo, but it goes straight to a message telling me the caller isn't available. It doesn't ring. There's no voicemail. According to my list of calls, this is my eighth attempt to get through in the past ten minutes.

The phone must be switched off, or set to reject all inbound calls. Either way, I'm not likely to get an answer.

There's nothing I can do but tap out a message.

Please don't hurt her. I'll do whatever you want.

I left the school as soon as I made contact with Sasha. It's fair to say she was surprised to hear from me.

I'm back on India Street now, but parked a little further along the street, the space I vacated earlier now claimed by the flashy silver Mercedes of one of the neighbours.

My gaze is drawn upwards again to the window of Hollie's bedroom. Was it really just a few hours since she was in there? It already feels like a lifetime ago.

I'm not sure why I've come home, exactly. I should still be out looking, but the photo message made it clear that I'm not going to find Hollie wandering the streets. She didn't run away. She isn't in a strop, teaching me a lesson.

Someone took her. Someone has her.

And I have no idea what she could be going through.

I got nothing from the cameras, although I didn't hang around long enough to really figure out how they worked. Sasha can take care of that. She'll know how to handle it. If there's anything on there, she'll let me know.

We're alike in so many ways, my sister and I, but dramatically different in others. She was always the wild child, never fully trusted by our parents, never fully welcome. They used to tell me she was 'troubled'.

They had no idea.

I haven't seen or spoken to Sasha since I cut her out of my life. She's got no reason to want to help me, and if I was the one in trouble, I wouldn't even ask.

But she'd do anything for Hollie. And I'd partner with the Devil himself if it meant getting my little girl home.

The clothes I used as an excuse to go out searching still sit on the passenger seat, Mr Floppsity now perching on top, glassy eyes staring blankly like he's suffering a PTSD flashback.

The box of cookies Clive gave me is there, too, though half of the contents are missing. I can taste the chocolate chips, so must've snacked on them, absent-mindedly, on the drive back. Stress eating has always been my problem.

One of them, anyway.

I stuff the clothes and the rabbit beneath the seat, then cram the box with its three remaining cookies into the glove compartment. The box is bulky, and it takes a bit of effort to force the door closed. Normally, I'd be worried about causing damage, but tonight, it's the least of my concerns.

It's almost eleven. I've been gone for close to two hours.

Clive is going to have questions.

I rehearse my answers as I pass the stone lions, enter the

building, and make my way up the stairs. I pause, just inside the door to the flat, when I hear Clive's voice from the living room.

It's quieter than usual. Not a whisper, but not a kick in the arse off it.

'No, it's fine. It's fine. She doesn't.'

A pause. A sigh of exasperation.

'No, I know, but I'm telling you, she doesn't, alright?'

I try to ease the door closed, but the mechanism makes a loud *clack* as it snaps into place.

Clive says something else, quieter this time, then I hear the scuffling of him heaving himself up off the couch.

He meets me in the hallway, all smiles and bluster.

'There you are! I've been phoning round looking for you. I was starting to think you'd got lost.'

'Phoning round? Phoning who?' I ask, my eyes darting to the door behind him. 'Who were you phoning?'

'Whom.'

I blink. Frown. 'What?'

'*Whom* were you phoning,' he says, then he winces. 'I think. I'm never sure.'

'Clive.' I stress his name. 'Who were you talking to?'

There's a hesitation, just for a moment. Something behind his eyes makes me think of Mr Floppsity, and then his grin widens and he claps his hands together with a *bang*.

'Doesn't matter, you're here now. All's well that ends well.'

He rests a hand horizontally across the tips of the opposite fingers, like he's a sports coach calling for a time out. It's his way of asking if I want a cup of tea, because apparently saying the words out loud like a normal person is too much trouble.

'No. I'm fine,' I say, and I squeeze past him into the living room, as if I might find the person he was talking to sitting there in my favourite chair.

I don't. Of course I don't.

He hasn't left his phone lying around either. It must be in his pocket.

If he doesn't want to tell me who he was talking to, then there's not a lot I can do to find out.

Not yet, anyway.

'You get Hollie her stuff?'

His voice is further away, calling to me from the kitchen. I don't reply, but he continues, undaunted, after sloshing some water into the kettle.

'Did she like the cookies?'

'Uh, yeah,' I mumble, as he pads into the room behind me.

'Suzie's mum alright with them having sugar and everything?' he asks.

He lurks by the door, like he wants to keep his distance from me. Or am I just imagining that?

'It's fine,' I say, dismissively. 'You were talking to someone when I came in. Who was it?'

'No one.'

He's trying to shrug it off.

Any other night, I'd let him. Any other night, I'd turn a blind eye to whatever he was up to, grateful for the roof over our heads, and for him never once lifting a hand in anger.

Any other night, I'd happily live in denial.

But not tonight.

Tonight, I'll allow him no secrets.

'So, you were talking to yourself? Is that what you're saying?'

'What? No. Don't be daft.'

He snorts with laughter. The water in the kettle rumbles away in the kitchen, as it hurries towards the boil.

'Who, then?' I demand. 'Who did you call?'

He searches my face, like I'm a stranger. 'Alan, alright?'

He turns on his heel and heads for the kitchen, just as the

kettle clicks off. I follow a few paces behind, mind racing, as I try to remember which one Alan is.

'The weird guy? From along the street?'

'He's not weird,' Clive protests, but he knows he doesn't have a leg to stand on. 'Alright, yes, he's a bit weird, obviously, but he's decent enough. He's always at the window. Does the Neighbourhood Watch. I just thought that maybe he might have seen you coming or going.'

I'm not buying it. It doesn't make sense.

'Why not just phone me, if you're that worried? Why not call me and ask?'

Don't get me wrong, I'm glad he didn't, but it's a legitimate question.

There's a goofiness to his smile, like he's embarrassed. He stops just short of *aw shucks*ing and shuffling his feet.

'Because I didn't want you knowing I was worried. I'm perfectly aware that you can take care of yourself, and I didn't want you thinking I didn't believe that. So, rather than call you, I phoned Alan.'

I still don't believe him. I want to demand he hand his phone over, so I can see for myself. Sasha would. Sasha would break his fingers to get it, if she had to.

But, for better or worse, I am not my sister.

Besides, he's a deep sleeper, and I know his passcode. If he's lying – if he's hiding something – I'll find out.

And then, I'll find out why.

TWELVE

SASHA

Well, this is quite the predicament.

I can see why Elizabeth panicked. Of course she did. Panicking is what Lizzie does best.

A looming English test used to send her into a spiral of anxiety. One wrong word from a boy she liked could render her housebound for days on end.

Accidentally killing a guy in a building she's broken into? Yeah, that's going to mess her up for years.

And so, it's Sasha to the rescue, once again. It's funny how you can be the black sheep of the family, until a black sheep is exactly what's needed.

When she called, I almost told her to piss off, but when I found out about Hollie, how could I refuse to help? The relationship between Elizabeth and me is complicated. My feelings for my niece, however, are simple. Elegantly so.

Mess with her, and you mess with me.

The old guy on the floor has the look of a grandpa about him. Not a nice grandpa, necessarily – not a grandpa you'd be keen to visit – but a grandpa, all the same.

I stand over him, my hands on my hips, mentally pulling together a To Do list:

Clean up the scene – including, but not limited to, the mound of still-warm vomit on the floor.

Deal with the body. Sticking him at the bottom of the stairs and faking a fall is one possibility, but there are scratch marks on one of his cheeks that would lead to an investigation. I can't take the risk of there being other forensic evidence linking Elizabeth to his death, so I'll have to get rid of him. Properly.

Great.

What else was there?

I hum below my breath as I try to remember Elizabeth's instructions. What was it again? What did she say?

'Cameras!' I say out loud, then I go back to humming as I step into the office. It's the theme to *SpongeBob SquarePants*. It's been going round and round in my head since I saw the sign out front saying 'Oakbridge School Gate', which scans remarkably well with the tune.

Whaaat saves all the kiddies from jakeys outside? Oakbridge School Gate!

Anyway. Where was I?

Oh, yeah.

Cameras.

I'm not familiar with this exact system, but they're all much of a muchness. My fingertips caress the keys, searching back through the last few hours of footage.

I follow Elizabeth's progress through the school in reverse, stopping just after she drags a frog-shaped bin away from the door, then moonwalks backwards out of shot.

Everything from then, until now, I delete with a couple of keystrokes, then I turn the cameras off so they don't see everything I have to do next.

That done, I scrub back further, past the teachers walking backwards into the building and shedding their jackets. Past my sister's frantic search of the corridors, past her pacing around in the hall.

Before I know it, the footage is teeming with costumed children, who all squeeze back into the spotlit darkness of the hall.

I slow the rewind to double speed and sing quietly below my breath.

'Oakbridge School Gate, Oakbridge School Gate, Oak-brii-idge School Gaaaaate!'

Damn, that's catchy.

I tap the spacebar, jolting the video to a stop. The cameras aren't great – even the fully lit ones are grainy, so the footage from the hall is a hazy, pixelated mess – but something on the screen catches my eye.

I spool slowly forwards, one frame at a time.

Tick. Tick. Tick.

A moment later, I stop.

'Well,' I announce to the world at large. I cross my fingers. Tap my toes. 'Well, well, well.'

After a quick search of the drawers in the room, I conclude that the dead man doesn't have what I'm looking for. I step over him and the cooling puddle of vomit, and go in search of the school office, which I'm sure I passed on the way up.

Sure enough, it takes me only a few seconds to find it, and less than a minute to find what I'm looking for in the secretary's desk. She's also got a KitKat in there. A four-finger one, at that.

Bonus.

'Want a finger?' I ask the dead man as I step over him, waving a stick of the chocolate-coated wafer in his direction.

If he does fancy a piece, he doesn't admit to it.

'No? Fine. Suit yourself.'

I'm humming again as I return to the security camera set-up, insert the USB stick I took from the secretary's desk, then start copying the files across.

I'd like to imagine Elizabeth will be grateful for all this, but I know better than to get my hopes up.

She's never grateful for my help. No matter what lengths I go to.

The computer that runs the security system is a few years old, and in need of an upgrade. It's practically wheezing with the effort of copying the video files to the memory stick. The process isn't going to be quick, but that's fine.

I do, after all, have a corpse to dispose of.

THIRTEEN

SASHA

It has been five years since I last cleaned up my sister's mess. Five years since that night. Since Kenny.

It's not something I ever expected to have to do again, but then, you never know with Lizzie. She struggles to keep her emotions in check. And, on occasion, her stomach contents.

It's all been cleaned up now, though. The footage has transferred, the surfaces have been wiped. I've done everything I've come to do.

Almost everything.

For the old man, I'm thinking the Union Canal. There are a few paths that connect to it just a little out of town, tucked away, hidden from view. Wrap him up, weigh him down, stick him in there, and Bob's your uncle. No more dead guy. No more problem.

I don't really want to load him into my car, but I didn't notice any others outside. And while he's got half a ton of keys attached to a loop on his belt, none of them seem to be of the vehicular variety. It seems, then, that I don't have a lot of choice.

I'll need to wrap him well, so his DNA isn't all over my boot and back seats. There's bound to be something around here I can use.

It takes me a bit of poking around, but between the janitor's office and the cleaning cupboard downstairs, I eventually cobble together my very own corpse disposal kit. It comprises the following:

1 hammer, for the removal of teeth and general destruction of the face.

1 saw, for cutting off fingers, limbs, or anything else.

20 black bags (approx). Always opt for extra thick. There's nothing worse than those flimsy, semi-transparent ones where the arse falls out as soon as you put anything in them. And when it comes to wrapping a body, that statement could end up being literal. Go heavy duty, or go to prison.

1 roll of duct tape. Or is it duck tape? I can never remember. Whatever it's called, I had an ex-boyfriend who used to say the tape is like the Force from the Star Wars movies. It has a light side, and a dark side, and it binds the universe together.

In hindsight, I don't know what I saw in him.

General fastenings. Rope is fine, but chains are better, because of the weight. Speaking of which...

Weights, assorted. Only necessary if you're dumping in a body of water. There's an art in when to attach them, though. You want to make sure the bugger sinks to the bottom, but you don't want to make him impossible to lift and manoeuvre on the way there. Timing is everything.

Cleaning equipment, because no matter how hard you try, and how careful you are, things *are* going to get messy.

Half a stolen KitKat (optional).

I secure his legs together first, wrapping the tape across his shins, pulling them together. The saw I found is a long one, so this way, I'll be able to cut off both feet at the same time.

Not that I'm necessarily planning to cut his feet off. Not

unless I find any distinguishing marks there. Still, it's a useful tip for future reference.

I don't bother tying his hands yet. They'll be going in a few minutes. Instead, I pull a black bag down over his face, and reach for the hammer. It's not that I mind seeing the damage – I'll have to check at various points to make sure he's as unrecognisable as possible – but the blood spatter is a problem I don't really want to have to deal with.

I wrestle the bag down past his shoulders, feel for the contours of his face to figure out exactly where I'm aiming, then raise the hammer above my head.

It's then, before I can strike, that he screams. His whole body jerks, kicking awake. A little curved indent appears in the surface of the bag, where he's tried to draw in a breath, but found only plastic.

Whoops.

I'm such an idiot. I took Lizzie's word that he was dead and didn't bother to check. In fairness, he looked pretty dead, and he was out for the count for a very long time.

I keep the hammer raised, considering my options. If I swing, the situation will return to the one I was in just a moment ago, with a dead guy to get rid of. It's a simple solution to an unexpected problem.

But, Lizzie seemed to think he might know something about Hollie. Something about wings in a drawer? She wasn't making a whole lot of sense.

I lower the hammer and pull the bag off with one quick, sudden yank. He coughs and splutters, like he's going to hack up his lungs. His eyes are wide, his irises like tiny islands in a sea of white.

Well, white with red flecks, technically.

'You alright there?' I ask. My smile, and the brightness in my voice do little to calm him. Quite the opposite, if anything. 'You're a proper Grandpa Joe, you are!'

The bag may be gone, but he's still coughing, still wheezing, still staring at me like his brain is lagging behind his body in the whole waking up situation.

'You know who I mean? Grandpa Joe. From *Charlie and the Chocolate Factory*?' I say, trying to bring him into the conversation. 'Lies around doing nothing for years, then suddenly – boom – one sniff of a Golden Ticket and he's up on his feet, laughing and joking, dancing around, doing cartwheels.'

I lean down so my face is right above his. Close enough to see his faded childhood chickenpox scars, and the dirt clogging his pores. Close enough to kiss him, if I wanted.

'Cartwheels,' I say, and I can feel the bile rising at the back of my throat at the thought of it. 'Can you believe that? There's Mr and Mrs Bucket, piss-poor, living in a hovel, working their fingers to the bone to keep a roof over everyone's head. Poor Charlie, not a penny to his name. Picked on at school for having holes in his shoes, and smelling of damp and BO. Because kids sweat, you know? They do. It's normal. Girls, too.'

The old bastard is still coughing in my face. Still gasping. His breath is like sour milk, his eyes, the saucers.

I hate him. Despise him. For what he did to Charlie. For everything he put them all through.

'And there you are, Grandpa Joe, fit and well, but hiding that fact. Lying to everyone.' I shout it at him. Scream it in his face. 'To your own *family*! You're a monster. You're a *disgrace*!'

He tries to sit up. I press a finger to his forehead, forcing him back down. He's weak. Or back pretending to be, at least.

I search his face, hoping to see some sign of contrition there. Some hangdog look of apology. But all I see is fear, and confusion. He has no idea what I'm talking about.

I blink. Once. Twice. Slowly.

What was I talking about?

I shut my eyes. Control my breathing.

Charlie.

No, not Charlie.

Paper wings.

A drawer.

'Hollie,' I mumble, and her name brings a smile to my lips.

I open my eyes. The old guy isn't smiling. Not by a long shot.

'Me and you are going to have a talk about Hollie.'

FOURTEEN

ELIZABETH

I'm propped up in bed, notebook in my lap, phone beside it, trying to make a plan to get my daughter back.

The notebook page is blank. I have no idea what to do.

The phone's screen is dark, but I can still see the picture of Hollie on that couch, like it's burned into the glass. When I saw the image, I swear I could actually feel her fear, like it was my own. It hasn't left me and sits on my chest like a weight. Like a cancer, chewing away at my insides.

What if they do something to her? What if I never see her again?

So many questions and *what ifs*, I feel like my head is going to explode with them.

There have been no more messages. No calls. Nothing. I've tried to contact them a dozen more times, but each call is cut off, and each increasingly desperate text remains unanswered.

My legs are restless below the covers. They're urging me to move, to get up, to go looking, but I have no idea where to start, and running around without a plan isn't going to do Hollie any good.

I need to think.

And I really need Sasha to come through with something.

I slide the pen from the spiral of metal that holds the note-book together, click the button on the bottom, then bring the point towards the page, willing something clever to appear.

The point rests against the paper, not moving.

'Come on,' I whisper, pleading with my brain to give me something. Anything. Some starting point I can work from. Some clue that will point me in the right direction. 'Come on, please.'

'You say something?'

Clive appears in the doorway, looking like he's in the grip of a full-scale rabies infection. He brings the toothbrush back to his teeth and scrubs at them, churning up more of the foamy white residue.

Despite there being nothing written in the notebook, I flip it closed in panic. His eyes dart to it, but he says nothing, just keeps brushing his teeth in the doorway.

'Sorry. Thinking out loud. I'm just making a list of things I need to do tomorrow,' I tell him, the lies coming as easily as ever. 'Busy day.'

He starts to reply, but there's too much toothpaste. He holds a finger up, then retreats to the bathroom. I hear him spitting and rinsing, then he reappears again, wiping his face on a hand towel.

'Sorry. So, what? You're not going to be around?'

I shake my head. 'Why?'

He tosses the towel back in the direction of the bathroom, pumps a fist like he's scored some impressive victory, then he crosses to the bed and sits his phone on the charging pad. A little *ta-daa* sound announces that charging has begun.

'No, I just thought we could have done something,' he says, pulling his pyjama top over his head to reveal his pale, blotchy torso. 'Breakfast. Lunch. Whatever.'

I wince, like I'm disappointed. 'Sorry,' I say, though I stop short of offering any explanation for why I can't.

What would I even say? I don't have a job or a social life. Clive has had the same cleaner come in twice a week since long before we met – a sixty-year-old Polish woman called Halina, who fusses over him like she's his mum.

When Hollie and I moved in, I offered to take over all the housework, but Clive couldn't bring himself to tell Halina that her services were no longer required.

And so, I was left with just one duty – to be a mother. To keep my daughter safe.

Even that, I've failed at.

He removes his pyjama bottoms, so he's standing there, naked and unabashed. I reach over and click off the bedside lamp beside me, plunging the room into merciful darkness.

'When are you getting Hollie back?' he asks.

Maybe it's just his voice coming at me out of the dark, or maybe there's something in the inflection, but the question seems off. Wrong, somehow.

'I'm... I'm not sure yet,' I admit.

It's probably the only true thing I've said to him all night.

All relationship, maybe.

He's shivering slightly when he gets into bed and wriggles himself up beside me to steal some of my warmth. His closeness makes the fine hairs on the back of my neck stand up, and though I try to stop it, I feel my body going rigid.

Not tonight. Please, God, not tonight.

Most nights, as long as I know Hollie is asleep, I can get through it. I can convincingly make myself seem like a willing participant, in fact, while I mentally run through my times tables, or imagine all the worse places I could be.

All the worse things I could be doing.

There's no way I could deal with that tonight, though.

He's so close I can smell the sour musk of his sweat. He's

tried to mask it for once with one of the many colognes I've bought him over the past year or so, in the hope he'll take the hint. The scent is mixing with his body odour, though, not masking it. The sum of their parts is sickly and cloying, and I'm forced to swallow back a mouthful of saliva.

He yawns. It's big and exaggerated, like something from a cartoon.

'Right, well, good night, babe,' he says.

He grabs one of my breasts, makes a honking noise, then grins at me like he's just won a comedy award, before flopping around to face the other way.

'Good night,' I say, and though it's loud and clear to me, I'm pretty sure he misses the relief in my voice.

It doesn't take him long to fall asleep. He makes it a couple of pages through his *SAS Bravo Six* nonsense, or whatever it is he's reading on his Kindle this week, before I hear the familiar thud of the eReader slipping out of his hand and onto the floor.

I give it another few minutes until he starts snoring, then I ease back the covers and creep around to his side of the bed, notebook and pen in hand.

The pulsing white glow at the top of the screen that indicates the phone is charging draws me in, like the light of one of those ugly fish that live near the ocean floor.

I crouch beside it and let the floorboards and my breathing settle. Clive's eyes are closed, and his face is slack, one side of it squished up against his firm memory foam pillow.

His mouth hangs slightly open, his breaths rattling in through his nose, before making a soft popping sound when they hit the back of his throat.

If he has a guilty conscience about something, then he's not losing any sleep over it.

Slowly, carefully, I ease the phone up from its charging pad. It emits a sad-sounding bleep that almost makes me drop it in fright. I freeze, clutching the mobile to my chest to hide the glow of its now fully illuminated screen.

Clive's snoring stops. We're face to face, less than a foot apart. His eyelids flicker. If he opens them, he'll be staring straight at me. He'll catch me clutching his phone.

I hold my breath. The room is silent. Not a sound. Even the distant rumble of late-night traffic on cobbled streets fades away.

And then, from beneath the covers, the unpleasant *parp* of a fart. Clive mumbles something incomprehensible, then the bandsaw of his snoring fires up again, and I almost sob with relief.

I still daren't move too much, for fear that he'll hear me, and I don't want to take the phone to the living room in case he wakes up and sees it gone. So, I quickly tap in the PIN code he isn't aware that I know, dial the brightness down a notch or two, then tap through to his recent call history.

I'm almost disappointed when I see the name at the top.

Alan from Number 32.

It was a fairly short call – just under four minutes. Outbound, so Clive was the one who did the phoning.

It's just like he said. He was telling the truth.

In case I need it, I take a note of Alan's mobile number, scribbling it down in my pad.

I'm just scrawling the last digit when there's a gasp from the darkness. I press the phone against my chest again, my mind already racing to find excuses and explanations for what I'm doing, though it's struggling to settle on anything in any way convincing.

Clive's weight shifts. He grunts, then he flops over onto his back, one arm sticking out of the bed, palm upwards, so close that his fingers are almost touching me.

In a second or two, he's snoring again, even worse than

before. It was too close a call, though. I turn down the volume so the phone doesn't do the same *ta-daa* as before, and reconnect it to the charger.

Then, pressing myself against the wall so as not to brush against his hand, I fetch my own phone from the other side of the bed, and tiptoe out of the room. Still holding my breath.

FIFTEEN

ELIZABETH

Clive's drinks cabinet is always full, and tonight is no exception. It's been years since I've touched a drop, but tonight I'm almost tempted. I stand with the lid of the antique-style globe open, my eyes drinking in the bottles. He classes himself as 'a whisky man' though there are far more gin liqueurs and flavoured vodkas here than there are single malts.

I close the lid on my temptation. Not tonight. Maybe, when I get Hollie back, I can have a drink to celebrate. For now, though, she needs me sober. She needs me sharp.

She needs me, full stop.

I click on the lamp next to Clive's armchair, then sit in his spot, pulling my bare feet up beneath me on the smooth, cool leather. There's a charging cable plugged into the wall right by the chair, so I take a moment to plug in my phone, then place it on the walnut side table between Clive's coaster and the TV remote.

The screen lights up. A gap-toothed Hollie smiles out at me from the background. The picture is a few years old, taken just before I met Clive. She's still got a bit of baby-cheek chubbiness about her, but the grin is unmistakeably hers.

The screen goes dark, and Hollie's face is lost again when the mobile returns to standby mode.

I don't know how long I cry for, I just know that by the time I'm finished, the muscles in my chest and sides hurt from trying to contain the sound. The top page of my notebook is dotted with the spots of tears, slightly blurring the number I scribbled down back in the bedroom.

I write it out again, more neatly this time, before the ink can spread any further.

I underline it. Once. Twice. Three times. Each line is more determined than the one before, like I'm summoning my nerve, building myself up to...

To what? I still have no idea what to do.

The thoughts I've been fighting to keep at bay start snuffling around at the barricades.

Hollie crying.

Hollie hurting.

Hollie calling out my name.

'No!' I say out loud. It's a sharp reprimand, like I'm chastising a misbehaving puppy. 'No.'

I sit straighter in the chair, gripping the pen until my knuckles are white, focusing on the notepad, forcing those mental images away. I can't think about them. I won't. Think about that stuff, and I'll be a basket case, rocking back and forth in the corner.

And what good will that do anyone?

I flip the notebook to the next blank page, and draw a line down the middle, splitting it into two distinct halves.

On the left, at the top, I write the word 'Questions'. On the other side of the line, I write 'Answers'.

It already feels overly optimistic, but I stick with it.

I spend the next few minutes writing down all the questions I can think of. Who took Hollie? Why? Where is she now? Who might have motivation? Who can I trust?

The pen scratches across the paper, the usually neat loops and whorls of my handwriting becoming sloppy and messy in my rush.

I pause halfway down the page, my list of questions almost exhausted.

There's one more, though. It's the one question that could help answer all the others.

The question that has been going round and round in my head since I received that photo of Hollie, with the two-word message propped up on the dirty couch beside her.

I etch the question onto the page, pressing hard, the lines heavy.

What do they know?

After a moment's thought, I underline the first word.

Whoever took Hollie believes they know something about me. A secret. But I have a lot of secrets, so which one have they discovered?

The side of my hand sweeps across the page, slightly blurring the line that separates both sides. I scan down the list of questions, pen held ready to fill in any answers.

I draw a blank on almost all of them. There's only one I feel confident in answering. Next to the one about who I can trust, I write my sister's name.

Then, after a moment's consideration, I score it out, and write, 'Nobody'.

I'm doing a second run-through of the list in case there's anything else I can answer, when I hear it. The creak of the building's main door being opened. The heavy thud of it closing again.

I check the clock. It's almost two. It's possible that it's just one of the neighbours coming back from a Friday night on the town, but they're all older, and not exactly into the Edinburgh nightlife scene.

I sneak into the hall, and up to the front door of the flat, listening for any further signs of movement. Hearing nothing, and seeing nobody through the peephole, I undo the locks and step out onto the landing.

Part of me – some desperate, pathetic part that still clings to the idea that Hollie simply ran away – half expects to see my daughter plodding up the stairs, cold and tired, but safe. Home.

There's no sound in the stairwell, though. No padding footsteps. No sign of movement. Nothing.

The motion sensor picks me up as I step away from the door, blinking on the wall-mounted lights. The old energy-saving bulbs take a while to warm up, and their low, orange-hued glow barely makes a dent in the darkness.

The metal railing is cold to the touch as I lean over and peer down through the gap in the stairwell. The lights haven't come on down there, meaning they haven't detected any movement.

Somebody must have moved, though. The door didn't open and close itself.

Even as I'm thinking it, the light behind me turns off with a loud, mechanical click. A few seconds of standing still, it seems, is enough to convince the sensor that you no longer exist.

I wave an arm. The light returns. Downstairs remains cloaked in shadow.

A breeze blows up through the stairwell gap, and swirls past me, through the wide-open doorway of the flat.

Shivering beneath the flimsy fabric of my pyjamas, I head back inside and close the door.

And a moment later, I hear the *clunk* of the light turning off, and darkness rushes in to fill the space I left behind.

PART 2

SATURDAY

SIXTEEN

ELIZABETH

The light is like thumbs pressing down on my eyelids and draws a groan of pain from my dry lips.

I'm back in Clive's armchair, both legs folded beneath me, a blanket draped across my lap. With some effort, I'm able to open my eyes and focus on the clock.

The realisation that it's almost nine in the morning makes me blurt out something that could be an obscenity, but might not even be a word at all.

Oh God. I fell asleep. Guilt stabs at me. How could I have let myself fall asleep?

The blanket wasn't me, was it? I don't remember. I throw it aside and rise to my feet, already calling out Clive's name.

My legs are too numb to support me, and I cry out in fright as I fall, face-first, to the floor. Between the shout and the clatter, Clive should have come running, but there isn't a sound from elsewhere in the flat.

I shake my legs just enough to stir some life back into them, then get up and hobble through to the bedroom.

Empty. Clive isn't here.

A quick check of the other rooms reveals he isn't anywhere

in the flat. He's gone. It's Saturday morning. Where the hell would he be?

Was he angry at me sleeping through in the living room? If he was, would he have covered me with the blanket?

A terrible thought slowly begins to occur to me.

The notebook. Where is the notebook?

If he's seen it, if he's read what I've written, then he knows. He knows that Hollie is missing. He knows that someone has taken her.

The muscles of my legs feel like they're burning as I race back along the hallway to the living room. My phone is still charging on the side table, but the notebook? Where is the notebook?

'Oh, God. Oh, God, no!' I cry, hysteria expanding my chest, squeezing out all the air.

He's found the notebook. He knows. He knows everything.

I grab my phone. Maybe I can still call him. Maybe I can explain and stop him doing anything stupid like going to the police.

I'm about to dial his number when I catch sight of the spiral of metal, the pen tucked back inside it. The notebook has slipped down the side of the armchair, wedged between the cushion and the arm. The pages have been creased beneath my weight, and the one I wrote my questions on has torn away from the binding at the bottom, but I don't care.

He hasn't seen it. He doesn't know. I can still fix everything.

I check the phone for any more messages from whoever took Hollie, but instead find an email at the top of my inbox. It's from Sasha. The subject line is blank, and all that's written in the message body are the words, 'You're welcome'.

There are several attachments. The first few just seem to be random files grabbed from the school server. There are employment records, résumés, timetables, staff appraisals, and financial statements for the last ten school years.

None of it, as far as I can see, tells me anything.

And then, I find it. The last attachment on the list.

A video clip.

I lower myself back onto Clive's armchair and tap the little triangle to make the footage start playing.

It's silent, even after I crank the volume, and I realise there's no sound on the clip. It's security camera footage from the hall the night before. A timecode at the bottom tells me it was taken near the end of the disco, right before home time.

Boys are running around, chasing one another with plastic weapons, costume capes billowing out behind them.

Girls hang together in various social groups, dancing in unison like they're performing for TikTok, or chatting in tight little huddles.

The clip lasts less than twenty seconds. I have no idea what I'm meant to be looking at.

I start it again, and this time I scan the screen for any sign of Hollie. It takes me a few seconds, but I finally spot what I think might be her up the back of the hall, picked out in the swooping oval of a disco spotlight.

I pinch and zoom in on that part of the video. The image expands, but the blurriness increases, too.

For a system that cost us so much money, the quality is abysmal.

I turn up the brightness and hit play again as soon as I reach the end of the clip. This time, I'm watching right from the start.

Hollie and a boy from her class stand huddled together. They're doing something. It's hard to make out, and I have to play through the whole clip again before I realise what they're up to.

They're swapping costumes.

I was right. Last night, I knew there was no way Hollie could get past me dressed as a giant butterfly.

And she didn't.

Because she wasn't.

She was dressed as Darth Vader.

But why? And who is the kid she swapped with? Two more questions to add to the list. I don't know the answer to either of them.

But I know someone who might.

SEVENTEEN

ELIZABETH

I'm out of breath when I reach the front door, the short hill on the way here having really taken it out of me. My muscles ache, like I've been working out – a hangover from sleeping awkwardly in the chair, no doubt.

Even if I didn't know which was the right building, the Roman numerals on the door would give it away. Everyone else on the street has normal, regular old numbers, but not this house.

Not her.

And it is a house, too. It's one of the few on the street that was never converted into flats. It's a sprawling, three-storey Georgian building in one of the posher parts of Edinburgh's West End, where the streets are cobbled, and the money, for the most part, is old.

I suppose, if you've got the sort of cash to own a house this size in Stockbridge, you can put whatever the hell you like on your front door.

I press the buzzer, then rattle the ornate door knocker that's shaped like some sort of bird's head. There's no noise from within. I noticed on the way over that their Bentley's not parked out front, either.

Please, be in.

I try again, clattering the door knocker. It echoes along the curve of the road like a burst of gunfire.

I'm about to try shouting in the letterbox when I hear an exclamation of, 'Good *grief!*' from within, and footsteps hurrying closer.

Locks are unfastened – several of them – and when the door is finally opened, I can only just see her through the gap allowed by a thick, heavy security chain that's drawn tight between the door and the frame.

Mabel Walker – the Uberbitch – stares at me. This isn't unusual, but for once, it's not with contempt. She's shocked to see me. Then again, I slung on yesterday's clothes, and did nothing to make myself in any way presentable. Both these concepts, I'd imagine, are completely alien to her.

'Elizabeth?' It takes her a moment to say my name, like she has to rifle through some internal Filofax to find it. She has an external Filofax, too, even though I had assumed they'd been discontinued years ago. Who the hell uses a Filofax these days?

Still, I'm glad she does. It's the reason I'm here. Much as it pains me to be coming to her for help.

She's wrapped in a plush, dark green dressing gown. There's a slight redness to her cheeks, and her hair is less sculpted than usual, suggesting she's been working out. Yoga, or Pilates, or some such nonsense, if I had to guess.

'What is it?' she asks. There's a note of caution in it, like my sweating, wild-eyed appearance is making her nervous. 'What do you want?'

'Darth Vader,' I say. It comes out as a wheeze. I grab my side and press in to try and stop the stitch that's building.

She blinks. 'Excuse me?'

'Darth Vader,' I repeat. 'Who was Darth Vader?'

It's possible that she frowns, but all the Botox makes it hard to tell. 'What is a *Darth Vader*?' she asks, and while she's not yet back in full-on sneering mode, she's headed in the right direction.

'Seriously, Mabel?' I say through a strained series of breaths. 'Darth Vader. From Star Wars. From the Star Wars films.'

She looks affronted. 'Is that the outer space thing? How would I know who he is? Is this some sort of joke?' Her eyes narrow, scrutinising me. 'Are you on drugs? Is that what this is?'

'For fu—' I take out my phone, open a browser, and search Google Images for a picture of the character. He's adopting his classic pointing-at-the-camera pose. I'm sure my late husband, Kenny, had the same picture in his bedroom way back when we first met.

I turn the phone so the Uberbitch can see it. She tilts her head back and peers at it along the length of her nose.

'Is it William Shatner?' she guesses.

'What?'

'He was in that, wasn't he? Or is that the other one, with the pointy-eared chap and the Chinaman?'

Mabel is lucky she kept that chain fastened. I squeeze my phone so hard it feels like the glass is going to shatter.

'Last night. At the disco,' I explain, forcing the words through gritted teeth. 'There was a kid dressed up as Darth Vader.'

'Oh. Right.'

Mabel stares blankly back at me, but I get the sense that something is going on beneath the surface. If there is, though, she's keeping it to herself.

'And?'

'And I need to know who it was.'

She considers me carefully. 'Why?'

I'm prepared for the question. 'I think Hollie and him got their jackets mixed up. I want to get them swapped back.'

'Can't it wait until Monday?'

I bite my tongue. Force a smile. 'I'd rather get it sorted today. Do you know who it was?'

She sighs, and I get the impression she's not about to tell me. But then, her eyes start flitting left and right, as if she's spooling back through her memories of the night before, when she was sitting at the table, taking tickets.

'Daniella Taylor,' she eventually announces.

I shake my head. 'No, it was a boy.'

Mabel tuts and rolls her eyes. 'His mother is Daniella Taylor. He's Conrad. You'll have her number, I'm sure.'

I am forced to admit that I don't. For some reason, this makes her look at me like I'm some sort of vermin. Even more than usual.

'Well, I'm afraid I can't give it out. GDPR regulations. Data handling. That sort of thing. You understand.'

She smiles, and before I can say anything more, the door closes in my face.

Through sheer force of habit, I turn away, not wanting to stand up to her, or to cause a scene.

As I do, I clock a figure standing at a window on the other side of the road. It's Weird Alan. He's wearing a shirt that's fully open at the front, showing the greying hair of his chest, and the curve of his belly button.

He's watching me, and though it's impossible to read his face from this far away, I'm suddenly hit by the feeling that he's judging me like some God on high.

I stare up at him, then come to a decision. Turning to the door, I hold my finger on the buzzer until I hear Mabel come rushing back along her grand hallway.

'What on earth is it now?' she demands, before glancing back over her shoulder. 'I'm in the middle of something.'

'I'm sorry. I just...' I pull together a smile. It's not much of one, but it's the best I can do under the circumstances. 'Hollie really wants her jacket back.'

I take a breath. I'm not good at confrontation. I'm not that sister. But I try, just this once, to channel my inner Sasha.

'And I'm afraid I'm going to need you to give me the address.'

EIGHTEEN

ELIZABETH

Daniella Taylor's flat is down a side street just off Stockbridge High Street, where the smell of artisan bakeries and second-hand bookshops lingers in the air.

It's part of a modern conversion of an old warehouse, or other industrial building, and though there are modern touches to the outside, like the blue doors and elegant balcony railings, it all feels sympathetic to the original architecture.

The flats form three sides of a cobbled courtyard that boasts one of those rarest of things – a decent number of parking spaces in Edinburgh city centre. They're all marked up as 'Permit Holders Only', but time is against me, and I'm prepared to take the fine.

I park as close as I can to flat 33, then take the stairs two at a time, ignoring the way my legs try to slow me down and drag me back. There's no bird-headed knocker on this door, so I rap my knuckles against the glossy blue wood, which triggers a mad fit of barking from a dog somewhere inside.

Big, too, by the sounds of it.

I step back and wait when someone shouts from inside.

'One second.'

The dog keeps barking, but it fades, like it's being shut away. I glance up at the sky, feeling the faintest suggestion of warmth from the early November sun, then turn my attention back to the door just as it's pulled open.

I didn't recognise Daniella's name, but I've seen her at the school gates. She's one of the younger mums. Mid-to-late twenties, with a fresh, smooth look, like she's only recently been plucked off the vine. Her hair is dark, a little curly, and hangs loosely around her shoulders like she doesn't quite know what to do with it.

There's a moment of confusion when she sees me, but she covers it with a smile. It's radiant. On another day, in another life, I'd want nothing more than to kiss her.

'Oh. Hey. Um...' She doesn't know my name, and I don't tell her. 'Hi,' she concludes, trying to cover her embarrassment.

Behind her somewhere, the dog is still barking. I hear a boy of around Hollie's age shouting at it to shut up, then the rat-tat-tat of gunfire from a TV speaker.

'Daniella. Hi. Sorry to bother you,' I say, like I've known her for years. 'I'm Hollie's mum. From...' I glance past her into the house, trying to remember her son's name. Mabel mentioned it less than twenty minutes ago, but I'm drawing a blank. 'Primary 5.'

'From Conrad's class. Yeah. Course,' she says.

Conrad. That's it.

'Yes. From Conrad's class. Is, uh, is he here?'

Her smile fades. Her body language shifts into something more defensive, one hand leaning on the door frame, like she's getting ready to block my path.

'Why?' she asks, all business. 'What's this about?'

I recognise the protective mother instinct only too well. There's no way she's letting me near her son. Not without a damn good reason.

So, I give her one. I've got no other choice.

'It's my daughter. It's Hollie,' I say. I falter, just for a beat, wondering if this is a terrible decision, but then push on through. 'She's missing.'

'Missing?' Daniella's eyes widen. 'What do you mean? Like... *missing* missing?'

'We haven't seen her since the disco. We're worried sick. The police are out looking, but I can't just sit around waiting and hope they find her. I'm climbing the walls.'

She's nodding before I'm even half finished, already imagining herself in my shoes and reeling from the horror of it.

'Oh, God. Oh, no, that's... I'm so sorry. Do you want to...?' She lowers her arm and steps back, inviting me inside. 'Come in. Please. I doubt Conrad knows anything, but we can ask him.'

'Thank you. Thank you so much,' I gush.

Then, the barking of the dog grows louder as I step into Daniella's cramped, cluttered apartment, and close the door behind me.

NINETEEN
ELIZABETH

Daniella's flat is nothing like Clive's, and a million miles away from Mabel's palatial home. The front door opens straight onto a cramped and cluttered living area where everything, through necessity, seems to double as something else.

A folded pile of clothes is stacked on an armchair. A couple of dresses are hung from the curtain rail. The corner of a crumpled sheet pokes out from the base of the sofa like the tip of a tongue, suggesting it sees regular use as a fold-out bed.

That last one makes sense, given that I can only see three doors leading off from this room. The dog is still barking behind one, the sizeable outline of it visible through the bottom half of the frosted-glass window.

There are no windows in the other doors, but I'm guessing they lead to a bathroom and the one and only bedroom. Conrad's, I bet. Of course Daniella would take the sofa bed. It's what I would do.

She seems nice. If things were different – if I was different – we could have been friends, I think. More, maybe.

A thought occurs to me then. A slow, creeping, horrible thought that fills me with dread.

'Has, uh, has anyone been to ask you about this already?' I ask, keeping my voice as level as I can.

Daniella shakes her head, frowning a little. 'The police?'

'Anyone?'

'No,' she says. 'No, just you.'

I relax. For now.

The boy sits, half swallowed by a beanbag, on a small square of available floor, less than two feet from the TV. He's leaning left and right, thumbs working away at a game controller as, on screen, he sprays death at a man dressed as a teddy bear.

'Hey, Con. Can you pause that?' Daniella asks. It's tentative, like she's worried he won't take the news well.

'It's a Battle Royale,' he says, not so much as glancing back at her.

Daniella smiles at me. It's a small, shy, sheepish thing, that makes me want to hug her. I don't, of course.

'No, I know, sweetheart, but it's important.'

'I'm down to the top twenty!'

His reply is a bark of indignation, like that should be the end of the matter. From the kitchen, the dog howls in agreement. I wish she'd shut it up.

'Con, please,' Daniella says, and for the first time, there's a note of authority in her tone. 'It's really important, OK? You can go back to your game in a minute.'

He ejects a cry of bitter frustration, stabs a thumb on a button until a menu appears on screen, then tosses the controller to the floor. His arms fold tightly across his chest, and he shoots me a look that could stop a clock.

Maybe I wouldn't take the pull-out bed, after all.

'Hi, Conrad,' I say, offering the horrible little toad my warmest, most grateful smile. 'Sorry to interrupt your game. Top twenty? That's impressive.'

Is it? I have no idea. He doesn't seem displeased by the

comment, although I have a long way to go before I've won him over.

Daniella picks up the bundle of clothes from the chair, looks around for somewhere to put them, then reluctantly settles for the floor. She smiles and gestures for me to take the seat, and only then seems to realise that the dog is still going bananas in the kitchen.

'Sorry, one sec,' she says, then she heads to the kitchen.

A moment later, the animal falls silent, and she returns to the couch, patting the next cushion over for Conrad to come and join her.

'Gave him a dog chew,' she says, tilting her head towards the kitchen. 'It'll keep him quiet for a bit.'

Conrad makes a performance of dragging himself up out of the beanbag and onto the couch beside his mum. He's still not happy about being forced to leave his game, and he's making damn sure we both know it.

'Hi, Conrad,' I say again. My tone is soft and soothing. I'm treading on eggshells. 'Do you know who I am?'

He looks me over, like he's trying to place me. Something flits across his face. His fingers tangle together.

He nods, but I go ahead and tell him anyway.

'I'm Hollie's mum. Hollie Jones. From your class?'

He nods again. I see his throat clenching as he swallows. I don't know him well enough to pick up on all his body language, but to an outside observer, he seems nervous.

'Don't worry, I don't think you're in any trouble,' I tell him. I have no idea if he thought he was, but it's good to at least put the thought in his head that he might be. 'I just want to ask you a couple of questions about Hollie. Is that OK?'

Daniella looks down at him. He's not a tall lad, and the top of his head barely comes up to her shoulder.

'You can help with that, can't you, sweetheart?' she says.

He nods in reply. It's slow and tentative. If I'm going to get anything out of him, I'll need to warm him up.

'Great,' I say, still urging him along with a smile. 'It's about last night. At the disco. I was on the snack table, remember? You bought... juice?'

Another nod.

'And Monster Munch.'

'Monster Munch. Yes. That was it, I knew there was something else,' I say, tapping myself playfully on the side of the head. 'Did you enjoy them?'

He shrugs, non-committal. In fairness to him, the PTA has had that box of Monster Munch kicking around for about three years. They're probably well past their sell-by date.

'Well, it was nice to see you there, anyway. I liked your costume. Darth Vader. You like Star Wars?'

He shrugs again, like he doesn't want to give too much away. Or maybe he just senses what I'm doing and knows what I'm building up to. His mum gives him a playful nudge with her elbow.

'What are you talking about? We love Star Wars, don't we?'

He looks down at his fidgeting fingers and shrugs again.

I've done all the softening I have time for, so I lean forwards a little, clasping my hands between my knees, and try to catch his eye.

'Do you know why I'm here, Conrad?'

There's no response this time. No shrug. No nod. No nothing.

'You and Hollie swapped costumes last night, didn't you? In the hall. You gave her your mask and your cape.'

'What?' Daniella blinks in surprise, then looks down at her son. 'You said you left them in class.'

When he fails to respond again, she leans away from him, so she's looking at his face rather than the top of his head.

'Con?'

'It's fine, Conrad. Nobody's angry with you,' I assure him. 'I don't care about the costume. I just want to know why you and Hollie swapped them. That's all.'

'Tell her,' Daniella urges. 'It's important.'

He glances up at her, then at me, then looks back at his hands.

His reply, when it comes, is so quiet I almost miss it.

'Dunno.'

'You don't know?'

Another shrug and shake of the head is all I get.

'Was it your idea, or was it Hollie's?'

A pause, then: 'Can't remember.'

'Well, *think*!' I spit the words at him, making him jump, then flash a smile of apology at both him and his mum. 'Sorry. Sorry, that was...'

I take a breath, composing myself. Daniella slips an arm around her son's narrow shoulders.

'Can you try and remember for me, Conrad?' I ask, forcing my voice back onto an even keel. 'It's really important. Were you the one who suggested swapping costumes, or was it Hollie?'

His tongue shifts around inside his mouth, like he's physically wrestling with his response.

'Hollie's,' he eventually mutters. 'It was Hollie's idea.'

I grip my knees, trying to keep my face as neutral as possible. It's not the news I'd been hoping to hear. I wanted him to tell me it was his idea, that it was all some stupid prank he'd cooked up for a bit of fun.

But, if Hollie suggested the swap, then it's possible that she deliberately planned to sneak past me. And all that does is open up more questions.

'Why?' I ask. Then, when he continues to look blankly back at me, I elaborate. 'Why did she want to swap costumes? Did she say?'

His fingers are writhing like worms now. He glances, just briefly, at his mum, then shakes his head.

'She didn't say why she wanted to swap? But you swapped anyway?' I press. 'Why would you just swap costumes if she didn't tell you why she wanted to do it?'

His head is lowered. He can't look at me. He shrugs again. 'Just a laugh.'

'A laugh?' I almost choke on the words. The pitch of my voice proves too much for the dog, and barking erupts from the kitchen again. It's just a few feet from where I'm sitting, and the racket is overwhelming.

'Sorry.' Daniella rises from the couch, her face a crumpled knot of embarrassment. 'I'll go give him another treat.'

Conrad looks up at her, watching her go. I wait for the door to close behind me, and for Daniella to start chastising the animal before I abruptly lean forwards, my voice a sharp whisper.

'Conrad, I need you to listen to me,' I tell him. 'I need to know exactly what happened last night. Everything Hollie said. I need you to tell me, because I found you, Conrad, do you see? I found you. I have a sister, Conrad. She's... not like me. And, if I found you, then she can find you, too. And you don't want her to find you, Conrad. Trust me, you don't.'

His eyes grow wetter and wider with every word I say, my words, and the urgency of them, draining all the colour from his face. He's scared. That's good. He needs to be. I don't feel great about it, but if he's scared, then he's listening. And if he listens, maybe I can keep him safe.

'But I can tell her not to come,' I continue. 'I can keep her away. Away from you... Away from your mum, Conrad. I can do that, but only if you tell me everything. I can only keep her away if there's nothing else for her to find out. So, will you help me, Conrad? Will you help me to keep you and your mum safe?'

Before he has a chance to reply, the kitchen door opens, and Daniella bustles back through. I can hear the hard scraping of the dog's teeth grinding against a bone.

'That should keep him busy for a while,' she announces, a little breathlessly. 'Sorry, he's all noise. Big softy, really, isn't he, Con?'

Conrad is still staring at me, eyes like saucers. I nod slowly, and he mirrors the movement.

'Now, where were we?' Daniella asks, sitting beside her son. She puts a hand on his leg and he grabs for it, holding it tight.

'We were just talking about how important it is that Conrad *really* has a think for me, weren't we?'

Conrad nods again. His mum gives his leg a squeeze.

'Well, Con?' she urges. 'Anything you can tell Hollie's mum?'

His mouth flops open. He swallows. I'm worried I've rendered him mute.

But then, a croak. A word.

No, not even that.

Two letters.

'DJ,' he says.

Daniella looks confused. 'DJ?'

Conrad swallows again, then clears his throat. This time, he forces out a full sentence.

'The DJ told her to swap costumes.' He flinches, like he's worried someone's going to shout at him. 'And he told her not to tell anyone.'

TWENTY

ELIZABETH

'I'm sorry we couldn't be of more help.' Daniella stands just outside the front door of her flat, hands tucked in the pockets of her jeans, her oversized checked shirt billowing, ever so slightly, in the breeze. 'Maybe it'll be helpful for the police, though? The stuff about the DJ?'

I smile, tight-lipped. 'I'm sure it will. Can you do me a favour, though?'

'Of course.'

'We're trying to keep this as quiet as possible. I, um, the police and I, we don't want it becoming public knowledge yet.'

Her eyebrows – gloriously dark and unsculpted things – twitch downwards, like this strikes her as strange, but she quickly nods. 'Of course. I won't say a word.' A thought occurs to her. 'Oh! But wait a sec.'

She turns and darts back into the flat. By the sounds of things, Conrad is already back at his game. Clearly, my outburst didn't traumatise him too much.

It's only been a few seconds since Daniella retreated inside, but I'm already growing impatient, desperate to get moving. I make the most of the time by opening up the internet app on my phone and searching for the DJ.

His decks were tucked right in the corner, out of sight of the camera. Whatever he said to her, there'll be no footage of it on the recording.

What was he called again? I close my eyes, trying to summon up the memory. *Cheesy* something? *Someone's Cheesy Something.* What was his name? Duncan? David?

Damn it.

I type in 'Cheesy DJ' and am presented with several hundred thousand search results. Way too many.

'Cheesy disco DJ Edinburgh' narrows it down, but there are still a lot of results in the list. I'm scrolling through them when Daniella returns with something in her hands.

The sight of it almost makes me drop my phone.

'Conrad came home with this. I'm guessing it's part of Hollie's costume?'

The silver balls bobble around on the end of the springs attached to the smooth curve of the headband. Her butterfly antennae.

Last night, before our falling-out, I put them on to make her laugh, and though she'd rolled her eyes a bit, she'd soon started giggling when I jerked my head around, making them jiggle and knock together.

The sight of them now – this tangible connection to her – is like a knife to the heart.

'They were in Conrad's bag. He said Hollie had let him borrow them. I didn't know they'd swapped costumes, though.'

I reach a hand out for them, fingers trembling. When I take them, I swear I can still feel my daughter's warmth on the headband.

'Thank you,' I mumble, my throat narrowing.

I want to turn away. Run away. Hide my grief and my shame.

But she's tried to help me. I owe her the same courtesy.

'Um, listen, someone else might come,' I tell her. 'Not the police. My sister. She's going to be looking, too. I've told her not to, but, well, it's hard to make her listen. I'm going to pass on what Conrad told me, so there's no reason for her to come here. But, if she does...'

I hesitate, scared of all the possibilities for what could happen.

'Just, tell her what you told me. Tell her the truth. Whatever you do, just tell her the truth.'

There's a look on Daniella's face that I can't quite identify. Her mouth is fixed in a half-smile, but the rest of her expression is tipping over into concern.

She's been so helpful, but she's looking at me now like she's wishing she hadn't opened the door.

'Like I say, you probably won't see her,' I add, trying to offer as much reassurance as possible. 'But, if you do, please, for everyone's sake, just be honest.'

* * *

I can feel Daniella watching me from her window as I make my way to the car. I slide in behind the steering wheel, and sit the antennae on the passenger seat, already back scrolling through my phone.

I find the name down near the bottom of the list. *Darren's Cheesy Tunes*. There's an address for an industrial estate just this side of Leith, and a two-point-three-star rating. Other than that, there's not a lot of information beyond a couple of slightly blurry photos of his decks and lights.

His company slogan is emblazoned across both photos – 'Easy Cheesy!' – in Comic Sans font that's the *precise* wrong colour to make it stand out from the backgrounds.

It's not much to go on, but it's something. I start the engine, but before I can pull away, my eyes are drawn back to the silver bobbles of Hollie's antennae. The sight of them, the thought of them, the memory of her wearing them, makes my breath go short and my head go light.

She must be so scared. So very, very afraid.

I want to scream and rage, but I can't afford to. Not now. Not yet. I grab the headband and open the glove compartment, but Mr Floppsity is in there, all squashed up, staring accusingly back at me.

'Shut up,' I hiss, slamming the glove box closed.

I throw open the door and try to jump out of the car, but the seat belt pulls tight, dragging me back. It takes a bit of fumbling before I'm free. Clutching the antennae, I rush around to the back of the car, feel for the button to open the boot, then toss the headband inside, out of sight before the boot lid has even finished rising.

I slam it back down again, and stand there, my hands pressed against the smooth metal, my breath coming in fits and starts.

Slowly, as my heart rate begins to settle, something starts to niggle away at me. A worm in my brain, wriggling and tunnelling, alerting me to something.

I slip a hand under the rim of the car's boot and slide my fingers back and forth until they find the button.

I press it.

There's a clunk as the locking mechanism disengages.

I let the boot lid rise just far enough before I put a hand on it to stop it lifting the rest of the way.

Just enough for me to see.

Just enough for me to understand.

A shape lies curled up on the floor of the boot, wrapped in black bags and heavily taped. It's a large shape. Squeezing it in there must have taken quite some effort.

A note is stuck to the top of it. I recognise the sharp, jagged spikes and erratic strokes of the handwriting.

Sasha.

Soz. Didn't have time to deal with it all. Will sort later. Xxx

I read the note again, then a third time, as if I'll find a proper explanation hidden in there. I don't, of course. There aren't enough lines to read between.

Instead, I turn my attention away from the note again, and take in the plastic-wrapped shape it's attached to.

The shape of the dead man in the boot of my car.

TWENTY-ONE

ELIZABETH

I barely remember the drive out to the industrial estate, thanks in part to the fact that the dead body of a human being lies folded up just a few feet behind me. It's amazing how that sort of thing can really demand your focus.

I can't believe she's done this to me. She was supposed to be helping me, but instead I'm carting around the corpse of a man I...

Not murdered. I stop myself even thinking the word. I didn't murder him. He fell. It was an accident, that was all.

Not like before. Nothing like before.

I'm still in a daze when I eventually pull onto Tennant Street and am confronted by a row of single-storey brick-built buildings with matching roll-up doors and sprays of colourful graffiti.

Back in Stockbridge, there's a lovely mural painted in an underpass, all complimentary cool blues and greens. It's art, unlike the obscenities and tags daubed on the walls and corrugated shutters here.

The rumbling of my stomach tells me it's after lunchtime, and the clock on the dash confirms it.

2:27 *PM.*

How is it so late already? The Saturday traffic was at its usual near-standstill coming out of town, but still. I'm moving too slowly. This is taking far too long.

I crawl along the street until I find a door with the home-made logo for *Darren's Cheesy Tunes* fixed to the wall above it and pull the car in at the kerb.

I check my phone and then try calling the number that sent me the photo of Hollie. As with all the other times, I hear only the low, solemn tone of a failed call.

According to my call history, I've now tried the number forty-seven times. I make it a round fifty, before giving up.

Why won't they answer? Why won't they communicate?

Is she already dead? Is that it? Or are they dragging this out to make me suffer?

I feel myself tearing up at the thought that I might be too late to save her but swallow it back down. All I can do is keep searching.

For an industrial estate on a Saturday afternoon, Tennant Street is fairly quiet. A quick glance at the signs above the doors on either side of Darren's confirms why. Both units are empty.

In fact, aside from a bouncy castle hire place I passed on the way in, and a run-down photography studio offering 'Buy Three Headshot's, Get One Free!!!' across the road, complete with an unnecessary apostrophe, the entire estate seems deserted.

The paint on the front door of Darren's building is bubbled and peeling. The lock is a sliding steel bolt with a heavy padlock fastening it in place.

There's a short, wide window at head height just to the right of the door, but the glass is thick with grime inside and out, and only further enhances the darkness the whole place seems draped in.

A few steps further along is his roll-up metal door. A warning not to park in front of it is stencilled on in yellow paint, but time has faded it, and the spray-painted outline of an enormous cock and balls has obscured much of the rest.

I grip the handle and try to lift it, but the door doesn't budge. I shake it and bang my fists against the metal. The sound booms like thunder around the inside, then fades, once more, into silence.

Empty. He's not here.

Is Hollie in there, though? Is he holding her inside? I hammer on the roll-up door again and shout her name. Tell her I'm here, and that she's going to be OK.

The only reply is a low rumbling echo fading back into silence.

The beam of my phone's torch barely makes a dent in the dark when I shine it through the window. I have to stretch on my tiptoes and practically press my face against the glass to see inside.

From what I can tell, the space is mostly empty. There's no couch, and the walls don't match those in the photo I was sent.

Wherever she is, wherever he's put her, it's not here.

I return to the front door, and to the sign above it. There's no phone number. There wasn't one on Google, either. What kind of way is that to run a business? How does he expect people to—?

The answer, I realise, is staring me in the face. Just below the words *Darren's Cheesy Tunes* is a logo so familiar that I initially failed to notice it.

Facebook. He must be on Facebook.

I have been careful to steer away from social media, so I don't have an account. Still, I'm able to find the DJ's Facebook page fairly quickly. A quick scan of his timeline shows some photos from the school disco last night.

Before that, though, up at the top, is a picture of him, thin-haired and grinning, as he sets up his equipment in what looks like a tent. It was uploaded a few hours ago, but nobody has interacted with the post. No shares, no likes, no comments. Nothing.

Above the photo, he's written a short message. It's littered with typos, and the only punctuation he seems aware of is the exclamation mark.

'Seting up for the Musselburgh Galla Day!!' it reads. He's managed to spell Musselburgh right but overshot the mark with the number of Ls in galla. 'Come allong and party on down with sum top Cheesy Tunes!!! LUVVIT!!!'

Musselburgh is only a few miles away. Twenty minutes in the car, maybe less if the traffic lights are in my favour. I do a search and find the address. The gala day is taking place on a sports field just to the south of the town. It's not a place I've ever been before, but I'll find it.

I'll find him.

And then, I'm going to find my daughter.

TWENTY-TWO

ELIZABETH

Something inside me dies when I see the mass of cars parked around the edges of the playing field and jamming the car park outside.

Several other parts of me join it when a young policeman steps out in front of me, one hand raised for me to stop.

I am suddenly, overwhelmingly aware of a smell inside the car. I'm not convinced that I'm not imagining it, since I'm only just noticing it now, but I swear I can smell the dead body rotting away in the boot.

When I bring the car to a stop, the policeman walks around to the driver's side. He expects me to lower the window, but if I do that, he'll smell the body. I'm sure of it. He'll smell it, then he'll find it, then everything will be over.

I'll never see Hollie again. They'll take her away from me.

They'll take her back.

He makes a winding motion with a finger. There's nothing I can do but open the window a crack.

'Sorry, madam, car park's full,' he tells me, like I couldn't have worked that one out for myself.

He's in his late thirties, early forties, I guess, and stands with his cap on and his thumbs tucked into a stab-proof vest that feels a bit much for a gala day. Even in Musselburgh.

'Sorry, yes. I see that. But I'm only going to be a minute,' I tell him.

'Oh. Right. I see. I didn't realise. Here, then, I'll direct you to one of the many available *I'm only going to be a minute* spaces.' He tips his cap back a little, then hooks his thumb on his vest again. 'That was a joke, ma'am.'

'Yes. I got that,' I say.

'No such spaces exist.'

'No.' I force a smile, pretending that I find him funny.

I look past him, to the field filled with wandering adults and running kids. There's a lot of activity happening around the base of what I assume is going to be a bonfire. It's a big stack of wood, with an effigy at the top that must be Guy Fawkes.

I'd wondered why the hell anyone would be throwing a gala day in Scotland in November, but now it makes a bit more sense. The community must be combining it with its annual fireworks display. There's probably not enough in the coffers to make them two separate events.

Whatever the reason, it doesn't matter. I can see the big marquee, the familiar strains of Rick Astley's 'Never Gonna Give You Up' belting out of it.

'I just... I need to find my daughter,' I tell him. It's not the full truth, but it's most of the way there.

The genuine emotion behind it must help me sell it, because he looks away for a moment, sighs, then points over to where his brightly marked police car is parked. It faces directly on to the road I've just driven up, like he's hoping to make a quick exit.

'You can pull in in front of me, but not for long,' he concedes, with a heavy stress on that second part. 'Just watch and don't scrape the concrete bollards at the side. They're heavy buggers.'

'Thank you, thank you,' I gush, crunching the car into gear.

He points at me. 'Fifteen minutes,' he says, then, he tucks his thumbs back into his vest and backs away, giving me space to turn.

The space is tight, and the manoeuvre is tricky. The fact that he stands watching me doesn't make it any easier. I half expect him to shout at me to stop, then go running over to the boot because he's spotted an arm or a leg that I've accidentally left dangling out.

Instead, when I eventually pull up nose to nose with his car, blocking it in, he taps at his watch, sniffs, then turns and saunters off in search of, if not trouble, then at least someone else to annoy.

I wait until he's too far away to strike up another conversation, then get out of the car, making sure that I lock it behind me. The police officer nods at me as I go scurrying up to the temporary fence that has been erected around the field, hundreds of metal frames held in place by breeze blocks.

On the other side of it, squealing kids jump around on a bouncy castle, go skidding along oily slides, and try their hands at all sorts of side stalls and games. The smell of frying onions hangs like a cloud in the air. Empty drinks cans and sauce-stained paper napkins litter the grass.

I'm planning on waiting until the police officer's back is turned, then hopping over the fence. He clocks what I'm doing, though, points over to the entrance, then stands with his arms folded, watching me until I make my way around to it.

The woman sitting at the table by the front gate initially seems reluctant to tear her eyes from the crime novel she's reading, but when she finally sets it down, she offers a big beamer of a smile as compensation.

'Sorry. Was at a good bit. A detective constable nearly got hit by a train.'

'Right,' I say. 'How much?'

'Three pounds, love,' she tells me.

I ask her if she takes cards.

She tells me she doesn't.

'I don't have my purse,' I say, only realising this as I speak the words. 'I'm just looking for my daughter. I'm only going to be a minute. Can I just nip in?'

She sucks air in through her teeth and shakes her head. 'Oof. Sorry, love. No can do. The grief I'd get, you wouldn't believe. They'd have my guts for garters on the committee.'

I simultaneously hate this woman and fully empathise with her. Chances are her committee has a Mabel Walker of its own. It wouldn't surprise me if it was the same one, in fact, given how much the Uberbitch enjoys sticking her oar in.

Thrusting my hands into the pockets of my jeans, I search for any stray change. A crumpled fiver, maybe, that's been through the wash.

There's a pen, a couple of sweet wrappers, and my car keys. No money.

'Please, I'm worried about her. I'll literally just be in and out.' I gesture around us. There's no queue. Nobody is coming or going. 'I won't tell anyone. It'll be our secret.'

She groans and shifts on her hard plastic seat, like something painful is happening in her lower intestines.

Then, her hand crawls across the table like a spider, and pulls her book back towards her. With a jerk of her head, and the turning of a page, I'm free to go.

As Kylie Minogue's 1980s cover of 'The Loco-Motion' comes blasting out through the open flaps, I head for the marquee, and for whatever awaits me inside.

TWENTY-THREE

ELIZABETH

The tent is an onslaught of colour and noise when I enter past the small crowd of smokers and vapers gathered outside.

The only lights in the place are from the DJ booth, the same sweeping multicolour spotlight set-up that painted the walls of the school hall last night. They swing wildly over the fabric and structures of the tent, ricocheting at wild angles, then racing off in another direction.

The speakers are too loud. My ears ring with them, and I can feel the bass notes buzzing through the ground beneath my feet. Worms writhe in the grass, drawn upwards by the vibrations. A few boys have grabbed a handful of them and are cackling maniacally as they chase down their screaming sisters.

The whole place feels like the inside of a migraine. Of a nightmare.

And there, at the back of the tent, stands the cause of it all.

Darren is in his forties, with a receding hairline and an expanding waistband. He could probably once have been described as baby-faced, given his high forehead, and the way most of his features seem to have sunk down to near the bottom.

Now, though, his dark eye bags, ice-pick acne scars, and heavy wrinkles would counteract any such description.

I stand by the entrance, watching as he poses for a photo with two young kids, like he's some sort of celebrity. He kneels down on the grass beside them, arms around them both, pulling them in close while their mum snaps off a picture on her phone.

My stomach twitches. I want to throw up. Instead, I clench my fists down by my sides, pull myself together, and make my way through the throngs of dancing kids and drunken parents.

He's on his own when I reach him, tucked back in behind his booth. I start to speak, but he holds a finger up, not even looking at me.

'One sec, darling,' he says. It's an English accent. London. Essex, maybe?

To my shame, I just stand there, watching in silence as he squints at a note he has pinned above his decks, then slides up the fader of his microphone and leans in.

'Alright, folks, we all having a good time?' he asks.

The response is enthusiastic, but clearly not enthusiastic enough.

'I can't hear you!' he roars, and my eardrums ring with the volume of the response. He pumps his fist in the air, triumphantly. 'That's what I'm talking about. We're keeping it cheesy for the next half hour with *Darren's Cheesy Tunes*, then it'll be time to head on outside for...'

He stabs at a play button. The word 'Fire!' blasts out, followed by the opening guitar riff of The Crazy World of Arthur Brown's song of the same name.

Darren looks immensely pleased with himself as he slides the mic fader back down.

'Not bad link that, eh?' he asks, turning to me. 'Now, what can I do for you, darling? You after a request? Not sure I'll be able to fit it in, I've got a few to work through, and I'm knocking it on the head soon.'

He looks me up and down, not even bothering to hide it.

'But I'm doing a pub in North Queensferry tonight, if you fancy coming along? Sure, I could fit you in there.'

My voice won't work. I'm standing there, right in front of him, and no sound will come out. My insides feel frozen. Locked up. It's like I'm trapped inside my own body, unable to make it work.

'You alright?' he asks. He looks me up and down again, but there's less of a leer to it this time. 'You having a stroke or something?'

He starts to laugh, but it turns into a cough. He doesn't bother to cover his mouth. I can smell his last cigarette on his breath.

A kid bumps into me. One of the worm chasers. It's enough to jolt me into life.

'Hollie,' I whisper. It's lost in among all the racket.

He taps at his ear and leans forwards. The smell of his sweat fills my airways.

'Sorry, say again?'

I swallow and force her name out again. Louder, this time.

'Hollie.'

Something happens behind his eyes, but it's gone before I can identify it.

'Holly? Like, Holly Valance, you mean?' He shakes his head. 'I don't have any of hers. But I can bring some tonight, if—'

'My daughter. Hollie. Where is she?'

He considers the question, then glances around at the horde of excited kids. 'Dunno. What does she look like?' He moves his microphone closer. 'Want me to put out a shout for her?'

I shake my head. This isn't going the way I hoped it would. I wasn't expecting an instant confession or anything, but he's too calm, too composed. Maybe he isn't connected to Hollie's disappearance, after all.

Or maybe, he's just been ready for this.

'No. Not here. At the disco last night,' I tell him. He doesn't react. 'She was... she was in the butterfly outfit.'

'Oh. Yeah. At the school? I remember,' he says. 'Nice costume. Did you make it?'

'Where is she?' I demand. 'What have you done with her?'

He gives a little snort that's only ten per cent amusement, and the rest confusion. 'You what?'

'Hollie. My daughter. What have you done with her? Where is she?'

'How the hell should I know?' he asks. His eyes dart around the place, like he's worried someone might be listening in. 'Watch what you're saying. I haven't done nothing.'

'You have,' I insist. I feel tears trickling down my cheeks, and almost choke my way through the next few words. 'You've done something. You've got her. Please, just tell me where she is!'

The effort of getting the words out has made my volume climb higher and higher. A few of the adults standing nearby look in our direction. Darren clamps his hands on my upper arms to try to steer me out of sight behind the DJ booth, but I shrug them off.

'Look, missus, I don't know what you're talking about,' he insists, stepping in closer. 'If your daughter's missing, if there's something I can do, then I will, but you can't just—'

'Her costume,' I say, cutting him off. 'You told her to swap costumes. You wanted her to change so I wouldn't recognise her.'

He blinks. He's shocked that I know. His mouth drops open, forming a little circle of surprise.

Then, just as I think I've got him, he does something unexpected.

He smiles.

'Oh, is that it? I always do that at Halloween discos. I say it to every kid who comes up to talk to me.'

I stay standing, even though I feel like my legs have been kicked out from under me. My mouth tries to form a few different words, then settles on a whispered, 'What?'

'Look on my Facebook, if you don't believe me. All last week, all the Halloween discos I did, I mention it loads of times, getting the kids to swap masks, and that.'

'But... but why?'

He shrugs his rounded shoulders. 'Just a laugh, innit? Bit of fun. A prank, sweetheart, that's all. Ask the other kids at the disco last night, I suggested it to at least half a dozen of them.'

'You're lying,' I tell him.

I want him to be. I need him to be. He has to be the one who has her.

If he isn't, then I'm no closer to finding my daughter.

And time is running out.

'Like I say, sweetheart, go and check Facebook. Follow me, while you're at it, I could do with the bump.' He checks the timer on his decks, then steps back in behind the booth. 'But do me a favour, eh?'

He looks me up and down for a third time. This time, there's nothing there but contempt.

'Don't bother coming to North Queensferry, eh? Psycho bitches really ain't my thing.'

TWENTY-FOUR

SASHA

My fingers click out an impatient rhythm while I wait for the door to open. There's a dog inside, going bananas. The heavy thump-thump-thump of approaching footsteps suggests that someone will answer the door soon.

I tilt my head back and look at the clouds bunching together overhead, drawing like a blanket across the city. It might rain. I'd like that.

The door opens.

'That was quick.'

It's a woman. There's a note of impatience in her voice, like she's fed up of me before she's even met me. It's hurtful, but I try to rise above it.

'Sorry,' I say, smiling at her. 'I was just looking up. We don't look up enough, do we? As a species, I mean. We should look up more often.'

She seems confused by the question. I'm disappointed in her already.

'Did you forget something?' she asks.

Behind her, a boy sits slumped in a beanbag, eyes trained on his screen, thumbs flicking and tapping away at the levers and buttons of a video game controller.

Elizabeth, it seems, has beaten me to it.

'No,' I tell her. 'I reckon you must be thinking of someone else.' I point to my face and twirl the finger around. 'My sister. She looks like me, but not as good. Mousier.' I show my front teeth, like I'm nibbling on something. Cheese. They eat cheese, don't they? Or is that just in the cartoons?

'She was probably crying,' I continue. The thought amuses me. 'Was she crying?'

I bet she was crying.

'What are you...?'

She searches my face, like she's playing spot the difference. It shouldn't be difficult. We're similar, my sister and I, but you don't have to look too closely to tell us apart. It's in our eyes. In our walk. In the way we hold ourselves.

Under the surface, we couldn't be more different.

'I don't understand,' she finally concludes.

I assure her that's fine. She doesn't have to. She just has to let me talk to her son.

She refuses. That's her first mistake.

Trying to close the door on me is her second.

The dog, locked in another room, goes bananas when I force my way inside, one hand on her throat, the other closing and locking the door behind us.

'M-mum?'

The boy on the beanbag cranes his neck to watch, his fingers now frozen on his control pad. He looks afraid and confused as I force his struggling mother down onto the couch and hold her there, pin her there.

How could he not be? How could he not be afraid of me?

I don't want to do this. I really don't. I'm not a monster, no matter what people might say.

But Hollie is in danger, and I can't trust my sister to bring her home.

Even if she's been here, even if she thinks they've told her everything, there's every possibility that they haven't. They could be holding back. They could have lied to her.

They won't lie to me.

I point to the boy, then to the spot on the couch beside his mother. My hand is over her mouth, fingers splayed, keeping her quiet. She's thrashing around, slapping at me, kicking at me, but she has no room to get leverage behind the blows, and I easily shrug them off.

'You. Sit here. Now,' I tell him.

The dog hurls itself against the other side of the door, its shape a big, bulky blur beyond the frosted glass.

The boy shoots a desperate look over at it, like it might be his best chance of saving his mother. Of saving himself.

'If you even think about it, I'll pop her eyes out and I'll make you eat them,' I tell him. I keep my voice light and I smile, though. I don't want to traumatise the little darling, after all. Not unless he leaves me no choice.

I'm not sure the approach is all that effective. He's already sobbing as he sets down his controller. He clutches at his groin, and the tang of fresh urine fills the air.

'Aw, now look what you've done, you dilly dumpling,' I tell him, nodding to the darkening stain on the front of his trousers. I point to the couch again. 'Sit there. Don't be scared. This'll all be over in no time.'

Slowly, tears and piss dripping from him, he gets up, abandoning the controller. On screen, his character dies a bloody and painful death in a hail of hot machine-gun fire.

I ratchet the smile up a notch or two as he lowers himself onto the couch beside his mum. She falls into a snivelling semi-silence, like she's too scared of what I might do to him to keep fighting back.

Good girl. Clever girl.

'Is there anyone else in the house?' I ask.

She shakes her head. I glance very deliberately at the boy.

'Are you telling the truth?'

She nods, or as much as my grip will allow, at least. I give her the benefit of the doubt.

'OK. I'm going to take my hand away now. If you scream, call for help, or make a sound, I'll slit your son's throat. I don't want to, but I will. Is that understood?'

There's no argument from her. She just reaches for his hands and nods, wide eyes brimming with tears that trickle down her face and tickle between my fingers.

'Look at me,' I say, even though she hasn't torn her eyes off mine. 'Do you believe I'll do it?'

She nods. No hesitation.

'Good,' I say, then I release my grip, wipe my hand on the thigh of her jeans, then stand over them, looking down. 'Right. So. First of all, I want to start by saying sorry about all this. This is not how I like to conduct myself at all, but sometimes, needs must. Like today, for example. Like right now.'

They're huddling together, both shaking, her arms wrapped protectively around him. I'm suddenly taken by the idea of what a good picture it would make, and I frame the shot in a rectangle I make with my fingers and thumbs, then *click* like I've pressed the shutter.

'That's a keeper,' I tell them.

'What are you doing?' she whispers. 'Why are you doing this? What do you want?'

I blow out my cheeks. A dry little laugh tickles the back of my throat. 'Wow. Now you're asking. I want a lot of things. I won't bore you with the list. Mostly, right now, though, I just want my niece back.'

'Your niece?'

'I want you to tell me everything you know about last night.'

She practically spits the words at me. 'I already told—'

'Not her. I don't care what you told her,' I say, shutting her down. 'I want you to tell me. And I need you to tell me *everything*. No holding back. No lies. Everything.'

I look over at the TV screen. A countdown ticks down the final seconds of the dying character's life.

An idea strikes me. An awful, terrible idea. Even the thought of it turns my stomach.

But, sometimes, needs must. Like today. Like now.

'And to make sure you're telling me the truth,' I say, turning back to mother and son. 'We're all going to play a little game.'

TWENTY-FIVE
ELIZABETH

Sasha would have made him talk. She wouldn't have let him dismiss her like that, or come scurrying back to the car with her cheeks burning, and her tail between her legs. Sasha has a way of getting what she wants from people.

Maybe she still will. Maybe she'll appear any minute now, storm in there, and drag the horrible greasy bastard out of the tent by what little's left of his hair.

I hope not, though. That, like Sasha, would be noisy. It would attract all sorts of attention.

Better to be smart. Better to play it cool. For now.

I sit behind the steering wheel, watching in my rear-view mirror as Darren loads his DJ gear into the back of a clapped-out old Ford box van. There's nobody helping him, so he's had to make three trips across the field and back, carrying various battered boxes and bags for life filled with spaghettis of cables and wires, chain-smoking every step of the way.

It's not warm, but he's sweating so heavily I can see a dark patch on the back of his self-promotional *Darren's Cheesy Tunes* T-shirt. I swear, I can smell him from here.

Although, that might just be the dead body in the boot.

The police officer has cleared off somewhere, thankfully. Had he been around when I'd returned without a child in tow, he might have become suspicious and asked some awkward questions.

Better not to have to deal with that right now. All being well, I'll be gone before he comes back.

'OK, OK. Here we go. You've got this. You can do this.'

I whisper the pep talk under my breath, urging myself on, then reach for the engine ignition button as Darren slams the back doors of his van, then trudges around to the driver's side.

I time the ignition with the closing of his door, hopefully disguising it. If he hears me, or senses something is up, he doesn't show it. I watch, hand on the gearstick, foot on the clutch, as he winds down the window, flicks a cigarette end into the wind, then drives off slowly, cautious of the rows of cars parked on the verge on either side that turn the road into a tight, narrow passageway.

Below my breath, I whisper a count of five, then throw the car into reverse and begin to follow. Almost immediately, I realise my mistake. I should have turned the car as soon as I got back. It would have increased the chances of him seeing me, but I could've kept low, or hid in the back.

Now, I need to turn the car around in the overcrowded car park, while kids and their parents crisscross in front and behind me without a care in the world.

'Damn it,' I hiss. Darren's van is already halfway towards the main road. If he reaches there before I can get after him, he'll slip away in the busy Saturday afternoon traffic.

There's no time for caution. No time to lose. Hooking an arm around the passenger seat, I crane my neck to look behind me, and hit the accelerator. The car lurches backwards, engine whining in complaint, wheels chewing up the car park's lime-stone covering.

He's indicating left. Slowing for the junction. I'm not going to make it. He's going to get away if I don't hurry.

I'm so fixated on him that I barely hear the reversing sensor scream at me from the dashboard. I hear the crunch, though, that precedes the sudden, jarring stop.

The impact slams me back in the seat, wrenching my shoulder, and driving the air from my lungs with a big, sudden *whumf*.

'No! No, no, no, no!'

I can't see it, but I know what I've hit. One of the bollards lining the side of the parking area has crumpled the back end of the car. I can see a dunkle in the lid of the boot, raising the metal to a ridge along the middle, like it's buckling itself in an attempt to fly open.

'Shit!'

The gearbox grinds as I shove the stick into first. I'm about to floor it out of the car park, but hit the brakes again just in time to avoid running straight over the policeman from earlier. He's just a few feet ahead of me, waving for me to shut off the engine.

Beyond him, several hundred feet away, Darren's van joins the endless procession of traffic heading back towards Edinburgh city centre.

Without a word, the policeman takes out his notebook, makes a note of my number plate, then continues around to the side of the car.

'You alright there, madam?' he asks.

There's a suggestion of sarcasm to it that makes me want to scream at him. I swallow the urge back down. I can barely keep my hand steady as I reach for the button to lower the window.

'Hi. Again. Sorry, officer, I just... I didn't see the barrier.'

'Evidently,' he agrees. He bends forwards and looks at the other seats inside the car, all empty.

'Did you no' find your daughter?' he asks. His gaze meets mine. An eyebrow rises. 'Or is she in the boot?'

My heartbeat strikes the wrong rhythm. A wave of hot, prickly heat rises up my neck and face.

'Ha. No. There's no one in the boot,' I tell him.

My voice is too thin. The words are too quick. His eyes flit across my face, like he's searching for something. He can tell something's wrong.

Oh, God. He knows. Does he know? How could he know?

Finally, he sniffs. 'Aye. Well, I hope not, for their sake.' He steps back and beckons me out of the car with a crooking of his finger.

He's out of the way now. The road ahead of me is clear. I could just jam my foot down on the accelerator. Just go, just drive.

But he has the car registration. His own car is already facing the right way, and is still fully intact. How far would I even get?

'Madam?' he says. 'Can you get out of the vehicle, please?'

'Sorry, I'm just a bit shaken up,' I say, as I unclip my seat belt.

'I'm sure you are, madam. Do you have your licence there?'

I'm fairly sure it's in the glove compartment, wedged under Mr Floppsity. But I shake my head, and mutter an apology.

'Left my bag at home.'

'Home. Right. And where's that?' he asks. 'You local?'

Some inner voice, buried deep, urges me to lie. The bubble of anxiety rising up my throat makes it impossible.

'Edinburgh, yes. Stockbridge.'

He whistles through his teeth. 'Nice. What's your name?'

The voice screams at me. I'm too terrified to do what it says, but he picks up on my hesitation.

'Name, madam?' he says, in a more officious tone than before.

'Elizabeth. Jones. Elizabeth Jones,' I mumble.

Half a dozen or so people have slowed on their way to and from their car, watching on and earwigging in. The policeman writes my name in his pad, then points to one of the rubber-neckers with the end of his pen.

'Jog on, folks. Nothing to see here,' he tells them, and they all pick up the pace again, like some cosmic fast-forward button has just been pressed.

He takes a few more details – full address and date of birth – then produces a breathalyser test and instructs me to blow into it.

'Is that really necessary? I just had a... prang.'

He looks at the boot, and at the shattered plastic of the bumper that lies scattered on the ground.

'Bit more than a prang, madam. And, aye. It is. One big, long breath, don't stop until I tell you.'

That little nagging voice falls into a sullen, contemptuous silence as I comply. The effort of blowing makes my head go light, and I have to lean on the roof of the car for a moment while he waits for the results.

'Good. Good news. Passed that test with flying colours,' he says, though I can't quite tell if he's pleased or disappointed.

'Great. I mean, yes. Of course,' I reply. 'Can I go, then?'

'Go?' He jabs a thumb back over his shoulder. 'In this? I don't think so.'

I try to offer up an argument – any argument – but it gets stuck in my throat when he turns and strides around to the back of the car, and I'm forced to scramble to keep up with him.

The damage is bad. About a third of the bumper has splin-tered around the impact site, and the number plate is hanging off at one side.

Worse than that, though – far worse – is the fold in the metal of the boot lid. It starts just to the right of the handle, and runs vertically upwards, mimicking the shape of the bollard.

The impact must have bounced the car forwards again,

though, because there are a few inches of space between where the concrete ends and the metal begins.

He runs a hand across the damage, and when his fingers brush against it, panic jolts through me like a bolt of lightning. I see a flash of a body, all bound and taped. Of a prison cell, with me in it.

Of Hollie, and all the terrible futures which could await her.

From the front of the car, deafening even over the sound of squealing kids just beyond the fence, comes the sound of my phone ringing. It's propped up on its cradle on the dashboard. The screen is lit up, but I can't see who's calling.

I take a step, but a warning from the policeman stops me.

'Whoa, whoa. Leave it. It can wait,' he tells me.

He nods down at the boot. I feel the blood draining from my face. I'm light-headed again, leaning on the car to stay upright. I know what's coming. I know what he's going to ask.

And I know what that means.

'Do you mind doing me a favour, madam?' the police officer says.

He steps back, giving me room. The ringing phone grows louder, more insistent.

'Do you mind opening the boot for me?'

TWENTY-SIX

ELIZABETH

It's been a lifetime since the police officer spoke. He's just staring at me now. Staring. Staring. Waiting.

I need to do something. Anything. Anything that doesn't involve opening the boot and showing him the dead man all bent and buckled inside it.

The phone keeps ringing. He's still staring. Staring. My mind is empty, but my head feels full, like there's a hurricane raging around inside it, smashing my thoughts to pieces, making them impossible to gather up.

'Sorry?' I say. A pathetic attempt to stall for time.

The phone gives a half-ring, then stops. Even as my brain desperately tries to drum up an excuse not to open the boot, part of it's listening for the *ding* of a new voicemail being received.

It doesn't come. Whoever was calling didn't leave a message.

'The boot, madam. Open it,' he says. It's not a polite request this time. He's not asking me, he's ordering me. He's not giving me a choice.

I should tell him. Tell him about Hollie. About everything. Face my fate.

But how can I, when it could mean damning her to a fate far worse?

My gaze creeps to the dent in the metal, and to the handle right beside it. 'I, uh, I'm not sure that's a good idea,' I say, swallowing back twin urges to scream and vomit.

He tucks his thumbs into his stab-proof vest and slouches his weight onto one hip. His eyebrows rise so high they disappear beneath the brim of his cap.

'Oh? And why's that?'

'I just... It, uh, couldn't it be dangerous?'

'Dangerous?' He considers this for a while. Considers me. 'Is there something in the boot, Elizabeth?'

My name from his mouth is jarring. It reminds me, once again, of just who holds all the cards here. He has my name, my address, my identity.

That nagging voice in my head whispers, pointing out that he hasn't passed that information on to anyone yet. I force the thought all the way back down again, too afraid to even contemplate what it might be suggesting.

'No,' I say. It sounds unconvincing, even to me, but I persevere. 'There's no one. Nothing, I mean. There's nothing.'

This time, he looks at me for a full five seconds. Then, still not taking his eyes off me, he shifts one hand to rest on the extendable baton that's holstered on his belt.

'I'm going to ask you again to open the boot, Elizabeth,' he says.

'There's nothing in there,' I insist. I'm trying to smile, but the muscles of my face have forgotten how it's done. 'I'm just... I'm worried if I open it, it'll do more damage.'

He steps forwards suddenly. I flinch back, like he's going to hit me, but instead he grabs for the handle, and there's nothing I can do but watch as the lid of the boot springs open and begins to rise.

I can't see inside it, only the look of surprise on his face.

'I can explain,' I begin, but a look from him silences me. He summons me over with a beckoning finger, and my feet shuffle me closer, unable to do anything but meekly comply.

'Well, well, well,' he says. 'You're in luck.'

The yawning, empty chasm of the car's boot looms directly beneath me. A deep, dark hole I could almost tumble down into.

'The damage seems to be mostly cosmetic,' he says. He takes his hand off the baton and runs it across the metal rim of the boot well. 'Frame seems undamaged.'

I know he keeps talking, but the words are just empty sounds that buzz around me like flies.

It's empty. The boot is empty. All that's in there is the antennae of Hollie's butterfly costume, and a half-filled plastic petrol container.

How is that possible?

Don't get me wrong, I'm not complaining, but I don't understand.

I swallow, but my mouth is so dry I almost choke on it.

'So, I can go?' I ask, talking over him, interrupting whatever he was saying.

'Oh, I don't think so, no,' he says, then he leans in and lifts up the little shelf that covers the hidden subfloor.

My whole body tenses. The space beneath the shelf is only a few inches deep, so the only way you could stash a corpse in it would be after you'd put it through an industrial blender, but I'm still terrified of what might be unveiled.

There are a couple of tools and a spray can that can be used to inflate a flat tyre in an emergency.

The police officer barely acknowledges those, and instead runs his hand along the inside, fingers massaging the exposed metal.

'You were lucky, though. Could've been much worse. I can call a recovery vehicle, get you towed.'

No. I can't let that happen. I need the car. I need it to find Hollie.

I curl my fingers up and dig the nails into my palms, forcing myself to focus. To calm down.

'That's... that'll take ages, won't it?' I point to the entrance road, throttled by the cars parked on either side. 'You'll have to shift all them.'

He follows my finger, and I can tell he doesn't like what he sees.

'You'll have to get people out to move them, and the DJ's away. He can't even do an announcement.'

I can practically hear his mind working, imagining the amount of effort that's going to be required.

'Isn't there a garage nearby I can just drive to? Save you all that hassle? There's bound to be one in Musselburgh, isn't there? I could drive straight there, then get a taxi home. You said yourself, it's all cosmetic. The frame's undamaged. It'll be safe to drive around the corner, won't it? I could just do that and save everyone a lot of hassle.'

I'm talking too much. Trying too hard. Still, he tears his gaze from the road and shifts his stance to face me, chewing thoughtfully on his bottom lip.

The nagging voice in my head falls silent. The muscles in my face finally remember how to smile.

'So,' I begin, giving my car keys a little jingle. 'What do you say?'

TWENTY-SEVEN

ELIZABETH

It's almost forty minutes later when I pull up along the street from the DJ's unit. The police officer watched me all the way to the bottom of the road, so I had no choice but to turn right, headed for Musselburgh, then take the longer coastal road back into Edinburgh.

On the drive over, I glanced into the rear-view mirror, and caught sight of Hollie's booster seat on the back seat. The emptiness of it, the memory of her, were a gut punch. An icy hand on my throat that made it so I couldn't swallow. Couldn't breathe.

I fought through it, blinking away the tears, until I arrived here. Now.

I had no idea where Darren might have headed to, and all I could think to do was come back here to the industrial estate, in the hope that Darren hadn't yet left for his evening gig over the bridge in North Queensferry.

I already googled a list of pubs in that area while stopped at traffic lights on the drive over, so I could be prepared if I got back to the estate and found that he wasn't here.

There was no need. I can see his van parked just along the

road, directly outside the unit with his sign emblazoned across the front.

Got him.

I check my phone and hit redial on the last number I called. It's the number that the picture of Hollie was sent from.

The same number that tried to contact me while I was talking to the police officer outside the car. They left no voice-mail, sent no more text messages, and every attempt to call them back just takes me to the same dead tone as before.

I've spent most of the trip here trying not to think what the consequences of me ignoring their call might mean for Hollie.

Trying, but failing. She has died half a dozen ways between Musselburgh and here, each one worse than the one before.

The street is still mostly deserted. I shut off the engine, pull on the handbrake, then step out onto the pavement. It's after five o'clock in Scotland in November, and night has almost fully descended. Only the lamp posts, and the occasional distant flash of fireworks, stand against it, and I skulk between pools of light and darkness as I make my way back to the DJ's building.

A strip of yellow light paints the pavement at the base of the roll-up door. I hesitate at it, watching for shadows to move through it from within.

Nothing.

The small, landscape window by the door shows light behind it, too, but what I thought was grime on the inside is now revealed as a sheet of frosted plastic affixed to the surface of the glass. It's impossible to make out any details, but I can see the bright glow of a monitor screen and get a sense of someone moving in front of it.

Darren is in there. This is my chance.

Returning quickly to the car, I open the damaged boot and lift the floor. The metal tyre iron is cool to the touch. There's a faint suggestion of condensation clinging to it, a newly formed crease in the metal clearly allowing moisture to creep in.

Tooled up, I return to the DJ's office, then pause at the door to collect my thoughts and make a plan. How should I play this? Should I knock? Should I smash the glass, turn the lock from the inside, then force my way inside?

What do I say to him? What am I prepared to do if he won't tell me where Hollie is? How far am I prepared to go?

My heart starts to race at the thought of it all. And, even more so, at the thought that he might have been telling the truth. He could have no involvement in Hollie's disappearance, and no idea where she is.

What then?

I push that thought away, raise a hand to knock, then change my mind and get ready to swing the tyre iron at the glass instead.

It's only then that I remember the door's sliding bolt and padlock. The padlock is missing, the bolt open all the way.

Keeping my weapon ready, I turn the door handle, and it opens with a click.

Open.

A moment later, I'm inside.

That's as far as my luck goes, though. The main door leads into a tiny entranceway that's about the size of a telephone box, with a second door standing dead ahead, and a narrow closet on the right.

I can hear movement from the door ahead, but there's a keyhole next to the handle of this one, and no windows to break. If he's locked it, and decides not to open up, the only way in would be to break the door down. It looks far too solid for that. And I'm far too weak.

But I have to know what's in there. I have to know if he has my daughter.

I squat down by the door, trying to see through the keyhole. It's blocked, though, either by a key, or some sort of cover. This close, I can hear him breathing in the room beyond. Heavy.

Rasping. The sound of it makes my skin shift sickeningly around on the back of my neck.

There's a tremor in my hands as I stand and reach for the scuffed metal door handle. A sense of dread lies leaden and heavy in my gut.

I push down on the handle. Slowly. Carefully. The low, guttural breathing continues, uninterrupted.

He's too focused on whatever he's doing to hear me.

My fingers tighten their grip on the tyre iron as I press my shoulder to the door, gently applying pressure.

To my relief, it inches inward.

His next breath has a quizzical note to it, and panic about him rushing to block the door urges me into action. I push on in, screaming blue murder, and flailing my makeshift weapon like it's a medieval mace.

He yelps in fright, eyes bulging as he rises from a computer chair, one hand still wrapped around the shaft of his erect penis, the other frantically grabbing for his jeans.

It's not *his* eyes that catch my attention, though. Instead, my focus is drawn to those of a young girl with blonde hair and dimples. She looks around the same age as Hollie – nine, maybe ten – but with shiny blonde hair that's tied in bunches on either side of her head.

She's beaming at me from across the room, her face alight with excitement.

Beside her, on screen, DJ Darren is pressed in close for a hug, the beam of his disco lights casting half his face into shadow, and painting the other in a devilish shade of red.

I recognise the marquee behind him, and the grass beneath the girl's feet. This photo is recent. It's from the gala day. From today.

'It's not what it looks like,' he babbles, hurriedly doing up his belt.

The wad of toilet paper and bottle of baby oil on the desk beside his keyboard tell me otherwise, damning him as a liar.

And as something far, far worse.

'Oh, God. Oh, God, what are you doing?' I shriek. 'What have you done? Where's my daughter? Where's Hollie, you sick freak?'

He stumbles towards me, head shaking so hard his saggy jowls flap around like they're filled with water.

'I told you, nothing. I didn't do nothing! I wouldn't touch the kids. I wouldn't. This isn't what it looks like, I swear.'

He's a couple of feet away, and closing, hands grasping, face red. The gap-toothed grin of the girl on the screen seems to egg me on.

I swing, hard and fast, bringing the tyre iron around in a wide *whumming* arc just as his head comes into range.

He ducks. No. *No!*

I feel his fingers around my wrist. His weight is on me, around me, pressing in, pressing down. The smoke-and-sweat stink of him fills my nostrils again. I choke on it.

I see a fist. Too late. Too late!

Pain, like the shockwave of a bomb blast, explodes across my cheek, filling my head with noise, and my mouth with the coppery tang of blood. The floor turns to quicksand beneath my feet, sucking me down, dragging me in.

I tumble to the floor, then fall right through it.

And I keep on falling, down, down, down, into the icy, smothering dark.

TWENTY-EIGHT
ELIZABETH

Black.

Cold.

Silence.

No pain. Not really. Not yet.

No nothing, in fact.

I am far below the surface of a vast, endless lake, cut off from the world above. Too deep. Too far gone for anyone to reach me.

Light – a suggestion of it, at least – flickers and darts across the surface, drawing me upwards, like a moth to a flame.

There's a sound, muted but urgent. A wailing. A screaming.

Not me. I don't think so, at least, though the weight and the pressure of the darkness around me makes it hard to be sure.

Hollie? Is it Hollie? Calling to me? I swim upwards, through the dark.

The sound grows louder, clearer, sharpening into a crescendo that propels me upwards on a rising current of bubbles, back towards the surface, back towards the light, back towards consciousness, and whatever might await me there.

As I break the surface, my whole body jerks violently, eyes flying open, fists lashing out to defend myself.

My knuckles strike glass. The pain comes then, harsher and more urgent than the dull throbbing on the side of my face.

I'm in a car.

No.

I'm in *my* car. I'm draped across the back seats, legs bent awkwardly and uncomfortably to fit me between both rear passenger doors.

Hollie's booster seat is on the floor, jammed upright. Empty. She's not here.

There's a smell I don't recognise at first, but which my befuddled brain rushes to identify.

Smoke.

The screaming is suddenly ear-splitting. It fills the car as a fire engine thunders past just a few feet away, lights flashing, horn blaring to announce its arrival.

A hundred feet ahead of me, through the windscreen, flames leap from the small, landscape window of an industrial unit.

Darren the DJ's industrial unit.

'Oh, dear God.'

I grab for the door handle, then stop. My head throbs as the misfiring synapses of my brain try to pull themselves together.

The last thing I remember is Darren's fist cutting through the air towards me, and the pain exploding across my cheek.

And now...

And now...

How did I get to the car? Not on my own, judging by how I've been unceremoniously dumped in the back. Not Darren, surely? He wouldn't knock me out, then drag me to safety, would he?

No. It wouldn't make sense. But then, nothing makes sense.

Almost nothing.

There is one possibility, but the thought of it scares me. I pat myself down, then scan the inside of the car around me, searching for a note, but finding none. There's only my phone, propped in its cradle on the dashboard, its screen dark.

Beyond it, along the street, a group of firefighters clamber from their vehicle, already pulling on their protective gear and hooking up their hose. The smoke coming from within is thick and black. It pours through the shattered window and rises through glowing red gaps in the unit's flat roof.

Did Darren do this? Was setting the fire an attempt to cover his tracks, before making his escape?

His van is still there, I notice. Parked out front. Unmoved.

Not much of an escape.

One of the firefighters returns to the truck, then emerges with an axe that, even from this distance, looks heavy. He takes aim with it at a spot near the door handle, then swings. Once. Twice.

I have to squint to see the hunk of metal falling away.

A padlock, I think.

Darren's padlock.

He must've left and locked up behind him.

He must have.

Otherwise...

I'm not sure why, exactly, but I feel my gaze being drawn to the phone mounted on the dash. I had it with me when I went to confront the DJ. Someone has taken it from my pocket and deliberately placed it here for me to find.

I stretch through the gap between the front seats, reaching for the phone. A police van comes howling past, the speed and close proximity of it shaking my car on its axles and making me scurry back down into cover.

I watch, my breath fogging the glass, as the van skids to a

halt behind the fire engine. Two police officers – a man and a woman – jump out and run over to help but are urged to stay back by one of the firefighters.

I'm too far away, and they're far too busy to notice me. With a lunge, I stretch through the gap, grab the phone, then fall back out of sight again, the mobile clutched to my chest like it's a precious and fragile thing.

Peering through the gap between the headrest and the chair, I watch to make sure nobody is looking in my direction. If they've noticed the car, they don't seem to be remotely concerned about it.

With a tap and a scan of my face, my phone wakes and unlocks, and I'm immediately presented with a photo I don't recognise. It looks like it's been taken accidentally, as it shows nothing but a blurry section of floor, and something that might be a pair of feet.

I'm about to swipe to see the next picture when I realise my mistake. It's not a photograph I'm looking at. It's a video.

From when I hit the play button, it takes me five or six seconds to figure out what I'm looking at. The moment I do, I turn the screen away, my thumb grasping wildly for the button that will make the screen go dark again.

Hot, bitter bile burns all the way up the back of my throat. Inside the car, the smell of smoke seeps in through the vents, painting the air in faint shades of grey.

Outside, further down the road, fire blooms like a flower through the collapsing roof of Darren's office building.

I stare in mute, disbelieving horror at the phone in my hand, the few seconds of footage I saw etched in deep, jagged lines on my memory.

'Oh, God,' I whisper. There's a hoarseness to it, as the smoke starts to take its toll.

But, no. That's not right. It wasn't God who did this. Not by a long shot.

'Oh, Sasha!'

A tear hugs the contours of my swollen cheek.

'What have you done?'

TWENTY-NINE

SASHA

'Aaand, I'm back!' I announce, twirling my sister's car keys around on my finger. 'Now she's out of the way, we can get back to it.'

He looks funny, down there on the floor. He's clutching at his thigh, close to the injury, but too scared to actually touch it.

I don't blame him. Knees were never meant to bend that way.

'I was rubbish at maths,' I tell him, with a sniff. 'Never paid much attention. Bored me senseless.'

I smile, as a memory comes back to me.

'There was this big test once. Fourth year, I think, and instead of answering anything, I was giving a handjob to Robbie Maitland up the back. Up the back of the room, I mean, not up his back. His cock wasn't fused to his spine, or... Anyway, doesn't matter. What do you call that angle your leg's at? Obtuse? Is that it? Is that a word? Equilateral? No, that's triangles.'

I smile down at him, and the glint in my eyes draws a sob from his bloated, bloodied lips.

'Will we try for a triangle, DJ Darren?' I ask, stooping to

pick up Elizabeth's tyre iron. It's lucky for her I got here when I did. Although, luck had very little to do with it. I'd been lying in wait for a while, watching. 'It'll take some doing,' I tell him, hefting the metal bar from hand to hand. 'But I'm game if you are.'

'P-please. Please, I'm sorry. I'm sorry. Don't hurt me. I don't know anything, I swear. I swear to God.'

I put a finger to my lips to silence him.

'God isn't listening,' I whisper. 'He's a busy man. Or... being. Or whatever he is. It's just you and me, DJ Darren.'

I let that sink in, then I show him what I picked up back at the car. His eyes are drawn by the sound of the sloshing liquid.

'Do you know what this is?'

His face crumples. He tries to back away, squirming across the floor, but his leg won't let him.

And besides, there's nowhere for him to go.

'Please, no, please! Don't! Please!'

I sigh. Heavily. Wearily. 'I asked you a question, DJ Darren.' I tap the plastic container in time with each word. 'Do. You. Know. What. This. Is?'

His breath goes short. He can barely get the word out. I'm confident that, if he hasn't already, he's on the brink of soiling himself.

Two in one day. Not bad. At least the last one had the excuse of being a nine-year-old.

'P-petrol.'

'Bing! Big hand for DJ Darren, ladies and gentlemen,' I declare, turning and briefly basking in the applause from the studio audience. Really milking it. 'Petrol is the right answer.'

I squat beside him, my game show host smile falling away.

'What do you know about petrol, DJ Darren?'

He shakes his head, his eyes still locked on the canister. 'Nothing. N-nothing.'

'Aye, you do. Come on. Think. Hit me with some facts. Petrol is...' I nod, encouragingly. 'What?'

Tears and snot threaten to choke him. A dark stain spreads across the crotch of his jeans, and drips down the crack of his arse.

Called it.

'Yes. Petrol is *wet*,' I declare, pointing to the rapidly expanding shadow of piss. 'Well done. What else?'

His reply is an indecipherable mess of sobbing. I help him by waving a hand in front of my face, wafting away the sour odour of his urine.

'Petrol is... What else? *Smelly*. It's smelly, isn't it?'

When he still doesn't respond, my temper gets the better of me. I lunge at him, grabbing a handful of his fine, thinning hair, and jerking his head back.

'Isn't it?' I spit, the words foaming between my gritted teeth.

He cries out in fright, and in shock, and in pain. Mostly in pain. His reply bursts like a bubble on his lips. 'Y-yes!'

'OK, that's two. He's on a roll, folks.' I let go of his hair, and gesture for the studio audience to give him some encouragement.

Up on the desk beside us, a little girl with dimples and a crop top watches silently on.

'Tough crowd, DJ Darren!' I tell him. 'So, what else? We can get through this. Wet. Smelly. What else?'

He swallows. I watch him trying to force all his fractured pieces back together, one ragged breath at a time.

'Please.' His voice is a whisper. A gasp. 'I didn't do anything. I haven't touched anyone. I wouldn't. I wouldn't, I swear. I swear to God.'

I sit in front of him, cross-legged on the floor, keeping my distance from the still-spreading puddle that forms a moat between us.

'Oh, DJ Darren,' I sigh. 'I already told you, God isn't listening. It's just us. It's just you, me, this petrol canister, and the truth.' A thought pops into my head out of nowhere. 'Actually, that's an idea.'

His gaze tracks my hand as I reach into my pocket and take out Elizabeth's phone. She's going to want to see this.

Well, maybe not *want* to, exactly, but she should. She needs to.

And, yes, the thought of her horror when she does really tickles my funny bone.

She's got face ID security, but given that, to the untrained eye, we look so alike, the phone springs open without a problem.

I hum below my breath as I search for the camera app, then I hit record, do a dramatic sweep up to reveal the bloodied, piss-soaked DJ on the floor, and then find a place to prop the phone that'll give the best possible view of proceedings.

'For posterity,' I tell him. 'I'll give it to my sister. Maybe there's someone on your side who'd want a copy, too? Your wife?' I look him up and down, then glance very deliberately at the child on his PC screen. 'No. Doubt that. Your mum, maybe? Do you live with her? Would she like a copy?'

'Please. *Please*,' he begs. 'I'll tell you anything you want.'

'Oh, I know, I know,' I assure him. 'Don't worry, I know you will.'

I smile at him, a warm and friendly one, then go back to humming as I remove the cap from the canister and slide the plastic funnel free from its housing.

'What else?'

'Look, maybe... Maybe I can help. I didn't hurt her, I swear, but maybe I can help you find—'

'My niece. Oh, you will. Relax.'

I screw the funnel into place on top of the canister, twisting it slowly, around and around.

'What else?'

His mouth is dry. The next word rasps like bone dragging on rough concrete.

'W-what?'

'Wet. Smelly. What else is petrol?' My smile falls away, my face slackening into a cold, dead-eyed stare. I have to bite the inside of my lip to stop myself laughing. 'Last chance, DJ Darren. Game's almost up.'

He doesn't want to give the answer, but something in my expression forces him into it.

'F-flammable.'

He jerks back at the shrill sharpness of my response. 'Ding-ding-ding. We have a winner.' I give the funnel one final twist, locking it into place. 'Petrol is *flammable*. Or maybe inflamma-ble? Do they mean the same thing? I don't know which is which. That's something for you to find out. Either way, we get the gist.'

I shuffle back a little, steering clear of the advancing puddle of urine.

'Good grief, DJ Darren, how much did you drink?' I ask him. 'Anyway, you could also have said "toxic", but you went for "flammable". Good choice. More visually spectacular.' I point to the phone, propped up, watching on. 'The camera is going to love it.'

'Please, no, please. I didn't do anything. I just... I just thought it'd be funny for them to swap costumes. I do it every time.' His head cranes back, following me as I get to my feet. 'Every Halloween, or fancy dress party. Ask anyone! Please. *Please!*'

I angle his monitor so the girl with the dimples is staring down at him.

'Sorry, DJ Darren, I didn't catch any of what you just said. I wasn't listening,' I tell him.

With a jerk of an arm, I slosh a few glugs of petrol across his legs.

'But I'm listening now. We're all listening now.' I gesture to the girl, to the phone, to the hushed studio audience somewhere in the shadows behind me. 'So, I suggest you tell us *everything*.'

THIRTY

ELIZABETH

I throw the phone onto the chair beside me and slide the window down to let some air into the car.

I'm half a mile away from the industrial estate now, but the smell of the smoke still lingers, even here.

The saliva in my mouth is so thick I have to chew it before swallowing it back down. I can't watch any more. I won't.

I refuse to watch a man being burned alive.

Because, I have no doubt, that's where the footage was going. Even if I hadn't seen the flames leaping from the roof of the building myself, I know what Sasha is capable of. I know the extremes she'll go to.

I can't watch.

I won't.

And yet...

What if there's something on there? What if there's information that'll help me find Hollie? Why else would she have left the phone there, so prominently on my dashboard, for me to find?

To torture me. That's a possibility.

But maybe to tell me what I need to do. Where I need to go. How to save my daughter.

Maybe that's on there, too.

No.

I can't.

I won't.

I have to.

I delay a few moments by calling back the number that sent me the photo of Hollie.

The flat, dead-sounding bleeps tell me nobody is going to answer.

Outside, a flash lights up the street. A *bang* erupts across the sky, then sparkles crackle as they fall from the heavens like fiery flakes of snow.

Fireworks.

My hands shake as I return to my camera roll. I can't look at the top row of thumbnails yet. My eyes refuse.

Instead, they lock onto the photos I took last night of Hollie in her costume, before we headed out to that damned disco.

I tap on one, then swipe slowly through them.

Looking at them, you'd never know she was annoyed at me, or that we'd fallen out. She looks so pleased, so proud, holding her arms out at her sides and turning to show off the full splendour of her wings.

It was just twenty-four hours ago. A lifetime.

An accidental swipe too far wrenches at my heart and draws a cry of pain from deep down in my gut.

The picture of Hollie, tied up and blindfolded, has automatically been added to the photos app. The shift from my daughter smiling and posing to this image hits me like an oncoming train. I can't breathe. Can't think.

My fingers tap frantically at the screen, backing me out of the image, saving me from it.

I should've gone to the police right at the start. Told them everything, to hell with the consequences. They could have protected Hollie, even when I was gone. They could have kept her safe.

But would they? Or would they condemn her to a hell even worse than the one she's in now?

I can't take that chance. I won't.

I force my eyes to look upwards, to the top row of the camera roll, where the latest thumbnails are.

The video I just watched is second in from the left. I'm about to tap play on it, when I realise there's a more recent one. At first, I think it's my face, but even at that size, I'm able to pick up on the subtle differences.

I tap on the thumbnail and brace myself as it expands to fill the screen.

The pupils of Sasha's eyes are twin dark pools as she steps out onto the street and pulls the door of Darren's unit closed behind her, trapping a cloud of black smoke inside.

'Alright, Lizzie?' she says, beaming from ear to ear. She stops at the door just long enough to slide the bolt across and padlock it, and to give it all a wipe with her sleeve. Once her fingerprints are cleared away, she starts to walk along the street, back in the direction where my car is parked.

I get a glimpse of the small window that looks into Darren's building. It's ablaze with flickering orange light.

'So, in case you've bottled it with watching the recording – and I know you will have – here's what you missed,' she continues, addressing the camera.

She draws in a breath and opens her mouth like she's about to make a big announcement, then grins.

'Nothing. He didn't know anything. Well, either that, or he is one stoic, hardy bastard, and I'm pretty sure it's not that.'

She keeps walking at a slow, deliberate saunter. Behind her, smoke rises from the gap at the bottom of the DJ's roll-up door.

'We went through his computer. There was a lot of very

dodgy stuff on there, let me tell you. Kids. Downloaded, mostly, but a few favourites he's taken himself at discos and parties.'

She shakes her head, almost like she's sensing the question that forms in my head.

'Nothing with Hollie in it. He insisted he had no idea where she was, and he stuck to that, even when I went out of my way to motivate him.'

She winces and shrugs, like none of this is any big deal, and I am reminded, yet again, of how different we are.

'Anyway, that's the story. Dead end, I reckon.' She chuckles, like she's just made a joke, then stops walking.

There's a jangling of keys, then the familiar *beep-beep* of my car being unlocked. The phone swings around. When it settles, it's mounted in the cradle, facing the empty driver's seat.

Sasha bends into view, then turns and peeps into the back seats. 'That doesn't look comfy,' she says, though her voice is muffled.

When she turns back to the camera, she's all smiles. She spots something down on the front passenger seat, reaches for it, and returns with one of Clive's cookies.

'Anyway, that's that,' she says, taking a bite and spraying crumbs everywhere. She swallows, and suddenly her face is serious. Terrifyingly so. 'I'll keep looking. I'll find her.'

The dead-eyed stare becomes a twinkling grin like a switch has been flicked. She blows a kiss to camera, then reaches for the phone to stop the recording, her finger expanding until it almost fills the screen.

A split second before she can press the button, though, she draws back.

'Oh. You might want to look into where your boyfriend went this morning,' she suggests.

Then, with a wink and a smile, she stops the recording, and silence returns to the car.

It wasn't him. I don't have to watch the footage myself to

know that Sasha is telling the truth. I believe her. If he was lying, she'd have got the truth from him. If he was hiding something, she'd have taken a slow, painstaking delight in uncovering it.

He didn't know anything. He didn't have Hollie.

I'm back to square one, and time is running out.

She could be anywhere. With anyone. Anything could be happening to her.

Pain pulls tight around my chest, stealing my breath away. A hundred unwanted thoughts and images fill my head. Tears fill my eyes, trickle down my cheeks. Something thick, and heavy, and wet sticks in my throat, choking me.

She could be anywhere.

With anyone.

Anything could be happening.

I shake my head, chasing those thoughts away. This isn't helping. This isn't getting me anywhere. I need to plan. Think. Act.

I need to find my baby girl.

There's only one lead to follow now. Sasha gave me it, but she shouldn't have had to. I was so relieved not to have to explain anything to Clive this morning, that it didn't occur to me how strange it was he'd gone out without so much as a word.

Where was he going so early? What was he up to?

A firework bursts overhead. I fire up the car's ignition.

And with the crackle of colourful explosions raining down from above, I head for home.

THIRTY-ONE

ELIZABETH

I'm just around the corner from home when my phone rings. It's hooked up to the car's sound system, and the sudden *burring* from all around me jerks the wheel in my hand, earning a horn blast from a car coming in the opposite direction who has to swerve to avoid me.

My heart leaps into my throat.

It's the same number as before.

It's them.

I wrench the wheel to the side, pulling me onto a set of double yellow lines. My hand is shaking so badly I miss the button to answer the call the first time and have to tap a second time before the ringing stops.

'Hello? Hello. Who is this?' I ask. My voice is pitted with potholes and cracks, barely holding together. 'Where's my daughter? Where's Hollie? What have you done with—'

'Mum?'

It's her. Oh, God, it's her. Scared. Muffled. But alive.

'Hollie?! Oh, Jesus, Hollie! It's OK, baby, it's OK, I'm here. Can you hear me? Talk to me, baby. Talk to me.'

I hear a thump. A click. My heart is a jackhammer inside my chest.

'Hollie? Hollie, can you hear me? Talk to me, sweetheart.'

The next voice I hear is not my daughter's. It's a man's, I think, though the electronic rasp of a voice changer makes it hard to be sure.

'Nice of you to answer this time. I was worried you were ignoring me.'

'No, no. I tried, but I couldn't,' I babble. 'Please, I tried to call back. Who is this? Don't hurt Hollie, please. I'll do whatever you want. Do you want money? I can get you money. However much you need, I can get it.'

He laughs. It's a sharp, staccato thing, and sounds slightly robotic through the voice changer, like I'm being taunted by the Daleks.

'I don't want your money, Elizabeth,' he says. 'This isn't about money.'

'What, then? Whatever you want, I'll do it, just don't hurt her, please. You don't need to hurt her.'

'The truth.'

He says the words so softly and matter-of-factly that I almost talk right over him. It takes a second or two for my adrenaline-charged brain to realise he's spoken at all.

'What?' I ask, and he laughs again. Even disguised, there's a sneer to it.

'Should have guessed. You don't even understand the concept, do you, Elizabeth? Lying's not just second nature to you, it's your only nature. It's all you can do. Lies, upon lies, upon lies.'

He's right.

'I don't know what you're talking about,' I insist. 'I just want my little girl home. I want her home with me.'

'She's never going to *be* home with you,' the caller tells me.

'No! Don't hurt her. Please. Please, don't hurt her.'

'That ball's in your court, Elizabeth. There are two ways this can go. In one, you confess to what you did, and I let Hollie go. She grows up safe. Maybe she'll come and visit you. Maybe, you can make her understand.'

He pauses, giving me a moment so his message can sink in.

'Nobody wants what happens with option two. Not you. Not me. Certainly not Hollie.'

'Please—'

'The truth, Elizabeth. That's all we want.'

'Yes, but—'

The line goes dead. The caller's number disappears, and my phone returns to the Home Screen.

'No, no, no!'

I call him back. There's silence for a moment, then the same flat, dead tone as before.

'No, no, don't do this. I need to know.' I scream at the mobile, my spittle flecking the glass. 'I need you to tell me. I need you to explain.'

I'll do what he says. Of course I will. If it means keeping Hollie safe, I'll confess to anything. Whatever it takes.

But I have done some terrible things in my time. There are a lot of skeletons in my closet.

I'll confess.

Whatever it takes.

But confess to what?

THIRTY-TWO

ELIZABETH

Clive isn't home when I arrive back at the flat, though his car's parked out front. Fireworks are screaming across the sky on all sides, so it's possible he's gone out to watch them somewhere.

Strange that he didn't ask me.

Strange that he hasn't called all day.

I'm still shaken from the call. Still shaking. I can hear her voice, hear all the fear and dread packed into the one short word she spoke.

Mum.

She cried out for me. The one person she thought she could rely on to keep her safe. The one person she should have been able to trust, and I've failed her. I've allowed this to happen.

No, worse than that. Something in my past – something I've done – has caused this to happen. This is my fault. Whatever happens to her, whatever they do, is on me.

Her bedroom is silent, like a crypt. The bright colours of the posters and artwork she's stuck to her walls seem darker, more drab, as if every moment she's gone is bleeding the vibrancy from them.

Her bed was messy when I last saw it, her outline still half visible in the creases of her sheets. Now, though, even that has been taken from me. The sheets are pulled tight, the duvet arranged neatly and tucked in at the bottom.

Of course. It's Saturday. The cleaner would've been in.

Was there evidence here? Should I have scoured through Hollie's wastepaper basket, or checked beneath her pillows? Would that have helped me find her? Would that have brought her home?

It's too late now. The room has been cleaned from top to bottom, all hoovered up and dusted down. Anything that was here, is likely now gone.

I sit on her bed, half hovering, barely letting my weight settle. Despite the tidy-up, I'm afraid I'll disturb something. That I'll crush some remnant of her, some memory.

She looks down at me from a photograph on a shelf. It was taken last summer, when we hiked to the top of Arthur's Seat, the extinct volcano in Holyrood Park that towers above Edinburgh.

It was a long, steep climb, and we didn't really have the shoes for it, but she didn't complain. Not once.

The smile on her face in the photo is just another wound on my heart right now, and I can't bring myself to look at it for more than a few seconds.

A confession. That's what they want from me. Can I do that? Can I spill my secrets, after all these years?

If it means saving Hollie, then yes. Of course. I'll admit to everything, even those secrets that aren't just mine to carry.

But I need to know more. I need to know exactly what 'truth' they're trying to expose. Once I know, then I'll do it. I'll own up. If it means saving my daughter, I'll face whatever consequences I have to.

But I need to be sure.

I open up my phone, and watch the video message from Sasha again, right up until her comment at the end about Clive.

Where did he go this morning?

Where is he now?

I get to my feet, smooth down the spot where I've been sitting on Hollie's bed, then make my way through to the bedroom Clive and I share.

When I step inside, I just stand there, by the door, looking the place over as if I'm only just seeing it for the first time. I take in the wooden headboard, with the spars he keeps hinting about handcuffing me to, and I've thus far been able to laugh off.

The bedcovers are neatly pulled together, the pillows plumped up in place.

His Kindle sits on his bedside table, beside a little tartan-topped lamp that would look more at home in a high-end tourist trap hotel.

I check the table first, sliding open the narrow drawer and having a root around inside. There's a bottle of 'intimate massage oil' with a sticky, filmy residue coating the outside. I prod it with a finger, pushing it aside, revealing a scattering of pens, batteries and old charging cables below.

The drawer shudders, like it's resisting me, as I pull it out as far as it'll go and bend lower, getting a good look inside.

There, tucked up at the very back, is a notebook, barely the size of a mobile phone, a pen fastened to it by a loop of elastic.

When I open it, I see a date at the top of the first page. It's from seven years ago, a good three years before I moved in with Clive. The entry below it, written in untidy script, like it was jotted down in a hurry, reads like a diary entry at first, until it becomes disjointed and nonsensical.

The next entries are about flying, and a monster, and being frozen in the bed while dark, humanoid shapes stare down from the shadows at the corners of the room.

Most of the pages seem to be blank. It's a dream journal, started years ago, before being abandoned. I flip all the way to the back to make sure there's nothing else there, then return it to the drawer.

There's a cupboard below the drawer. I open it and root around. It's mostly John Le Carré books, an old electric razor in a battered cardboard box, and a set of pink furry handcuffs I had no idea he owned.

Nothing else, though. Nothing incriminating. Not even when I check between the pages of the books and run my hand along the underside of the drawer above.

Whatever I'm looking for, or hoping to find, it isn't there.

I turn my attention to the bed, and the cluttered space beneath. It's a graveyard of old trainers, hot water bottles, and spare pillows, all enrobed in a covering of dust.

There are a few cardboard boxes, too. Shoe boxes, mostly. I pull one out and open the lid, revealing receipts, warranty information and manuals for every electrical appliance in the place, and several more that have, presumably, long since been carted off to the dump.

There's not a lot more of interest in the other boxes. One contains old ticket stubs and photos from Clive's younger days – the contents of a memory scrapbook he's never quite been arsed enough to get around to making.

I find his passport, birth certificate, and the old paper part of his driving licence in another box, along with funeral cards for his mum and his dad, and copies of the photos used in each. There are handwritten eulogies for both of them, carefully folded up, but I have neither the time nor the inclination to read them.

I shove it all back and lift the mattress.

Nothing.

I check the wardrobe.

Nothing.

I still don't know what I'm looking for. Why would Clive be behind all this? He loves Hollie like she's his own daughter, and, despite all my best efforts, she loves him, too. Even if he had been hiding some grudge against me, he wouldn't hurt her, would he?

Unless...

What if he wanted her in his life, but not me? He knows Hollie's dad is no longer around. If I was out of the picture, she'd be taken into care. At least, as far as he knows. He's a stable father figure. They already have a relationship. He could push for custody of her. He could take my daughter from me.

It's a stretch. There's no saying it would ever go through. And Clive has given no sign to suggest he knows anything about my past that I haven't told him. And I've been careful. I've been meticulous. All he knows about me is what I've allowed him to know.

Unless it isn't.

The whole thing feels... flimsy. I'm clutching at straws, I know it. But flimsy is all I have left.

Abandoning the bedroom, I head for the living room, and rummage around in the drawers and cabinets there. All I find is the same familiar junk that has been knocking around forever. Packs of batteries, old playing cards, picture frames, board games, novelty birthday mugs – the day-to-day detritus of an unremarkable life.

Hollie's voice from the call replays itself in my head, begging me to keep looking, to not give up. I scream an obscenity at the room around me, then whip round on the spot, scanning for anywhere else I haven't looked.

I have no idea where else to search, or what I'm hoping to find. I'm racing towards a dead end, full speed, with no brakes and no seat belt. I have no more leads. No more clues. All that's left is for me to go to the police station and tell them everything.

To confess. Finally, to confess.

My gaze flits past the newspaper rack tucked down next to Clive's chair, then returns to it a moment later. It's crammed full of old papers, TV guides, magazines and junk mail he's held onto for reasons best known to himself. None of it is new. I haven't seen him buy a newspaper in months, let alone read any of the ones wedged in the rack.

A memory seeps in, like a drop of blood in a pool of water. It was back in the early days, after we'd just moved in, and I was guiltily following the old Polish cleaner around, feeling like I should be doing something to earn my keep.

I'd asked her whether she wanted me to empty the rack into her box of recycling.

She'd shaken her head emphatically and told me that Clive instructed her never to touch the contents of the rack.

'Important papers,' she'd said, wagging her finger. I'm still not sure if she was addressing me, or mimicking Clive talking to her. 'No touch.'

I have to move the armchair to free the rack from behind it. It's heavy, the three separate sections packed so tightly that you'd be hard pressed to squeeze even one more sheet of paper into any of them.

At first glance, none of it seems all that important. The newspapers are a few years old. It's only when I see the dates that I'm able to link them up with the funeral cards in the box below the bed.

I bet, if I flick through the pages, I'll find obituaries or death notices for Clive's mum and dad.

I sit them to one side, and rifle through what's left. There are a lot of old bills, council tax statements, and NHS letters about test results and check-ups. For every one of those, though, there's a Tesco Clubcard statement, or a flyer for a local pizza company, or an invitation to switch mobile phone providers addressed only 'To the Resident'.

There's a Christmas edition of the *Radio Times* from three years ago, a colourful pull-out listing all the horses running in the 2022 Grand National, and a fold-out map showing the locations of 'Fun Days Out with the National Trust'.

'It's all junk. It's nothing,' I declare to the room at large, spreading it out on the floor around me, hunting through the...

Wait.

An image, half hidden by a Waitrose recipe card, stops my heart. Stops me breathing. I feel like I've taken a plunge into an icy bath, and all my blood is rushing to my core to protect my vital organs.

My head feels light. My fingers tingle. I slide the recipe card aside to reveal an image of a middle-aged man holding up a tiny tiddler of a fish and beaming like he's just landed the Leviathan.

The person taking the photograph is reflected in the mirrored lenses of his sunglasses. I recognise her at once, although I'd know who she was, even if the reflection wasn't there.

Because I remember that moment.

I remember taking that picture.

And I know the face of the man smiling back at me. I still see it, most nights, when I close my eyes.

Kenny. My late husband. A man that Clive has never known.

Has he?

There's a creaking of a floorboard from behind me. I snatch up the photo like I'm afraid it'll disappear if I don't keep track of it, and turn to find Clive looming in the doorway.

'Elizabeth?' There's an edge to his voice. A sharpness. 'What the hell do you think you're doing?'

THIRTY-THREE
ELIZABETH

He's wrapped up, jacket on. The padding makes him seem larger, more imposing. The lines of his face are drawn downwards into a scowl.

For the first time since we met, he actually makes me feel something.

Fear.

'Clive, I—'

'That's my private stuff. Why are you rummaging around in my private stuff?'

The unzipping of his jacket is like an underscore to the question.

'I know, I'm sorry, I was just looking for... something.'

'What?' he asks, shrugging off his jacket to reveal a colourful knitted jumper. It's one of his better ones. The sort of thing he'd class as 'Sunday Best' if he was into any of that stuff.

I almost say, 'Nothing.' I almost tell him it doesn't matter, that I made a mistake, that I shouldn't have been looking in there.

I almost offer to make it up to him.

But the smiling dead man in my hand seems to taunt me.

I swallow back my fear and get to my feet. 'What... what is this?' I ask, turning the picture for him to see.

Now that I've stood up, he's able to get a better look at me. The scowl on his face is suddenly tempered by concern.

'What happened to your face?'

My fingers brush against the bruising on my cheek. The flesh feels pillowy beneath my fingertips.

'Car accident. Someone rear-ended me in Sainsbury's car park,' I tell him. 'I didn't have my belt on while I was manoeuvring. It's fine.'

'It's not fine. You're hurt. What about the car, is it—?'

'It's fine, Clive,' I insist, then I direct his attention back to the picture in my hand.

His eyes seem reluctant to leave mine. Eventually, though, they look down at the photograph.

'I don't know. It's some guy. Fishing. Why?'

'Why do you have it?'

He's back looking at me now. Staring. I can smell smoke from him. Not cigarettes, but the thick, woody tang of a bonfire.

'I don't know.'

My fingers tighten like pincers on the photograph. The absurdity of his reply emboldens me. 'You *don't know*? You don't know why you have a photograph of this man you've never met in your "private stuff"? Seriously?'

I realise my mistake almost as soon as it's out there. Confusion creeps down his face with the pace of a thawing glacier.

'How do you know I've never met him? Do you know who it is?'

I silently curse myself. Idiot. *Idiot*.

'Why do you have it?' I press, ignoring his question.

He glances around us. Either a thought has occurred to him, or he's actively seeking an excuse to change the subject.

'Where's Hollie?'

'She's still at Sarah's. Answer the question.'

He blinks. His frown fully settles into place. 'Sarah's? You mean Suzie's?'

I don't hesitate. Hesitation is weakness. Hesitation gives him an opening.

'Yes. Suzie's. She's there.' I hold the photo higher, so he has no choice but to look at it. 'Why do you have this picture? I need an explanation, Clive. Please.'

He tosses his jacket onto the couch, sighs, then takes the photo from me and studies it. He turns it over to check the back, then, finding it blank, he shrugs.

'I think it came in with the junk mail. Put it aside to see if you knew what it was. Forgot to ask you.'

I think of the flyers and mailshots tucked into the rack alongside the picture.

It's a plausible answer, but I don't believe it. Not yet.

'When?' I ask. 'When did it come in?'

He puffs out his cheeks. 'Dunno. Last week sometime? It was just on the mat with some local takeaway stuff. Thought maybe it was some viral marketing thing.'

'For what? Fishing?' I ask.

'Well, I don't bloody know,' Clive snipes back.

The aggressiveness of his tone makes me retreat a pace. He sniffs and looks away. There's something different about him tonight. Something I can't quite put my finger on.

'Have you been drinking?' I ask him.

'One or two, aye,' he confirms, without batting an eyelid. 'Went to the bonfire to check out the fireworks. Was hoping we could all go, but I didn't know where you were.'

'You didn't check,' I point out. 'You never called me to ask.'

He shrugs. There's something petulant and sullen about it. 'You always moan if I do. Accuse me of checking up on you.'

He's right. I do.

'I don't,' I protest, but he just laughs and shakes his head.

'Whatever you say, Elizabeth.'

He puts a hand over his eyes, then runs it down his face, like he's trying to wipe off his expression. I get the sense that he's about to tell me something, but then he bites his lip, shakes his head again, and turns the photo around to face me.

'So, who is it, then? Who's the fisherman?'

'I don't know.'

'Bollocks!' he snaps. 'Yes, you do. You wouldn't be making all this fuss if you didn't. And you said he's someone I've never met. How would you know that if you didn't know him?'

I consider telling him the truth.

But only for a moment, and even then, not seriously.

Instead, I give him the official story.

'It's Hollie's dad.'

'Your ex? Oh.' He turns the photo back so he can take another look. 'Wait, what? I thought he was—'

'He is. This is an old picture.'

'Right.' He glances up at me, but then returns to the photo again. 'So... what? Why would someone stick a photo of your husband through the door?'

'*Late* husband. And, I don't know,' I say. Although I have my suspicions.

'You sure he's dead, aye?' Clive asks. A little smile tugs at the corners of his mouth, like he's trying to make a joke of it all. 'He's not come to steal you back?'

'He's dead,' I reply.

Definitely, definitively, indubitably dead.

'Right. So... what's this about?' He flicks the photo with a finger. The *crack* of it makes me jump. 'Seems dodgy. I don't like it. Should we talk to the police?'

'The police? And say what?'

He scratches at the back of his head. 'I mean... It's weird, though, isn't it? We should say something to someone.'

His anger about me poking around in the newspaper rack seems to have dissipated.

'I don't think anyone will be interested,' I tell him, trying to steer him away from any thoughts of the authorities. 'I just... Can you remember when it arrived? What day?'

I'm not sure that detail matters, but it might. If I'd seen it at the time, I would've taken it as a warning. I'd have been on my guard.

'I'm not sure,' he admits.

'Think, Clive,' I urge. 'Please.'

He chews on his bottom lip, like he always does when he's concentrating. His eyes dart left and right, scrubbing through some internal calendar or timeline.

'Wednesday,' he declares, with a firm, confident nod. 'It was Wednesday. I remember, because I'd come back from the bank, and that was Wednesday morning. So, before twelve on Wednesday.'

Wednesday. Two days before Hollie was taken.

I want to grab Clive by his stupidly cheerful jumper and shake him. If he'd showed me this, if I'd seen it, Hollie wouldn't have been at that disco. She wouldn't have been at school. We wouldn't have been in this country.

If I'd seen it, I could have protected her, kept her safe.

But this *idiot*, this *cretin*...

I swallow back a swill of bile and a surge of rage. It's not his fault. He didn't know.

Unless he did. Unless he's lying.

'Where were you this morning?' I ask.

The question catches him off guard. He chews on his lip again, then, as soon as he realises, makes a conscious effort to stop.

'What?'

'This morning. You were out early.'

'You were asleep on the chair. I didn't want to disturb you,' Clive says. 'I pulled a blanket over you in case you were cold.'

None of that answers my question. I stare at him until he buckles.

'Fine. I was at the gym.'

'The gym?' I look him up and down, as if to highlight his physique. 'You don't go to the gym.'

'Aye, well, I thought it was time I started,' he says.

'Which gym?'

'The, uh, the big one. Up by the Western General.' He picks up his jacket and takes it out into the hall. 'It was mobbed. I felt properly out of place, too. They were all ultra-fit, and here's me wheezing away.'

When he returns, I'm still standing there, arms folded. 'All day? You were at the gym all day?'

'No. Course not. I came back here,' he says, then something flashes behind his eyes. Panic, maybe. 'I went out for a bit. Round to Alan's.'

'Weird Alan's? You went round to *Weird Alan's*? Why?'

His feet shuffle on the laminate flooring. He scratches at his head again but manages to stop himself biting his lip.

'Warhammer,' he says.

He winces, like he's bracing himself for my reaction. The word means nothing to me, though.

'You know, the wee figures? Knights, and goblins, and dragons, and that? Tabletop gaming.'

'What, like... Dungeons and Dragons?'

'Sort of. Same idea. Similar,' Clive continues. 'Alan's big into them, and I mentioned I was thinking of giving it a go, so we've been talking about it. He got me over to look at his undead army. It's impressive.' His enthusiasm wanes under the heat of my stare. 'If, you know, you're into that sort of thing.'

'Undead army?' I practically spit the words back at him. 'You were round at Weird Alan's playing with his *undead army*?'

He smiles. It's thin, and weak, and a hair's breadth away

from becoming a cringe. 'Not playing with it, no, just... just looking at it. There's a shop in town. Over on Castle Street. He reckons they're the best place to go to get started. He used to go there, back in the day, before he became, you know...'

'A weirdo hermit who never leaves the house?'

I realise, then, what's going on. A new hobby. A sudden interest in the gym. His Sunday Best jumper, and a spray of cologne.

I suddenly see him for exactly what he is.

He's not a kidnapper. He hasn't taken Hollie.

He's a man in the grip of a mid-life crisis.

And that makes him useless to me.

There's nothing he can tell me that will help me find my daughter.

But I have learned one thing.

I now know for certain what I'm supposed to be confessing to.

THIRTY-FOUR
ELIZABETH

Fettes Police Station is just a short drive away from the flat. I considered walking, given that it's late, and the back lights of my car are no longer functional, but eventually decided just to drive. A fine, or points on my licence, are the least of my worries.

The station is a grim, concrete block, probably built back in the 1960s. It's surrounded by a metal fence, the black-painted bars blistering with rust. The automatic gate doesn't open as I approach, and there's no obvious way to signal to anyone inside. I reverse up, park on the road, and walk the rest of the way to the front door.

The wind whips at me, swirling around, encasing me in the smell of cordite, or gunpowder, or whatever it is they use in fireworks these days. A few spots of light rain dapple my forehead. The opening salvo of an oncoming storm that's accompanied by bursts of fire and whistling screeches from on high.

This is the right thing to do. It's the only thing to do. They want me to confess, so I will. I'll tell them what I did.

What we did.

Sasha won't be happy, but maybe I can get her to understand. Not for my sake, but for Hollie's.

Hollie.

Her name tightens my throat and burns at the corners of my eyes.

What will happen to her? Will they let her stay with Clive? Will he want her to? He's a good man. He didn't bat an eyelid when I told him about her. He grew to love her almost right away. She doesn't call him Dad, but maybe one day she could.

If not him, then it'll be the care system. Foster families, maybe. A procession of strangers and part-timers. A lottery of good ones and bad.

There is another alternative, of course. Far, far worse than either of those. The thought of it makes me stop twenty feet from the police station's front door.

I can't let her be taken there. I won't. Better she die than go back there.

I force my legs into action. Plod forwards. One step. Two.

They don't know about that. Nobody knows. As far as anyone's concerned, we're a normal family. Those secrets are safe.

Anyway, it's irrelevant. Clive will fight for her. I know he will. He's told me himself, more than once, she's the daughter he always wishes he'd had. You can see it in his eyes, too, when he looks at her. In his smile. In the way he is with her. He'd do anything for her.

Anything.

For all his faults, I know I can rely on him to keep her safe.

From anyone.

I'm ten feet from the door. My legs seize up again.

Why wouldn't he show me that photo when it arrived? Why not leave it out, at least, so he didn't forget? Why stuff it down with his parents' obituaries in the newspaper rack?

Why get so upset when he caught me snooping?

Even though I had discounted him having anything to do with Hollie's disappearance, my mind races back to my earlier theory, and starts revising it based on what I now know.

What if Clive knew about Kenny? What if whoever gave him the photo told him what I did? He'd be scared. For himself, yes, but maybe for Hollie, too. He couldn't confront me about it for fear of what might happen – I could disappear into the night with her.

Or, I could do something worse.

I can rely on him to keep her safe. From anyone.

Even me?

If he wanted Hollie, but wanted rid of me, then this would be the perfect way to do it. He didn't try and stop me when I said I was heading to bring some more clothes over to Suzie's. He didn't volunteer to do it, either.

Does he know? Is he fully aware that she isn't there, that there is no Suzie? Does he know that I left to come out here, to confess everything to the police?

Is this, all of this, part of his plan?

The door to the police station stands dead ahead. There's a light on inside. I can see the front desk, though there's nobody standing behind it. They'll be through the back somewhere. One press of the bell on the counter, and they'll come through.

And, then, I can tell them.

And my life, and Hollie's, will be torn to pieces.

Warhammer.

Undead army.

A shop on Castle Street.

There was too much detail when Clive was telling me where he was. Too much information, even for him. I should've recognised that at the time.

I know a lie when I hear one, after all.

I take out my phone, open up the notes, and find the number I took from Clive's call history the night before. If Clive is telling the truth about where he was today, Weird Alan should be able to confirm it.

I copy and paste it into my phone app, then hit the button to start calling.

It rings. Once. Twice. The repetitive *burring* goes on and on. Ten seconds. Twenty.

'Come on. Come on.'

There's movement inside the police station. The boom of a firework from a few streets over ricochets off the concrete, the explosion reflecting off the glass like a camera flash.

The phone keeps ringing. Over and over.

I'm about to hang up when there's a click. A voice answers.

'Hello?'

I've never talked to Weird Alan before, or even heard him speak, but I know, right away, this isn't him.

It's a woman.

'Who is this?' I ask.

There's a pause. A drawing in of breath so subtle I might have imagined it.

And then, the line goes dead.

I hit the redial button. This time, there's no sound from the line, just a hollow silence that eventually gives way to a robotic-sounding voicemail greeting.

'Damn it.' I stab my thumb against the screen and am about to eject some further obscenities when I see a woman in police uniform standing in the doorway of the station.

'You alright, love?' she asks. She smiles, but her eyes are studying me, sizing me up. 'You need something?'

I look down at the phone in my hand. Glare at it, like I'm accusing it of some terrible, heinous crime.

'You need help with something, love?'

I think of the voice on the phone.

I think of the possibilities.

I think of my daughter.

'No, it's fine,' I tell her, returning the mobile to my pocket. 'I think it's better if I just handle things myself.'

PART 3
SUNDAY

THIRTY-FIVE
ELIZABETH

Clive was asleep when I came home. I could hear the bandsaw of his snoring as soon as I entered the flat.

After the police station, I drove home, then walked the streets of Stockbridge for a while, hoping that inspiration as to Hollie's whereabouts would suddenly strike, or that one of my calls to the kidnappers would be answered.

Neither happened.

A couple of times, when I saw police cars passing, I considered flagging them down and throwing myself at their mercy.

Confession may be the best way of getting Hollie back safely, but something tells me it won't be. An instinct, a feeling in my gut, insists that whoever has her won't just let her go, no matter what I own up to. They can't afford to release her, in case she identifies them.

That's what I tell myself, at least. It helps soften the edges of my guilt.

It was later than expected when I got back home. After two. Not sure how that happened. My whole body was vibrating with the cold when I finally returned.

Once again, there had been no calls or texts from Clive to check my whereabouts, or to make sure I was OK. It isn't like him. He's definitely up to something.

I couldn't face getting into bed beside him, and my body has been aching ever since I woke up on the armchair yesterday morning, so I slipped into Hollie's room, and slept on top of her bed, a pair of her pyjamas clutched in one hand, and one of her teddies hooked beneath my arm.

It took me a few hours, but I eventually cried myself out enough for exhaustion to take hold and drag me down into sleep.

The sleep was fitful, haunted by dreams of Hollie. Nightmares, mainly, that slicked my body with sweat and twisted the bedsheets into knots.

And now... voices. Low. Male. Clive, I think, and someone else. Someone I dimly recognise but can't yet place.

I'm still fully dressed from last night, so I quietly swing my legs out of bed, then creep up to Hollie's bedroom door. Pressing my ear against the white-painted wood, I hold my breath and listen.

They're in the living room. I can't fully make out what they're saying, but I pick up the odd word here and there.

Concern.

Accident.

Hollie.

I check my watch. It's almost nine. Based on when I last checked during the night, I've been asleep for three, maybe three and a half hours. Judging by the state of the bedcovers, it was a fitful, restless three hours, at that.

Clive's voice grows a little louder. At first, I think he's raising it in anger, then realise he's moving across the room, getting closer to the living room door.

My phone rings. It's so close, and so loud, that I jerk

forwards in fright, the side of my head knocking against the door.

Clive's name is on the screen. Even as I see it, I hear him calling me from the other room.

'Elizabeth? Are you here?'

Footsteps draw closer. I run a hand through my hair and smooth down my crumpled clothes, then pull open the door, a big smile as fake as Monopoly money plastered across my face.

'Morning. Yes, I'm here,' I trill, stepping out into the hallway.

Clive aborts his approach to Hollie's room, drawing up short just before he walks straight into me. I glance past his look of surprise to the living room door but can't see whoever else it is that's in there.

'Where have you been?' he asks. It's part confrontational, part concern, but it's difficult to quantify the ratio. 'I was worried sick.'

Not worried enough to try and get in touch, I almost point out, but I don't. Instead, I just tilt my head back to indicate the room behind me.

'I stayed out to watch some fireworks,' I say, using his own excuse against him. If it's a weird claim for me to make, then it asks questions about his usage of it, too. 'You were asleep when I got back. Didn't want to disturb you.'

He searches my face, considering the explanation, then slowly points a thumb back in the direction of the living room.

'Right. Fair enough. Well, there's someone here to see you.'

A knot of dread sits like a weight in my stomach. I have no idea who's in there, beyond the fact that it's a man. And there are no men I can think of that I'd be happy to see right now.

'Who?' I ask, but the word sticks in my craw. I clear my throat and try again. 'Who is it?'

I hear the creaking of a footstep on a loose floorboard. A shadow moves across the living room wall.

The knot pulls tighter, grows heavier, as a figure appears in the doorway, toned and handsome in his tight-fitting running gear. It's no wonder all the mums love him.

'Morning, Elizabeth.' It's Mr Wilkinson. The teacher. 'I just thought I'd pop round to say hi to Hollie.'

THIRTY-SIX

ELIZABETH

Clive gestures for me to enter the living room, and I'm suddenly ten years old again, being escorted into the headmaster's office, head down, shoulders slumped, feet dragging along the floor.

He closes the door behind us, which immediately makes me uneasy, makes me feel trapped. Clive never closes the living room door, much less stands in front of it with his arms folded, like a bouncer at a nightclub.

My heart begins to thrum inside my chest. A subway map of lies and excuses starts to plot out all the possible conversational routes inside my head.

'You forgot these,' Mr Wilkinson says. There's a slight stutter when he spots my black eye, and the purple bruising I'm able to see on my swollen cheek.

'Had a prang in the car,' I say, offering up an explanation before he has a chance to ask about it.

He holds out a carrier bag, a handle in each hand, and angles it so I can see inside. Hollie's shoes lurk down at the bottom.

'Thought she might be needing them,' he says, closing the bag and sitting it on the floor at his feet.

'She's got others. She'd have been fine,' I say. 'You shouldn't have come all this way just for that.'

He waves, dismissing the remark. 'It's fine. I run past this way, anyway. It's on the way to the gym.'

Of course he runs. He and Clive must be about the same age, but Mr Wilkinson could be Clive's younger brother.

His *much* younger brother.

'The gym near the hospital? Clive goes to that one,' I say, trying to take charge of the conversation.

'Oh?' Mr Wilkinson shoots a glance in Clive's direction. 'I don't think I've seen you there. Have I?'

'I just recently started. I'm pretty new to it,' Clive explains, then he pats his stomach as if offering supporting evidence for this claim. The haste with which he blurts it all out further convinces me he's lying about the whole thing.

Before I can think any more about the *why* of that, though, the teacher hits me with a sucker punch out of nowhere.

'Clive tells me that Hollie has spent the last couple of nights staying with... Suzie?'

Oh, God. Oh, no.

'That's right,' I say, because what other choice do I have?

'I don't know a Suzie,' Mr Wilkinson continues, his brow furrowing like he's really racking his brains. 'Is she from the school?'

'She's in Hollie's class. Lives on Rose Street, doesn't she?' Clive chips in.

Is he trying to be helpful, or is he stitching me up?

'Rose Street?' The teacher purses his lips together and moves his mouth from side to side, like he's chewing over this new nugget of information. 'I'm not sure of everyone's address.'

He clearly knew ours, though.

'Do you mean Sophie?' he asks after some more thought, and I make a frantic grab for this life ring I've been thrown.

'Yes. Yes, that's it. Not Suzie, *Sophie!*' I cry, striking myself on the forehead with the palm of a hand. 'Oh, my God. I've been calling her Suzie. Oh, that's embarrassing. I'm going to have to apologise to her and her mum for—'

'Sophie's away this weekend,' Mr Wilkinson says. 'They've been away all week, in fact. They're on holiday. Florida, I think. Not due back until Wednesday.'

The subway map in my head shunts me onto a different track.

'Actually... was it Sophie?' I mumble, narrowing my eyes and staring off into space. 'Maybe it's not Sophie, then. Are you sure there's not a Suzie? Suzanne? Maybe it's a nickname...'

A look passes from the teacher to Clive. I suddenly get a sense of what's coming next, and a vertigo-inducing void opens in the floor beneath me. It feels like that, at least, but without the escape possibilities that a real hole would offer.

'You told us on Friday that your partner came to pick Hollie up from the disco and took her home,' Mr Wilkinson says. 'But he tells me that's not the case.'

'It isn't. I didn't collect her. I was at home,' Clive insists. He turns to me. Turns *on* me. 'What the hell's going on, Elizabeth? Where's Hollie?'

'Hollie's fine,' I say. I try to laugh it off, but it's the last bray of a dying hyena. 'She is. She's fine. This is silly.'

'I'm sure you understand, Elizabeth, that as Hollie's acting head teacher, I have a responsibility for her welfare. We care about Hollie. *I* care about her. We want to make sure she's safe.'

'It's the weekend.'

'That's irrelevant.'

I stab a finger against my chest, furious about what he might be implying.

Even if it's correct.

'I'm her mother. Her welfare is *my* responsibility.'

The teacher holds up his hands. 'Of course. Absolutely. Couldn't agree more. But...' He shoots another look at Clive. I don't see how it's returned. 'Please try and see this from my perspective. You were panicked on Friday that something had happened to Hollie, then you assured us that she had been collected and taken home. But it seems that isn't the case.'

'You lied to me about where she is,' Clive adds.

I spin round, practically at him. 'It's none of your business where my daughter is.'

He blinks rapidly, like I've swung a fist at him and stopped just short of connecting. Every time his eyes flick back open, I can see more hurt behind them.

'But it *is* mine,' Mr Wilkinson says. 'Like it or not, I have a duty – I have a responsibility to Hollie – to follow up on any welfare concerns. And, well, I'm not going to lie, Elizabeth, I'm concerned. I'm really quite concerned. Right now, I'm considering making this a police matter, unless you can provide a good explanation as to—'

'My sister.'

I hear the words coming out of my mouth at the same time as the men do. I'm as surprised by them as they are.

'Your sister?' Clive asks.

'Is this Hollie's aunt she's spoken about? That Miss Goodall mentioned on Friday? Sarah, was it?'

I shake my head. Slowly. Dumbly. 'Sasha.'

'Hang on. You said your sister was a psycho?' Clive reminds me.

I try to hide my wince behind a little laugh. 'I was exaggerating. Obviously, she's not a *psycho*.'

'You said those exact words to me. "She's a psycho." That's why she's not part of your life, you said.'

'Jesus, Clive. Again, I was exaggerating.' I try to laugh it off. It's paper thin. One-ply. Fully see-through. 'Relax.'

'What are you saying?' the teacher asks. 'Hollie was picked up by her aunt on Friday night? And she's staying with her now?'

'Yes. Exactly. I just...' I sigh, trying to sell the deception. 'Yes, I'd bad-mouthed my sister to Clive a few times, but she's getting better. She's doing better. Hollie loves hanging out with her, so I agreed that she could stay for the weekend. I didn't want Clive worrying, after the stuff I'd said, so... I lied. I'm sorry. I shouldn't have. It was stupid.'

I smile at both men, but neither of them returns it.

I can tell from the teacher's face that he doesn't believe me. Of course he doesn't. Why should he? Even if he thought it was a plausible reason for not telling Clive the truth, it doesn't explain my lying to him and Miss Goodall, or my total freak-out when I discovered that Hollie was missing.

There's no way out of this. There are no more lies I can tell that will explain it all away.

Luckily, I don't need to. Mr Wilkinson runs a hand down his face and sighs, like he's fighting against his better judgement.

'OK, here's what's going to happen,' he says. 'I'm going to see Hollie back in school tomorrow morning. Nine o'clock, if not before. Not a minute late, though. A minute late, and I've got no choice but to turn everything over to the authorities. It'll be out of my hands. Is that clear, Elizabeth?'

'Of course. Yes. No problem. She'll be there,' I say. 'Not a problem.'

'Good. Because, again, if she isn't, it's out of my hands.' He bends, picks up the carrier bag containing Hollie's shoes, and holds it out to me. 'Tomorrow morning. Nine sharp. That's' – he checks his watch – 'just under twenty-four hours. Whatever you need to do to make sure she's there, whatever that may be, I *strongly* suggest that you do it. Otherwise, I'll have no alternative but to call the police.'

THIRTY-SEVEN
ELIZABETH

I stand in the living room, listening, waiting, as Clive sees Mr Wilkinson out. Their conversation at the door is short and muttered. I think I hear the teacher stressing the importance of Hollie being back tomorrow, and Clive assuring him that she will be.

I wish that promise was within his power to make.

There's a tension in the air when he returns. He doesn't close the door behind him this time but remains standing in front of it. The only way out is through him.

If it comes to that, then so be it.

'Well?'

It's just one word. Barely a question, at all. And yet, it's one that's all-encompassing, asking *everything*.

'Well, what?'

'Liz, come on.' There's an incredulous note to his voice. 'What are you doing? What the hell's going on?'

'Nothing's *going on*, Clive. Hollie's at my sister's.'

'Which is where, exactly?'

I sigh and roll my eyes, like he's the bad guy. Like he's the one in the wrong.

'Let's go get her. I'll drive. I want to meet Sasha.'

I snort at that. 'No, you don't.'

'Why not?'

'Because she'd despise you, Clive. She'd think you're a joke.'

I watch the pain register on his face. He recoils, like I've physically struck him. 'I'm a joke, am I?'

'What? No. I don't think that, I'm saying *she'd* think that, because she's...'

'A psycho?'

For a moment, I almost tell him the truth. I almost tell him exactly what Sasha's like, and the things she's done.

The things she's made me do.

I'm about to, in fact, when he butts in.

'Is this about that photo?'

I flash back to a picture of Hollie, tied up and blindfolded. The thought of it almost drops me to my knees, but I push on through.

'What photo?'

He tuts, exasperated. 'You know what photo, Liz. The one of your dead husband.'

'Oh. No. No, of course not.'

I look away, but I can feel him looking at me. Scrutinising me. I hear a few intakes of breath as he works up the courage to ask his next question.

'How did he die?'

I'm not ready for the question. The answer is committed to memory, word for word, but it still catches me off guard. '*What?*'

'Your husband. Kenny. You never told me what happened to him.'

'I did. I told you.'

He shakes his head. 'You said it was "an accident". That's all. You never elaborated.'

'It's... painful. I don't like to talk about it,' I tell him, but he continues to stare at me, unmoved.

He's not letting me out of this.

'He lost control of his car. In the Highlands. It rolled a few times, then caught on fire. He... couldn't get out.'

His eyes widen a fraction. His dry lips make a slight popping sound as they pull apart.

'Jesus,' he whispers. 'Anyone else involved?'

I shake my head, my face a mask of practised grief. 'No. Just Kenny. There was nobody else around.'

I hope that's the end of it, but he's like a dog with a bone, refusing to drop it.

'Nobody? But, I mean, how does that happen? Rolling a car like that?'

'I don't know.'

'Well, what did the police say?'

'Nothing much.'

'Didn't they investigate? They must have investigated.'

'Yes. Obviously. The results were "inconclusive".'

I sigh, making clear my reluctance to continue this conversation.

Obviously not clearly enough.

'A guy rolls his car and burns to death, and they can't find *any* reason for it at all?'

'Maybe he was just being careless, Clive,' I cry, my patience snapping with such force that I swear I hear the *twang*. 'Maybe, he was too focused on something that was none of his damn business, and things got out of control.'

The only sound in the room is the unsteady rasping of my breath, and the low internal rumblings of my insides puckering up.

What have I said? Too much. Far too much.

'The hell's that supposed to mean?' he mumbles.

'Nothing. It doesn't mean anything,' I insist. I move to leave, but he's still blocking the door. 'Can you get out of the way, please? I want to go. I want to leave.'

He stands over me, arms folded, peering down. I think he might be about to refuse, but then he shakes his head and stands aside, and I hurry back to Hollie's bedroom to grab my phone and put on my shoes.

I'm just wriggling my foot into the second one when I hear the flat's front door slam closed. Hollie's bedroom window overlooks the street, and so I lurk behind her curtain, watching until I see Clive emerging from the building. He has no jacket on, and I expect him to get straight in his car.

Instead, he stops just a few paces past it, and shoots a look back up at the flat. I step back into the shadows and let the net curtain do the rest of the work. His eyes dart from window to window, then he hurries on towards the corner, headed for the main road.

It's November. In Scotland. A fine autumn drizzle is painting puddles on the ground. Stroppy storm-off or not, where the hell is he going without a jacket?

Not Weird Alan's. That's along the road, in the opposite direction to the one he's headed in.

Where, then?

To do what?

My foot slips all the way into my trainer. I unplug my phone from Hollie's charger, and pocket it. I grab my jacket.

And then, I hurry down the stairs, out onto India Street, and, with icy spots of rain dappling my skin, I lower my head and I follow.

THIRTY-EIGHT

ELIZABETH

India Street sticks out like an appendage from a circular street called Royal Circus, which is nearly bisected by Circus Lane. Seen from above, India Street looks a bit like the handle of a magnifying glass although, admittedly, you need to use a bit of imagination.

I expect Clive to take a left at the junction with Circus Lane. Left leads downhill, to where the artisan bakeries and *oh so Instagrammable* cafés of Stockbridge all lie.

Instead, though, he starts angling right, headed uphill, towards nothing of any real note. No bookshops. No award-winning craft beer microbreweries. Not even the gym he's claiming to now be a member of.

Nothing but residential streets for a good half mile, with the odd boutique hotel or two dotted in among them.

What is he up to?

He glances back at the corner, but I'm ready for it, and safely hidden behind one of several Range Rovers in the permit-holders' parking bays. He's looking up at the flat, anyway, checking to make sure I'm not watching from the window as he disappears around the corner, out of sight.

Emerging from cover, I hurry after him, only slowing when I reach the gable end of the first house on India Street. I creep along it, one hand trailing across the weathered grey stone, then peek round the corner when I reach the end.

Clive is marching up the hill, shoulders hunched against the wind and the rain. His head is down, and his hands are buried in his pockets. He gives the impression of a man trying very hard to turn himself invisible.

Traffic is crawling in both directions along the road, the Edinburgh traffic lights already orchestrating their usual stop-start dance.

There are only a couple of vehicles parked up by the pavement. Not a lot of cover. If I follow now, and he turns around, he'll be looking straight at me.

I have no choice but to let him pull ahead. I count to ten, then to twenty, then decide on a full thirty seconds before I risk falling into step behind him.

I underestimate his pace, though, and I have to hurry up the incline to stop the gap between us widening too far.

In moments, my legs and my lungs both feel like they're burning. All the stress and the effort of the last few days was already making my limbs feel heavy, so it's a relief when the road levels out a little, and I'm no longer dragging my arse uphill.

A horn blares close by on my left, making me jump. I turn in time to see a variety of rude gestures pass between a couple of drivers, and then the one who'd been dawdling at a green light floors the accelerator, just as it turns to amber.

The driver of the car that gets blocked by the change to red bellows a loud, clear, 'Twat!' out of his window, but the target of his rage is already too far away to hear him.

I look ahead again, half expecting to find Clive stopped there, staring back at me, his attention drawn by the horn or the shouting.

But he isn't. He isn't standing there. He isn't walking, either.

My gaze flits across to the opposite side of the road, searching for him.

I don't see him. He's not there. How can he not be there?

Pointlessly, I check behind me, in case he's somehow snuck past in the opposite direction. A young couple walk hand in hand up the hill a fair stretch back, but, of course, there's no sign of Clive.

I hurry on, picking up speed, a stumbling, fast walk that turns into a run. Even as I race along the pavement, though, my brain settles on the only possible solution.

He's hung a right back onto Royal Circle. He's re-entered the Circle. It's the only explanation.

And it makes perfect sense. He stormed off in a rage with no plan and no jacket. One short walk around the block, and he'll be heading back home. Maybe he was giving me a chance to leave without any more confrontation.

Or maybe, he just couldn't bear to stay there with me a moment longer than he had to.

Either way, he must be returning home now, approaching the flat from the opposite end of the street, no doubt expecting me to be gone. And he'll be right, of course.

I slow a little when I reach the corner, then proceed along the bend until the front of the flat comes into view again.

I still don't see him. There's no movement on the street. Not that I can see, at least. But I hear a sound from close by. A snatch of a woman's voice. The closing of a door.

A door with a row of brass Roman numerals.

Mabel Walker's.

The Uberbitch.

THIRTY-NINE

ELIZABETH

Like all the front doors on India Street, Mabel's is thick, heavy, and apparently impenetrable by sound. I can't hear a thing from inside, even when I creak open the letterbox and jam my ear against it.

Her husband's Bentley isn't parked out front, suggesting he isn't home.

I rifle through all the explanations for why Clive might have gone into Mabel's house. Any other day, there'd only be one. Today, though, there's another possibility. Something else that might explain it.

Something worse.

I try to remember the details of the voice of the woman who answered my call to what I thought was Weird Alan. Could it have been Mabel's? Her usual haughty tone was absent, but then she generally only uses that when she's talking to me, or the other junior members of the parent council.

If she was using a different phone, and didn't have my number stored, she'd have had no idea who was calling her.

So, maybe, then. Not impossible.

I consider just knocking on the door, but what if they don't answer? They'll know I'm here, and I'll be no further forward.

Instead, I creep around the side of the house, to where a tall wooden gate blocks access to the back garden. I try the handle, but it's locked from the other side.

The clamber over isn't graceful or pretty, but by using the recycling bin as a stepping stone, I'm able to haul myself over the top.

There's even less style to the landing, and it's something of a miracle when I escape with only a few minor grazes and no broken bones. The bruising around my eye and the puffiness of my cheek from where the DJ hit me yesterday is bad enough. It throbs as I pull myself back to my feet.

Mabel Walker's back garden is like something from a life-style magazine. A monstrous glass and metal extension opens onto a herringbone wooden decking, with grey wicker furniture and a slatted-roofed pagoda. Or pergola. Or whatever the hell this one's called.

A wide, brick-built barbecue and burnished metal fire pit stand off to one side, on a checkerboard of black and grey stone slabs. Behind them, raised off the ground, is a long row of wooden boxes with the sprouts of winter vegetables poking up through the well-tended soil.

An eight-feet-high fence surrounds the whole thing, shielding it from the prying eyes of neighbours. It's overlooked, though, by the two upper flats in the next building along, and I can only imagine how engorged with rage Mabel must regularly become about that fact.

I can't see any movement through the glass of the extension. It's a cross between a dining room and a lounge, with a rectangular archway leading through to a black marble kitchen that looks from here to be more than half the size of Clive's whole flat.

The double doors that lead out onto the decking aren't locked when I try the handle. Despite their weight, they glide effortlessly aside without a sound, allowing me to slip inside.

Into the lair of the Uberbitch.

I'm not sure if it's the building itself, or my own baggage with Mabel, but the place feels cold and unwelcoming. I'm gripped by a sense of dread as I tiptoe across the extension and into the sort of kitchen a minor royal wouldn't mind whipping up a pheasant sandwich in.

There's still no sound from elsewhere in the house. I hold my breath and creep to the door, expecting to hear the murmur of voices from one of the adjoining rooms.

But no.

Nothing.

The whole place feels deserted, and had I not heard Mabel's voice and the door closing from outside, I'd have sworn the house was empty.

The living room, with its red leather couches, wood-burning stove, and cluttered bookshelves, is empty. The room across from it – a second lounge, or maybe even a third, if you count the extension – is, too. There's an enormous wall-mounted TV and a games console in this room, and I get the impression this could be where Jessica hangs out, packed off out of sight of her parents.

I can't say I blame them.

She's not here now, though. No one is.

A staircase leads up from the hallway by the front door. It's in the same position as the one back at Clive's block of flats, but while that one has been stripped back to stone, this one retains all its original tilework, painstakingly restored to its former glory.

The weak November light, filtered through the small, net-curtained windows, doesn't do a whole lot to drive back the darkness. I plod upwards, slowly and cautiously, into the gloom, ears tuned for any signs of life.

The house spans three storeys. There are four doors on this floor. Is it possible that Hollie is behind one of them? I think back to the filth and squalor of where she was being held in the photo her abductor sent me, and can't imagine for one moment that any part of Mabel Walker's house looks like that.

I listen at a few of the doors on the first floor, and peek in at one or two.

Nothing.

The second staircase doesn't have the same tiles as the first. It's more modern, made of smooth, curved wood with bronze detailing on the banister. I continue up it to the third floor, keeping my weight as close as I can to the wall to avoid any give-away creaking.

I slow to a crawl at the top of the staircase. At the top of the house. They must be here. There's nowhere else they could be, unless Mabel has a secret room somewhere.

God. What if she does?

I glance back down the stairs I've just walked up. What if there's a hidden room where Hollie is stashed?

If I stopped to think about it, I'd realise there isn't a single good reason why Mabel would be involved in Hollie's abduction, but my hatred of her fuels my suspicion. Is my daughter tied up somewhere in this building? Could she be right beyond one of these doors?

This time, I don't even bother to listen. Instead, I barge straight into two bedrooms, a small study, and a bathroom with a free-standing tub.

All empty.

All clear.

So, where the hell are they?

I'm about to head back down to recheck the floors below,

when I hear it. A soft, low whimper of fear. Pain, maybe. It sounds close. Just a few feet away.

But, how?

It comes again. A hiss. A sob, stifled and strangled.

And that's when I realise. The sound isn't coming from around me.

It's coming from above.

Slowly – ever so slowly – I turn my eyes towards the ceiling.

FORTY

ELIZABETH

After some searching, I find the staircase behind a set of double doors in one of the bedrooms. There are eight steps, all steep, almost a ladder, leading to a dimly lit attic space above.

Here, this close, there's no doubt about the whimpering. I still can't tell if it's fear or pain but suspect it's a little of both.

I put my foot on the bottom rung, testing my weight on it. It makes no sound to give me away.

I move onto the next step. The next. Climbing steadily, hands grabbing the steps above and ahead of me for support.

The sharp ring of a slap stops me. The breathless sobbing cuts off, choked into silence.

'Shut your mouth, you snivelling little bitch.'

Mabel's voice is a hiss, thickened with contempt.

'Stop crying for your mummy.'

Anger drives me on. Hatred drives me up. I explode up into the attic, fists clenched, ready to swing.

I stop when I see the restraints. When I see the handcuffs. When I see the gag.

When I see the quivering, naked body of Clive, lying flat on his back on the floor, head tilted back in ecstasy as Mabel bounces violently on top of him. Her bare expensive breasts jiggle excitedly when she whips him with a short leather riding crop she clutches in one hand.

Clive's wide, watery eyes meet mine. He tries to speak, but the ball gag jammed into his mouth relegates it to a series of guttural, gasping, choking sounds.

Mabel, unfettered by any such contraption, screams out my name like it's some terrible curse. She jumps to her feet with an impressive turn of speed, pointing the riding crop at me like a sword.

Somehow, despite my shock, I have the presence of mind to take out my phone and start snapping off photos.

Mabel doesn't know which part of her naked body to hide first, so she falls back, scrambling for the clothes that lie, folded neatly, on a chair just to the side of where the action had been happening.

'How dare you? How *dare* you?' she shrieks, like I'm the one in the wrong here.

Clive, meanwhile, seems to be struggling to breathe as he fiddles frantically with the strap of his gag. His face is a slick of tears and snot. His pale, hairy body wobbles like half-set jelly.

The moment I heard the front door close, I started to suspect an affair. Coming in and catching them together would not have come as a surprise.

This, though? This is unexpected.

'What the hell is this?' I ask, even though the list of things it feasibly could be is staggeringly short.

Clive's ball gag hits the floor with a thud.

'Liz! Liz, listen,' he pleads. He tries to get to his feet, but he grimaces in pain and drops back to his knees, sending a ripple through his pale, pasty flab.

'Is this what you've been up to?' I ask. There's no emotion in it. No hint of the hysterical wronged partner.

The truth is, I really don't care what Clive's been doing. I just need to know what he hasn't.

'This is where you've been going, is it? Not the gym? Not Weird Alan's? You've been coming here. With her?'

'I'm sorry. I'm sorry. Liz, listen, please, I'm so sorry. None of this is real. It means nothing.'

There's a look of hurt on Mabel's face that, any other day, I'd take delight in. Right now, though, I feel nothing. She's not an irritant. She's irrelevant.

'Answer me!'

The sharpness of my tone startles them both. Clive cowers back. Mabel glances at the tiny VELUX window like she's considering a risky escape attempt.

'OK. OK, y-yes. I'm sorry. Yes. God. I was here. But it means *nothing*, Liz. *She* means nothing. I was just... curious. I wanted to experiment, and when you weren't interested, I thought—'

I cut him off with a look, not prepared to let him shunt the blame for any of this onto me.

I don't actually give a damn about his explanations, or his apologies. I care only about one thing.

'She's not here. You don't have her,' I whisper through the cracks in my voice. I'm not really aiming it at them. I'm not really aiming it at anyone. It's just a statement of fact I put out into the world.

Clive answers, regardless.

'We don't have who? What are you...? Hollie? Do you mean Hollie? You said she was with your sister.'

There's an accusing note in his voice, like he's chastising me, painting me as a terrible mother.

He's not wrong, but I'm in no mood to take it. Not from him.

'Are you seriously trying to take the moral high ground right now, Clive?' I ask.

I don't do confrontation well, so my voice is an angry squeak, like a mouse with ideas above its station. I gesture to his naked flab, and to the studded leather collar around his neck.

'Honestly? Like this?'

'What the hell are you even doing in my house?' Mabel demands. She's fully dressed, stripped of her additional appendages, and already hurtling back towards being her old self. 'You're breaking and entering. That's a criminal act. I'm calling the police. Give me my phone.'

She's asking me to get her mobile. No, not asking, *telling* me. She actually thinks she's within her rights to boss me around, even now. And she thinks I'm going to listen.

And, to my shame, I almost do. My instinctive need to people please almost makes me go scuttling off to fetch it for her.

But I don't. Instead, I swallow, clench my fists, and finally – *finally* – stand up to her.

'I tell you what. I'll get your phone, Mabel. Then we'll call your husband. We can video call him. Maybe send him some of the photos I took,' I tell her.

My heart races, skipping half a dozen beats. I'm babbling, my nervousness making me rattle the words out quickly, before I can change my mind.

'How do you think that'll go? You think you'll still get to live in this big fancy house, spending all his money, when he knows what you get up to?'

A moment ago, her face was beetroot red with embarrassment and, I assume, the exertion of giving my live-in boyfriend an absolute pummelling. Now, though, all that colour drains away.

'In fact, maybe we'll send them to everyone,' I suggest, feeling emboldened by the change in her expression. 'The school. The parent council. Whatever weird little country clubs you and Malcolm belong to, because there's bound to be some.

How about we do that? We could print them out, stick them up around town with your name and phone number underneath it.'

I bite my tongue, feeling like I've gone too far.

She stares back at me. For the first time since I've met her, she's been rendered speechless.

Of course, it doesn't last.

'You wouldn't dare.'

Her shriek of outrage makes something inside me snap. I meet her eyes and hold it.

And to think, all this time, I was actually intimidated by her.

'Dare? Oh, I'll dare. I will sell those pictures as T-shirts and tote bags. I'll wallpaper the Royal Mile with them,' I tell her. 'You think you know me, but you have *no idea* of the things I'm capable of.'

The warning is aimed at the Uberbitch, but I glance at Clive, making it clear I'm saying it for his benefit, too.

'So, for all our sakes, keep your nose out of my business, and stay the hell out of my way.' I pause a moment, before starting back down the steeply angled steps. 'Or I won't be held responsible for my actions.'

FORTY-ONE

ELIZABETH

I'm halfway down the final set of stairs when my phone rings. In my rush to pull it from my pocket, I fumble with it, and can only cry out and watch in horror as it bounces twice on the tiled steps, then lands, screen down, on the welcome mat at the front door.

'No, no, no, no, no.'

I race the final few steps and snatch up the still-ringing mobile. The top right corner of the screen is a spider-web pattern of fine cracks, but I barely notice, because it's *him*. It's the kidnapper. It's the man who took my daughter.

The timing seems suspicious, but I can hear Clive and Mabel screaming at each other up in the attic, so I doubt that it's either of them.

I swipe at the button to answer the call, but nothing happens. The screen doesn't register my touch.

Oh, God. No, please.

The phone keeps ringing, but it's been twenty seconds now, maybe more. Any moment, it'll go to voicemail, and there's no saying I'll ever hear from them again.

I try again, pressing harder. This time, the slider moves. I'm already replying before I can bring the phone to my ear.

'Hello! Yes. I'm here. I'm here!'

'Mummy, please. Please. I want to go home.'

I don't feel myself sliding to the floor until I hit the cold tiles. The muffled sound of Mabel and Clive's arguing is drowned out by the ringing in my ears.

'H-Hollie? Sweetheart, where are you? Mummy's here, baby. Tell me where you are, and I'll—'

'We had a deal, Elizabeth.'

It's the same voice as before. Cold. Unnatural. Electronic.

'Please, just... let her go. Please. Take me. We can swap. You can take me. I'll come quietly, I promise.'

'Why would I want you, Elizabeth? The people close to you only end up getting hurt.' Even through the voice changer, I can hear him smirking. 'Besides, Hollie is much more fun.'

'Don't you hurt her!' I hiss. 'Don't you lay a damn finger on her!'

'Or what? Or you'll kill me, like you did your husband?'

Just like Mabel a few minutes ago, I'm struck dumb. I was right about the photograph, then. About what all this is for.

'Cat got your tongue?' he asks, and I babble out a reply that barely makes sense.

'He was... It was... The whole thing... It was an accident. The police looked into it. We didn't... *I* didn't...' I draw in a breath, composing myself. 'I didn't do anything to him. I didn't do anything wrong, it was an accident, the police said so.'

'Wrong!' His voice crackles as he screams the word down the phone line. '*Inconclusive*, Elizabeth. That's what they said. Not that it was an accident. Because it wasn't an accident, was it?'

'It was! It was, I swear. Please, just let her go.'

'You knew what you had to do. You were told. We warned you.'

'Wait, "we"? Who are you?'

I look back up the stairs. Mabel is still shouting. Clive's voice is lower, like he's trying to calm the situation.

Whatever sordid nonsense they're up to, there can be no doubt now that they're not involved in Hollie's disappearance.

He hesitates before replying to my question. There's a pause where the line goes silent, like he's hit the button to mute his end of the call.

'It doesn't matter who we are. All that matters is you doing what you're told. You were told to confess.'

'I went to the police station,' I tell him. 'Last night. At Fettes. I went out there.'

'But you didn't tell them what you'd done, did you? You didn't follow through.'

The comment catches me off guard. How do they know that? Were they watching me? Are they tracking me somehow?

'Because I didn't know what I was supposed to be confessing to,' I insist. 'I haven't done anything.'

He sighs. The voice changer turns it into a low, flat, droning sound.

'Oh, Elizabeth. What are we going to do with you? Oh. Wait. I know.'

There's a rustling sound, like the phone is being moved. I hear my daughter's cries ramping up, becoming hysterical.

'No, no, don't! Mummy, Mummy, please, Mummy!'

'Hollie? Hollie?' My shouts are loud enough to silence the arguing upstairs. 'Stop, please, please, stop! I'll do it! I'll do it! I'll do whatever you want!'

Hollie falls silent. His voice returns.

'That's more like it. All you need is the right motivation, isn't it, Elizabeth?' He's smiling again. I can hear it. 'I want to see you on the news by this time tomorrow. Otherwise, you start getting bits of your daughter through the mail. Toes, then fingers, then ears, then whatever else I can carve off her.'

He goes silent for a few seconds, really letting that image sink in.

'Do we understand each other?'

'Yes. Yes, we do. We do,' I say. Even to me, my voice sounds like it's coming from somewhere far away. 'I'll do it. I'll admit to anything. I'll tell them whatever you want.'

'Good girl,' he tells me. 'Twenty-four hours, or we hurt her for real.'

And then, with a *click*, the line goes dead.

FORTY-TWO

ELIZABETH

I throw open the front door and stumble outside. The front step catches me by surprise and I fall, flailing, crashing to my knees on the pavement. I don't have the strength to stand, and the world is spinning too fast for me to even attempt it.

So, I stay there, on my hands and knees, choking on my tears and swallowing back wave after wave of hot, acidic nausea.

There's nobody out on India Street. Nobody to see me.

Except...

Damn.

I look up at the house across the street, expecting to see Weird Alan standing there again, watching from his window, like he always is.

Not today, though.

The big bay window on the first floor is empty. The curtains are open, but there's no sign of Weird Alan. No sign of anyone.

I'm relieved. The last thing I need is him squinting down at me in silent judgement.

Judgement.

That's what I feel every time I see him. Whenever I walk

past, either alone, or with Hollie, and see him looking down, I feel like he's judging me, and finding me wanting.

Like he can peer right into my soul and see all its many shades.

Or maybe, he just knows something.

He's always there. Always.

But not today.

I don't know if it's the adrenaline, but I'm up and running like a sprinter off the blocks.

It takes me just a few seconds to cross the road and up the flight of three steps leading to the front door. I try the handle. Locked. I find the intercom button for flat 2 and jam my thumb against it.

From upstairs, I can just hear the sharp buzz echoing through Weird Alan's flat.

I hold my thumb there until I have no doubt he's heard it, then release it and wait.

Wait.

Wait.

There's no crackle from the speaker. No reply from above.

'Come on!'

I press his buzzer again, holding it for longer this time.

I wait.

Minutes pass. Hours.

Nothing.

'Screw you, Weird Alan,' I hiss, then I press the buttons for the ground- and second-floor flats instead.

Just a few seconds later, a man's voice emerges from the wall-mounted speaker. He sounds older. Seventies, maybe. I get the impression of an old army sergeant major.

'Yes? What?'

I waste a second composing myself, before replying. 'Yes. Hi. Hello. Sorry to bother you. I'm a friend of Alan's. On the first floor? I'm trying to get hold of him, but he's not answering. Could you maybe...'

'Good grief. Again?'

'Sorry? I don't—'

The door emits a mechanical droning sound, and a lock shunts aside. I push on in before it can slide back into place again, shouting a 'Thank you' as I race up the smooth stone staircase.

There is a sour smell in the air when I reach the first floor. The source of it is immediately obvious. Half a dozen black bin bags are stacked in the corner next to Weird Alan's front door.

The sight of them takes me back to the body that appeared, just briefly, in the boot of my car, all wrapped in plastic and bound with tape. I still don't know exactly how it got there, or where it went.

I don't think I want to.

I knock on Alan's door, big fist pounds that should echo around his flat. Instead, there's a faint squeak as the door swings a few inches inward.

Placing the palm of my hand against it, I push it open all the way. The floor of the hallway is carpeted in old newspapers. The walls are bare plasterboard, daubed here and there with splodges of paint, like he was trying to settle on a colour, but never quite could.

And then, there's the smell.

Outside was bad enough, but in here, the odour of festering rubbish has been distilled down, concentrated into its purest form. I gag and have to back up a pace or two into the stairwell to swallow down some fresher air, before I can tackle the flat.

With the crook of an arm wrapped over my mouth and covering my nostrils, I venture inside.

My whole body feels like it's pulsing. Racing. My footsteps are slow and steady, but the world itself is moving too quickly, too fast.

I pass the open door to the kitchen, and the sight of it makes me retch. It's like a full-colour advert for squalor. Food lies rotting in takeaway trays, mould spilling over the edges. The sink is stacked with dirty plates, but a barricade of bulging bin bags would make it impossible for anyone to reach the taps.

A clear, viscous liquid has seeped from the bottom of one of the bags, and pools around it on the scuffed, filthy lino.

Orange-brown grease marks cling to the tops of the walls and stain the high ceiling nine or ten feet above. I pull the door closed to try and shut in the stench, but it has already permeated the fabric of the flat, and seeps from its every fibre.

Weird Alan.

You can say that again.

I'm almost too afraid to open any of the other doors, but I have to. I must.

The next one opens onto a bedroom.

His bed is a bare mattress on his bedroom floor, all piss stains and pastry crumbs. There's no sheet that I can see, just a couple of pillows and a scratchy woollen blanket.

Dozens of dried-out tissues lay scattered on the floor around it. I gag again but force myself to step inside and look around the rest of the room.

The only other 'furniture' in the place is made from repurposed cardboard boxes. Manky, threadbare clothes spill out of the tops of them, like the contents of the world's worst Lucky Dip.

Creeping back into the hall, I close this door, too, and cross to the one facing it. This flat isn't exactly like Clive's – it's smaller, for one thing – but it's not far off. Based on the layout of that one, the room across the hall should be the living room, where I've seen Weird Alan standing watching me and the rest of the world, so many times before.

I listen at the door but hear nothing. The whole place feels empty, but I am still half expecting to find a dirty green couch waiting for me when I step into the living room.

I don't. And the wrenching pain in my chest makes me realise how much I'd been hoping I would.

There's a grey, sagging old sofa with a patchwork of repairs on the arms, and a pile of books where a leg should be. It would have been a quality piece of furniture once, but the ravages of time and neglect, and years of food spillages have rendered it only fit for the dump. I can't imagine touching the thing without rubber gloves on, let alone sitting on it.

Over in the corner, there's a TV – an ancient boxy thing with a metal coil on top for an aerial. Even if it was plugged in, which it isn't, I can't imagine it would work. There's a thick layer of dust on the screen. In it, someone's finger has etched a couple of dots and the downwards curve of a sad face.

Once again, the floor is covered in newspapers. Peering down, I find the date on one. 15 October 2011. To be fair, I've had carpets that didn't last that long.

There are several stacks of newspapers at the far end of the living room, taking up maybe a fifth of the room's space. I get the impression that they were arranged quite neatly, once upon a time, but subsidence has struck at some point, and several dozen editions have spilled onto the floor.

Paint the whole thing green, and it would almost look like a rolling hillside in the Highlands, or the Lake District.

Somewhere far, far away from this place.

But I'm not there. I'm here, and rapidly coming to the conclusion that Hollie isn't. There's no sign of Alan, either.

For a weird, reclusive shut-in, he is notable by his absence.

There's no sign of any little painted goblins, knights, or undead armies, putting to rest any doubts that Clive might have been telling the truth about coming round here. Not that there were any such doubts lingering. He already admitted where he'd really been, and a man of Clive's delicate disposition wouldn't set foot in a place like this.

And Alan, as far as I've always been aware, would never set foot outside it.

So, where the hell is he?

There's only one room left. Unlike back at Clive's, the bathroom is tucked up at the end of the hall. The door is slightly ajar, but the narrow gap reveals only a strip of darkness beyond.

There's no light switch on the wall on this side of the door, just a cord dangling down from the ceiling on the inside. I reach through and pull it without stepping inside. A fluorescent strip light flickers, goes dim, then bursts into life.

There's no newspaper on the floor here, just the same rotting lino as in the kitchen. The toilet is filthy, the yellowing porcelain spattered with caked-on blobs of brown and black that burn my nasal passages, even with my arm blocking most of the smell.

My eyes water as I retch, but I nudge the door with my foot, opening it all the way.

I see a pair of pyjama bottoms lying tangled on the floor.

I see a razor blade, one corner embedded in the lino beside it.

I see a naked elbow, sticking out over the edge of a bath.

And then, only then, do I see the blood.

There's no big crimson spray on the grubby tiles or mould-flecked paintwork. Instead, Alan lies in a hazy red pool, like he slit his wrists open underwater to stop the blood arcing across the room.

I'd say he might have done it in consideration for whoever had to come in and clean up the place but, given the state of the rest of the flat, I very much doubt it.

He's sunk down so the lower half of his face is hidden beneath the surface. His eyes are open, gazing vacantly at his knobbly knees which stick up like the humps of the Loch Ness

Monster. There's no shine in his eyes. Whatever life had been in him upped and left a while ago.

Moisture plasters his usually wild and flyaway hair to his head, sticking it down. He looks nothing like the man who used to watch me from the window.

But it's him. There's no doubt about it.

I'm about to stagger back out into the hall, out of the flat, out of this building, when I see the note. It sits on the filthy toilet cistern, a torn page from an A5 notebook.

Carefully, watching where I stand, I inch my way over until I'm close enough to read what's written there.

Two things strike me, almost immediately.

This is a suicide note. It speaks of his pain and misery, and desire to no longer be around. That's the first thing I notice.

The second thing I realise is that Alan didn't write this. It isn't his handwriting. I haven't seen his handwriting before, but I know this isn't it.

Because I recognise it as soon as I see the sharp, jagged lines.

It isn't Alan's handwriting.

It's Sasha's.

FORTY-THREE
ELIZABETH

I scan quickly through the note, searching for something in there that will tell me if she did this to him, or if she found him in this state.

Those are the only two alternatives, because my sister was here. There is not a doubt in my mind about that.

There's nothing obvious on my first skim-read. It looks just like a suicide note.

> *Hello.*
> *Every day of my life was lonely and miserable.*
> *You have no idea what it was like.*
> *Sorry to whoever had to find me like this.*
> *I didn't know what else to do.*
> *So, I have ended my life.*

That's as far as I make it through the lines of text before I see the pattern. It's the same technique we used to use when sharing secret notes with each other as kids – the first letter of every line spelling out new words.

In this case: *HEY SIS.*

I scan on through the rest of the page, ignoring most of what Sasha wrote and instead just moving my gaze vertically down the left-hand side, reading only the first letter of each line.

HEY SIS DONT FREAK OUT I WILL SORT S

Don't freak out?
Don't freak out?!
How the hell does she expect me to not freak out? This is the second dead body I've been faced with in just over thirty-six hours. Don't freak out? With this, on top of everything else that's happened, it's a miracle I'm not having a breakdown.

A hundred and one questions all rush to the forefront of my mind, battling to be first in the queue.

When was she here? What led her to this flat? Did she kill him? Did she encourage him to kill himself? Or did she find him like this, the deed already done?

Not that last one, surely? She'd have snuck away and not bothered with the note. She was involved. Somehow, she was involved.

Oh God, Sasha. What have you got us into this time?

I scrunch up the note and shove it in my pocket. I can't leave that around. If I cracked the code, so will the police. It's not exactly a clever cipher. But then, Sasha was never the brains of the outfit. Of any outfit, really.

The muscle, yes. The raw, uninhibited rage. But never the brains.

Suddenly, the voice on the intercom makes sense. 'Good grief. Again?' That's what he said. Sasha must've used the same trick to get in as I did.

That's not good. It means the upstairs neighbour can place two women at Weird Alan's flat on the day he died. Worse – if he got even a quick look at us both through the window or stairwell railings, he might even think I was here twice.

Oh, God.

What am I going to do?

'Right. Enough. Calm down, Elizabeth,' I say, chastising myself out loud.

I take a breath, which is a mistake. A rush of vomit surges upwards but meets a surge of pressure coming the other way as I desperately swallow it back down.

Weird Alan isn't my problem. Or, not my main one, at least. Hollie. That's what I need to focus on – getting Hollie back safely. Everything else is a distraction.

Besides, from what I knew of him, Weird Alan taking his own life isn't entirely beyond the realms of possibility. Looking around the place, knowing about his shut-in lifestyle, it's almost a miracle he's lasted this long.

Maybe the police won't investigate. Maybe they won't even bother to talk to the neighbours.

Maybe. But unlikely.

I'll cross that bridge when I come to it. For now, though, I need to get out of here. The sight of the blood, and the smell of... well, everything... is making my head spin. It's felt like it's been spinning since Friday night, of course, but the last half hour has ramped things up considerably.

I feel the weight of it all crashing down on me. The pressure of it coming rushing in.

'Calm down,' I tell myself. 'Calm down. You can deal with this. You can do it.'

But I don't know if I can. Part of me wants to lie down on the floor – even this floor – curl myself into a ball and wait for it all to be over.

It's the scared part. The selfish part.

But the rest of me overrules it. The rest of me is going to get my daughter back.

I retreat out of the bathroom and make my way back along the hall towards the front door.

It's only when I'm reaching for the handle to open it that a terrible thought starts to gnaw at me.

Fingerprints.

I've touched at least three doors, and I think I might have leaned against the wall in the living room while leaning in to look around.

Would the police check for prints if they thought it was a suicide? Probably not.

But if they thought it wasn't? If they had reason to believe someone else had been with Alan in his flat?

Maybe.

Almost certainly.

Damn.

There's no way I'm going back to the kitchen to fetch anything, so I pull my sleeve up over the heel of my hand and return to each of the doors I touched. I wipe the handles, then hurry through into the living room.

I can't remember exactly which spot on the wall I touched, so I take an educated guess, then wipe a wide area around it. Dust forms little rolls between my sleeve and the raw plasterboard, before plopping onto the top edge of the skirting board.

It's only then, when I see the clean patch among the grime, that I start to wonder if I've made a mistake.

Will the fact that there are no fingerprints on the door handles make the police even more suspicious? Is that what'll trigger a full investigation that could link both Sasha and me to Weird Alan's death?

'No,' I say out loud. 'No, no, no, no!'

There's nothing I can do about it now. Although, for one brief moment of madness, I wonder if I can drag Alan's body along the hall, touching all the handles.

Fortunately, I dismiss the thought almost immediately. Even if I had the strength to do it, which I don't, it would cause a lot more issues than it would solve.

Besides, given how this weekend is going, what's one more dead guy to add to my list of problems?

I head back to the front door, remember the plastic dongle on the cord of the bathroom light switch, and give that a wipe, too.

Then, when I'm as sure as I can be that no trace of me remains in the flat, I slip out into the comparatively fresh air of the landing, and ease the door closed at my back.

FORTY-FOUR
ELIZABETH

I have no idea if anyone saw me leaving Alan's building, or watched me hurrying, head down, back to Clive's flat, but I can't afford to worry about it.

Clive is still out when I get home. I slide the security chain into place and flick the snib of the lock so he can't open it from the outside. It's his flat, and I have no real claim to it, but I'm damned if I'm letting him in right now.

I waste a full minute or so just pacing up and down the hallway, gripping my head with both hands, and ejecting random expletives at the flat's fixtures and fittings, before concluding that it's getting me nowhere.

When I stop, though, the flat feels too silent. Too empty. Like the whole place is holding its breath, waiting to see what I'm going to do.

I wish I could tell it.

Turning the TV on helps a little. The murmur of background noise stops the quiet feeling so dense and overwhelming.

But I still have no idea what I'm going to do.

I should make contact with Sasha, but the thought of it scares me. She's behaving even more erratically than usual, taking things into her own hands. She seems to be on her own quest to find Hollie, and if she does...?

Well, if she does, maybe things will be different between us. Maybe I can forgive her for the sins of our past. Maybe she can be part of our lives again.

Maybe.

But I can't rely on her. I can't rely on anyone but myself.

There's a roar of excitement from the TV. My eyes are drawn to the screen in time to see some footballer or other sliding on his knees before a cheering mob of supporters in the stands.

I never understood why, given everything going on in the world, part of every news broadcast should be dedicated to people kicking a ball around a pitch. It's bad enough at the best of times. Today, though, it feels so trivial that it's actually offensive.

I consider changing the channel, but then the newsreader pops up, smiling down the lens of the camera, and handing on over to 'the news where you are'.

I go back to pacing. I'm not sure it helps me think, but I'm far too wired to sit down.

I need to straighten things out in my head. Figure out what I know and try to get a glimpse at the full picture.

There are two deadlines, a couple of hours apart. The first is tomorrow morning at just before nine, when Mr Wilkinson and the staff at the school are going to be waiting for Hollie to come in. If she doesn't, I have no doubt that they'll get the police involved, with all the complications that will bring.

I think back to the information attached to the email Sasha sent me yesterday. Along with the video, there was a whole raft of information on the school staff. Nothing jumped out at me as being of interest, but maybe there's something in there I could use against Mr Wilkinson. Something I can blackmail him with.

Although, what good will that do me, when the kidnapper's deadline is just a couple of hours later? If he is to be believed, then he – or they – won't harm Hollie until around 11 a.m. tomorrow.

After that, though?

Well, after that doesn't bear thinking about.

The latter deadline is by far the main one, but miss the first, and the police involvement could well derail my chances of hitting the second.

If I even have a chance.

I have no idea what to do.

Do I go ahead and tell the police that Kenny's death wasn't an accident, like Hollie's abductor wants me to? Or do I figure this out? Do I find them? Do I bring her home without police involvement?

Is there a way that I can save her from her current nightmare, without plunging her straight into a potentially worse one?

I come to a decision. I'll give myself today to find her. If I haven't rescued Hollie by tomorrow morning, I'll confess. They want it public. They want it on the news.

I'll give them that. I'll make it so the whole world sees.

But if I don't want it to come to that, then I need to think. I need to plan. Like I said, Sasha was never the brains of the outfit. I am. Thinking is what I do. Granted, I tend to overthink everything, but maybe that's exactly what Hollie needs right now. Someone who'll obsess over the details. A worrier.

And let's be honest, when it comes to things to worry about, I'm spoiled for choice.

'Plan,' I say out loud. 'Think.'

It's not much of a talking-to, but it does the trick. I grab my notebook, then perch myself on the edge of the couch, ready to write.

The reporter on the TV talks about some upcoming changes to short-term holiday let accommodation. The mundanity of it is almost soothing.

What do I know?

Hollie was taken on Friday night from the school, after sneaking past me dressed as Darth Vader. It's entirely possible that the disguise and the sneaking past me was all just part of a prank, and Sasha found no reason to think otherwise after talking to Darren, the DJ.

Talking. I force myself to think of it as just that. It's cleaner that way.

The abduction, of course, wasn't a prank. I know my daughter, and I know how she sounds when she's scared. Genuinely, honest to God, deep down in the pit of the stomach scared.

And her voice on that call was the most frightened I've ever heard her.

So, someone took her at the school. Not Donnie, the janitor, though. There's nothing to indicate he was involved. Hollie had already removed her wings before leaving, so his story about picking them up is likely legitimate.

And, of course, he's been dead for two days, meaning he couldn't possibly be the man on the phone.

That poor man did nothing. He *died* for nothing.

I set down the notepad and pen, having not yet written a single word. Despite the time of year and the outside chill, the temperature in the room suddenly feels stiflingly hot. I wrestle the old sash window up a few inches, before it sticks in the frame.

Donnie's death was an accident. It wasn't my fault. He... he was coming at me. I'm sure he was. It all happened so fast. I didn't mean to hurt him.

He was in my car. Locked in the boot.

How was he in my car?

And where the hell did he go?

'Not my problem,' I declare, before picking up the notebook again.

It very much *is* my problem, of course. It's quite near the top of a long list.

But it isn't the most pressing one.

Kenny is the key to all this. My ex-husband. *Late* husband, I mean.

Could it be him? Somehow, could he have been lying in wait all these years, biding his time, getting ready to destroy my life?

Technically, I never saw his body. He was identified by dental records, after the police decided the fire had made him 'visually unidentifiable'. Nobody had asked if I'd wanted to see him, and I hadn't pushed it.

What if there was a mistake? What if it wasn't him?

What if he's been out there all this time, and knows what we did?

What *Sasha* did, I remind myself. I didn't make the alterations to his car. I didn't fix things so he lost control at just the wrong moment. My sister did that, not me.

It's a comforting thought, but it's not the truth. Not really. Sasha may have been the one to do the dirty work, but I was the one who gave her the idea. She was just the weapon – I was the one who aimed and pulled the trigger.

But I had to. He didn't leave me with any choice. He found out about Hollie. About everything. He was threatening to use it against me. He'd have blown my whole life apart, and condemned Hollie to suffer without me.

I don't regret it. I'm haunted by it, yes – every night for weeks on end, sometimes – but I don't regret doing what had to be done to protect my daughter.

And Sasha? Well, I don't think Sasha has the capacity for regret or remorse, so it doesn't bother her in the slightest.

That was the end of our relationship, though. The day Kenny died was the day I told her she could no longer be part of my or Hollie's lives. She didn't take it well, but, in the end, I didn't leave her with much choice.

I write Kenny's name at the top of the list and add a question mark after it.

Then, I add another question mark, and underline the whole thing.

What are the chances that he survived, then lay in wait for several years, before striking out of the blue?

Slim. Very slim. Non-existent, or near enough to it.

I don't score the name off the list, because I'm still not quite ready to rule it out completely – at least, not until I have better options – but I write a big X next to it and move on.

If not Kenny, then who? He had no siblings. His parents were both dead. He had a few friends, but most of them were just hangovers from his uni days, and he saw them maybe once or twice a year. Less, even.

Work colleagues? He was middle management at Lidl, with limited prospects for promotion, and a team of staff members who likely never gave him a second thought as soon as they left the building.

In his last staff review before he died, his performance was marked as 'adequate', which he was both pleased with and relieved by.

He wasn't exactly the type of colleague to inspire fanatical loyalty or devotion. I'm not even sure anyone from his work turned up at his funeral, because there were some hot new 'Middle of Lidl' deals released that day, and it was all hands on deck.

Not them, then.

So, who? Who cared about Kenny enough to resort to kidnap in order to avenge his death?

No one. I'm sure of it. Not a single living soul.

So, if they aren't looking for justice for Kenny, is this about me? Is it someone with a grudge who somehow found out, or even just suspects, the truth behind the accident?

That's feasible. It's likely, even.

I have never gone out of my way to hurt anyone, but I've had my share of secrets to protect over the last decade, and there have been casualties along the way. I have talked my way out of most situations, though, and when I haven't...? Well, Sasha sometimes took it upon herself to step in.

And for the past few years, since Kenny, I've kept my head down and my mouth shut. All of my secrets have remained just that.

Or so I thought.

The pen hovers over the paper. Who from my past could have done this? Who'd be willing to go to these lengths to hurt me?

Who would have no qualms about harming a child to do so?

Who would be willing to harm Hollie, specifically?

The temperature in the room climbs another few degrees. I glance at the TV, and the screen is a wall of flame that makes me jump to my feet in panic, before the footage pans across to a fire engine and several police cars.

I recognise the building, or what's left of it. DJ Darren's sign hangs from one bolt above the door, scorch marks obscuring most of the text.

Suddenly, the room isn't just stifling, it's shifting around me, the floor rumbling beneath my feet, the walls closing in.

I make it to the TV, slide my hands along the bezel, hoping to find a power switch and then, when I don't, pull the cable out of the back.

The room becomes darker. Becomes silent.

But the temperature continues to climb.

There is someone. Two people, in fact, who fit the description.

Two people who would hate me enough to do this.

Two people who would not hesitate to do harm to Hollie.

They're the reason I haven't gone to the police. They're the living hell I can never – will never – let my daughter be dragged back to.

Her parents.

FORTY-FIVE

ELIZABETH

On the one hand, it has been years since I've thought about Hollie's biological parents. Space in my brain is limited, and I decided, long ago, that they weren't worth a single cell of it.

And yet, in some respects, they've always been there. The spectre of them has been lurking in the shadows of my subconscious, and skulking around the edges of my thoughts.

I can barely remember their faces, but I can sometimes feel the shape of them, just out of reach, like figures from a bout of night terrors, looming just beyond the edges of my sight, where reality and nightmares mix.

I have often wondered if they ever looked for her. If they even noticed that she'd gone.

If they even remembered she'd existed at all.

I'm not convinced. If they did, though – if they searched for us, found us, and dug around in my past – could they have done this?

Would they kidnap Hollie, in order to get her back?

The voice on the call was a man's.

We. He'd said *we*.

Could it be them? Is that possible?

I pace the floor again, not yet writing anything down. There are holes in this. Lots of them.

If they'd found us, why not just go to the police? Why go through all this, when a simple DNA test could back up their story? Why try and manipulate me into a completely unrelated confession?

Maybe they don't want Hollie? Maybe, they just want to punish me. Maybe they want me to know the pain of having my daughter taken away from me and being powerless to stop it.

I snort at the thought. They didn't give a damn about her. She was just an inconvenience, standing in the way of their next fix.

I didn't steal her. I would never steal a child.

I saved her.

But that was a lifetime ago. How could they have found us? They didn't see me taking her. I've changed her name, been careful to make sure the paperwork is all as legitimate as possible.

Hollie Jones – my daughter – exists. She's in the system. She's *real* and she's mine.

Their daughter, whoever she was, is long gone.

I don't remember their faces, but I know their names. They're committed to memory, filed away, in case of emergency.

Sally Ferguson.

Hughie Green.

I fetch the laptop from the bedroom and make Facebook my first port of call. Both names produce several hits in the search results, but none of them remotely resemble the people I'm looking for. They're all too foreign, too young, too old.

I find one that could be a match for Sally – she's the right sort of age, and she at least lives in the UK, if not the right part of it.

A snoop around in her profile, though, shows her as a bright and breezy teenager and twenty-something, not the heroin-ravaged, child-neglecting piece of dirt the one I'm looking for would have been at that time.

I try a couple of other social media sites, but find nothing, then do a wider Google search.

I scroll through dozens of results before one stops me in my tracks.

A funeral notice.

Five years ago.

Hughie Green.

Suddenly and unexpectedly, our beloved son, brother, and partner, Hughie, passed away aged 22, at his family home in Aberdeen, on 12 August, 2019.

Though not without his troubles, Hughie's vibrant spirit and his humour and compassion will be deeply missed by all who knew him.

Hughie is survived by his devoted parents, Moira and Duncan Green, his sister, Donna Green, loving girlfriend, Skye MacPherson, and an extended family of friends and loved ones who mourn his loss.

A private family service will be held at a later date. In lieu of flowers, the family kindly requests that donations be made in Hughie's memory to Aberdeen Support for Recovery, a charity dedicated to helping those affected by addiction in our community.

Rest in peace, Hughie. Your light will never fade.

I read the notice again, trying to reconcile that description of the man with the one I met. Humour? Compassion?

I laugh out loud at the description of him. The sound is sharp and sudden and takes me by surprise. The echo of it rings in the silence, and I can't help but notice how cruel it sounds.

It's him, though. It has to be. The age fits. Location, too. The mention of 'his troubles' and the drug charity are the icing on the cake.

There's no mention of a daughter. Of course there isn't.

There's no reference to Sally Ferguson, either. Clearly, Hughie had moved on. Just not fast or far enough to break free from the life he'd trapped himself in.

Clearly, then, Hollie's biological father wasn't the voice on the phone.

Though he's ruled out, Sally isn't. I turn my attention to her and scroll through screen after screen of search results before I find anything of note.

It's a news article from the *Edinburgh Evening Times*. I click on the headline – *Toddler Group Raises Funds for Panto Trip* – and tap my fingers impatiently while I wait for the page to open.

I have to battle my way past dozens of irritating pop-up adverts that all load at different times, shunting the short blocks of text ever further down the screen.

Eventually, though, I'm able to read enough of the story to get the gist. A group of three-year-olds and their parents at a toddler group in Muirhouse did a sponsored walk to buy tickets to a panto at Christmas last year.

There's no mention of Sally's name in the article, so I hit the Control and F keys, and search within the page.

I find it tucked away in a caption below a photo. As soon as I spot the highlighted text, my eyes flick up to the picture.

And there, like she's stepping out of the shadows of a suppressed memory, is Hollie's biological mother.

She looks old. Older than me. Older than she should. Her clothes hang from her brittle-looking frame, and her smile is more gaps than teeth.

But it's her. After all these years, it's her.

Though Muirhouse might feel like a million miles away from leafy, upper-middle-class India Street, it's anything but.

Two miles. Maybe three. That's all that has been separating us. If I'd known, I'd have bundled Hollie up and moved us on. I'd have taken her far away from here.

But I had no idea. How could I have been so careless?

Hollie's biological mother has been living less than a ten-minute drive away for at least a year, and I didn't have a clue.

I commit her face to memory.

I close the lid of the laptop.

And I fetch a knife from the block in the kitchen.

FORTY-SIX

ELIZABETH

I start with the playgroup. According to the article, it's based out of the Muirhouse Millennium Centre, a low, squat building not much larger than Clive's flat. The community centre is plonked slap bang in the middle of a housing estate, facing a row of terraced houses, and overlooked by a couple of tower blocks.

It's also shut.

Part of the metal fence around the building is badly buck-led, as if someone attempted to drive their car into the side of the place but was abruptly thwarted.

I walk up the short path, confirm with the list of opening times on the door that the place is closed all day, then cup my hands against the glass and peer inside.

I'm not sure what I'm expecting to find. Whatever it is, I don't.

The rasp of laughter from somewhere nearby makes me turn and tighten my grip on the handbag I've brought with me. There's not a lot in it worth stealing – a few quid in loose coins, several pens, a small notebook, and half a bag of Mint Imperials covered in bits of fluff.

And a kitchen knife with an eight-inch blade.

I hang by the door, watching as a group of five teenage lads go strutting past, tracksuit bottoms tucked into grubby white socks, eyes scanning the area like predators in search of prey.

'I heard you did. I heard you totally fingered her.'

'Shut it. Seen the size of her? I'd have lost ma whole hand up there.'

'I'm just sayin' what I heard.'

Their body language, and the sneering tones of their voices, roots me to the spot in fear. It takes all my courage just to shuffle a pace or two back into the doorway, where I try very hard to turn myself invisible.

'Aye, well, I heard your mum fingers your dad, and he loves it.'

They don't seem to have noticed me. Or, if they have, I'm not worthy of their attention.

That suits me fine.

It's only when they've disappeared down an alleyway between two blocks of houses that I feel myself starting to relax.

What the hell has happened to me? I've lived on estates like this. I've dealt with kids like that. By rights, I should be more comfortable here than I am on India Street.

Has the middle-class lifestyle I landed myself in really made me this soft?

Of course, Sasha would say I've always been like this. That I've always considered myself better than those around me.

And maybe she's right. I always had her to rely on to do my dirty work, after all.

There are half a dozen notices in the windows of the community centre, advertising AA meetings, benefits advice, drug counselling, and the centre's food bank. It makes for grim reading. And yet, it also feels all too familiar.

It's in the last window on the right that I find the notice for the playgroup. It runs three days a week – Tuesdays, Wednesdays and Fridays – for two hours at a time. Even if I knew for sure that Sally was going to be at the next meeting, it would be too late. I need to find her today. Now.

There's a phone number at the bottom of the handwritten poster. I punch it into my phone, then call it as I make my way back towards my car.

I'm unlocking the door when the call is answered. The muffled voice takes me by surprise.

'Alright, aye, bloody hell. Fine, go and do what ye want!'

It's a woman, I think. There's a rasp to the accent. I'm about to ask her what she means when I hear a child having an absolute meltdown in the background and realise that she wasn't talking to me.

'Hello?' she says. 'Whit?'

'Uh, hi,' I begin, and then I realise I have absolutely no idea what I'm going to say.

When I started calling, I think I just assumed it would be Sally that answered, but this woman sounds far older. Fifties or sixties, maybe. The accent doesn't fit, either.

Of course, even if it had been Sally who answered, I still don't know what I'd have said. Now, though, one step removed from even that scenario, I'm at a loss.

'That you, Billy?' the woman demands. 'I telt ye, if ye don't stop calling, Gary'll come round there and put your teeth in, ye creepy wee bastard!'

Sensing she's about to hang up, I blurt out a quick, 'Hello!' that stops her in her tracks.

'Who's this?' she demands.

'Um... Hi. Hello. Hi,' I say, in what feels like an obvious stalling for time. 'Is, uh, is that the playgroup?'

There's a rustling sound down the line, then I hear just the faintest suggestion of a swear word. I imagine the woman on the other end of the line covering the phone with her hand to eject the expletive, before returning it to her ear again.

'Yes, this is she,' she says, in a voice that bears almost no relation to the one she was just using. 'I mean, this is... it. Yes. Are you wishing to enrol your kiddie with us?'

My mind darts ahead, skipping through all the potential conversational avenues that branch off if I say yes, trying to figure out if any of them leads me to Sally Ferguson.

If they do, I can't see it.

I try a different approach.

'Uh, no. I'm with the *Edinburgh Evening Express*. We did a piece last year about your fundraising efforts for the panto.'

'Oh. Aye,' she replies, her plummier phone voice returning to its previous rasp.

There's a whiff of contempt to it – even more so than when she thought I was some seedy silent caller.

'Whit d'ye want?'

'We were just, um, looking to do a follow-up story.'

'A follow-up story?'

'That's right.'

'In November? Eleven months after the first one?'

I wince but lean into the lie. 'That's right. We're looking ahead, now that panto season is coming up. It felt like a good time to check in.' I slide into the driver's seat of the car, then make my play. 'I don't suppose you've got a couple of hours to chat today?'

'A couple o' 'oors?' she splutters. 'Naw. I don't. How d'ye need a couple o' 'oors for? Last time, that camera guy just came oot and took some photies. In and oot, five minutes. Job done. *A couple o' bloody 'oors?*'

My lies continue to spill forth, undeterred.

'I thought it would be nice to do something more in-depth. Really look at the impact the group is having on the local community. Given how tough things are at the moment, I think our readers will find it inspiring to see a grass roots group such as yours helping to transform—'

'Awright, Mother Teresa, calm doon.' She sighs. It's a heavy, weary thing, like the air behind it has been a burden to carry. 'I cannae do a couple o' 'oors. I'm rushed aff ma feet here wi' the weans.'

As if on cue, a child goes running past, roaring at the top of his lungs.

'Will you shut it?' his mother roars back. 'I'm oan the phone.'

I pull the car door closed and place the handbag down on the passenger seat.

'Sounds like you've got your hands full, right enough,' I say, plastering on an understanding smile in the hope that she hears it. 'Is there maybe someone else I could talk to?'

I take a breath, building up to the question that could change everything.

'I think there was a Sally Ferguson mentioned in the piece. Is, uh, is she maybe available?'

'How should I know? I'm no' her keeper.'

I keep the smile plastered on. 'Ha! No. Do you have her contact details, though?'

She goes quiet. It might just be my imagination – my paranoia – but I'd swear there's suspicion in her silence.

Before either of us can say anything, I hear the murmuring of a little girl's voice. Four years old, I'd guess. Maybe five. I don't hear what she says, but her mother helpfully summarises in a much louder voice.

'On the walls? What walls? What do you mean? Why's he put shite on the walls for?'

'You're, uh, you're obviously busy—' I begin, but she cuts me off before I can say anything more.

'You know Birnies Court? The flats?'

My eyes flit to the windscreen, and to the tower blocks looming half a mile directly ahead, casting their shadows across the buildings below.

'I can find it,' I tell her.

'Sally lives there.'

'Right. Thank you. What number?'

'Mam!' the little girl squeals in the background. 'He's putting it on the carpet.'

'Aw, for—' Her voice becomes a guttural growl. 'You're a reporter, aren't you, hen? Ask aroond.'

The line goes dead.

I switch to the maps app, punch in the name of the flats, and confirm that it's one of the cluster standing directly ahead.

With a stab of a button on the dashboard, I start up the engine.

And the knife just lurks there, hidden, waiting, inside my bag.

FORTY-SEVEN

ELIZABETH

Birnies Court is one of six tower blocks on a complex built back in the 1960s which together form a development called Muirhouse View.

Why anyone thought that was a good name is a mystery. It's not exactly a selling point, since Muirhouse is the sort of place that people tend to want to look in the exact opposite direction of.

Birnies Court is one of the two tallest towers, topping out at fifteen storeys. It's also one of the worst-looking, all weathered grey cladding and rusted metal balconies with washing hung over them to dry.

A Union Jack is draped over one of the higher balconies, which would feel like a bold move even in the more gentrified parts of the city.

Sure enough, on the floor above, someone has scrawled the words 'TORY SCUM!' in red paint on a bedsheet, with an arrow pointing downwards.

There's usually a sense of community in blocks like these, though I suspect relations between those two particular neighbours are frosty at best.

The main entrance is via a security door, but wires sprout from the frame where the remote electronic locking mechanism should be. I push on inside and am assaulted by the smell.

It's not one particular scent, it's dozens of them, hundreds, all roiling and broiling together to form something truly indescribable. It coats the back of my throat, and permeates the fibres of my clothing, and I feel like I have to bend forwards slightly to push through it, as if walking into a stiff wind.

It's curry, and chip fat, and rubbish, and piss. It's all that, and a hundred other things.

My eyes are watering and I'm swallowing back saliva as I approach the closest door and rap my knuckles against the wood.

'Jesus Christ,' I wheeze, when a door opening several floors above wafts more of the smell down through the gaps in the stairwell.

Wet dog. Dirty socks. Dishes left festering in a sink.

Weird Alan's flat was bad enough, but this? This is something else entirely.

I'm doing my best not to gag when the door opens to reveal a man in his forties with a beer belly and a budding set of man-breasts.

He's wearing nothing but a pair of dirty boxer shorts and mismatched socks but doesn't appear the least bit perturbed to be standing there talking to me like this.

'Alright?' he asks.

He scratches at his belly as he looks me up and down. His nostrils flare. I'm not sure if it's something about my appearance, or if the smell has just hit him.

'What you want?'

'Uh, hi. Yes. Hello. I'm hoping you can help,' I say. I smile, turning on the charm. He seems impervious to it. 'I'm looking for Sally Ferguson. Do you know what flat she's in?'

He chews on something, his eyes narrowing. It takes me a

few seconds to realise that the thing he's chewing on is his tongue.

'Who wants to know? You police?'

He gives me another look up and down, then shakes his head, coming to his own conclusions.

'Nah. Not police. Council?' He stands up a little straighter, like he's about to square up to me. 'Social? You with the social? I don't know who you're talking about, love.'

'No, I'm none of those,' I say, blurting the words out to stop him closing the door in my face. 'I'm with the *Evening Express*. We're doing a piece on Sally's playgroup. How it's of such benefit to the community, and... Well, the woman I spoke to on the phone told me to come here.'

'What woman?'

'I... I didn't catch her name,' I admit. Even to me, the story sounds made up.

The man in the doorway stops scratching his belly and has a go at his balls instead. My eyes instinctively follow the movement, then hurriedly look away.

'Oh aye? So, how come she didn't tell you what flat she was in, then?'

'She was in a rush. One of her children was... playing up.'

He snorts. It's clear that he doesn't believe me. 'Yeah, well, I can't help you, love. Sorry.'

The door starts to close. My foot lunges, all on its own, jamming the door open.

'Wait, please. It's really important that I talk to her.'

He hasn't exactly been giving off warm, friendly vibes, but his demeanour becomes darker. More sinister. His eyes are two piggy little slits, his voice the hiss of something cold-blooded and venomous.

'Move your foot, sweetheart, or I'll move it for you.'

'Please, I just need—'

He yanks the door all the way open, his face twisting in

rage. I feel the wind of it whipping around me, like it's trying to pull me into the flat.

And then, the door is swinging back towards me, full speed, all his strength behind it. I barely have time to pull my leg back and stagger clear before it slams shut just centimetres from my face with a *bang* I'm sure must echo all the way to the uppermost floor.

I can hear him storming off, muttering to himself. It's clear I'm going to get no further with him. Sasha might be able to persuade him, one way or another, but the best I can do is move on to another flat and see if someone there can help. If I have to go through all fifteen floors to find her, then so be it.

I'm headed for the door across the hallway when a little girl of around three years old comes running in the front door, all smiles and sticky fingers. She stops dead in her tracks when she sees me, and backtracks a pace or two, only to be urged on by a woman with a baby slung across her chest, who is lugging two big bags of shopping behind her.

I smile at the girl, trying to show her I'm nothing to be afraid of, then I hold the door for her and her mother to come in.

'Cheers,' the woman says.

She glances up at me and flashes a smile.

More gaps than teeth.

The bags under her eyes indicate a lack of sleep, but the eyes themselves – two deep, dark wells – show so much more. So much worse.

A band tightens across my chest, so it feels like I can't breathe.

I remember.

I remember her face. Not just from the photo in the paper, but from back then. From years ago.

I remember who and what she was.

I remember what I did.

I remember the knife, tucked away in my handbag.

'Uh, Sally?' I ask. Her name is bitter on my tongue. Acid in my throat.

She doesn't stop walking, not even for a moment. 'No, sorry,' she says, and she ushers the little girl towards the stairs, carefully avoiding my eye.

It's her. I know it is. She's lying.

And I'm going to find out why.

FORTY-EIGHT

ELIZABETH

'I know it's you, Sally,' I say, following her towards the stairs.

The little girl looks back at me, then up at her mum, her eyes wide with worry. She's got bunches in her fine blonde hair, tied in place with two bright green scrunchies.

Sally trudges on up the first few steps, the baby asleep against her chest, the heavy bags pulling her down at the shoulders.

'No, sorry. She's away, I think. I'm not sure.'

Her voice sounds like her throat is lined with sandpaper. There's a nasal quality to it, too, like half the words are missing her mouth completely and coming out of her nose.

'I'm not... You're not in trouble, Sally,' I tell her. 'I'm from the newspaper. It's about the playgroup. I just want to follow up on the panto story.'

She reaches the halfway point in the staircase, before it turns in the opposite direction and continues up to the floor above. She hesitates, though I'm not sure if it's because of me, or so she can adjust her grip on the bags. Either way, I take advantage.

'I called the number we had, but the woman I spoke to was

having some, um, issues with her kids. I think one of them had smeared, um, poo on the wall.'

Sally's daughter's eyes widen further, and she has to fight back a giggle. Sally looks down at me, standing on the second step.

'She, uh, she sounded a bit stressed,' I say, offering up a smile. 'So she told me to come and talk to you.'

I can tell she still isn't convinced, but she's swaying.

'Big Ange?'

I take a swing.

'Uh, yes. That might have been it. There was just a number in the notes. But that rings a bell.' I smile at her, and at the girl by her side, hoping to charm, or at least disarm, them. 'Do you mind if I come in for a quick chat? It'll only be a few minutes.'

My whole body tenses, but I try not to let it show on my face. The next words out of her mouth will decide everything. Whatever happens next – whatever I'm forced to do – hinges on the next choice she makes.

Eventually, she sighs. 'Fine. A few minutes, just,' she says, then she sets one of the bags down on the floor. 'But you can make yourself useful and carry that for me.'

'No problem,' I say.

I swing my handbag onto my shoulder. I grab the bag of shopping.

And then I follow Sally and her children up the stairs.

FORTY-NINE

ELIZABETH

Sally's flat is on the third floor. She sets down her bag while she unlocks it. Her daughter's eyes remain fixed on me, one finger hooked in her mouth, pulling her lip down.

I don't want to – I try not to – but I can see Hollie in her. Not exactly. Not all the way. But there's a definite similarity.

The door opens. Sally gives a little groan as she bends at the knees to lift up the bag. There's nothing of her. I'm amazed her stick-thin limbs managed to carry her up the stairs, let alone with the added weight of a baby and a bag of shopping.

The girl runs inside, and Sally trudges after her. I follow, though I don't know why.

What am I doing here? There was no flicker of recognition on Sally's face when she saw me. No surprise, or shock.

She lied about who she was, yes, but she probably thought I was from the council, or social services, or maybe a bailiff chasing up an overdue debt. Once she bought the journalist cover story, she was willing to let me into her home.

Surely she wouldn't have done that if Hollie had been stashed away in here?

The flat isn't in great condition, but it's better than Weird Alan's. And it's a world away from the place Sally was in when I last saw her.

The woodchip wallpaper is partially stripped in the hall, several generations of inexpertly applied paint making the whole removal process far more difficult than it otherwise might have been.

The carpet in the long, narrow hallway is thin and thread-bare, but it's clean. Sally calls after her daughter as she goes steamrollering along the hall, whisper-shouting so as not to wake the sleeping baby.

'Katie. Shoes.'

The girl somehow manages to kick her shoes off mid-run, without breaking her step, then vanishes through an open door on the right.

A moment later, the sound of the *Peppa Pig* theme tune comes tinkling from the TV.

Sally rolls her eyes and smiles at me. 'Kids,' she says, and then she hands me the other shopping bag and nods at a door on my left. 'Kitchen's in there. Just stick it on the counter and I'll sort it. I'm going to put the wee man down.'

I take the bag without a word. The weight catches me off guard, but I manage to keep my balance as Sally turns and heads through a white-painted door that's scraped and peeling away in patches.

The kitchen is a small, galley-type affair, with cupboards lining both sides. There's a shiny, slightly plasticky-looking sink and draining board on one side, and an ancient-looking four-hob cooker on the other.

Every surface is cluttered with baby milk cartons, bottles, boxes of crisps, multipacks of Capri Sun, and a couple of boxes of cereal.

It's all as neatly arranged as it can be, given the lack of

space. The surfaces are badly scratched, and the fixtures all worn, but other than a couple of crumbs near the microwave, and two plates drying on the draining board, it's immaculate.

None of this is what I expected.

I heave the bags up onto the only bit of spare space on the counter and have a quick snoop around inside them. If I'm expecting to find something incriminating, I'm disappointed. It's mostly stuff for the kids, plus a couple of packets of mince and some vegetables, all marked with yellow discount stickers.

The sound of her footsteps behind me makes me jump away from the bags, and I'm all smiles again when she bustles into the kitchen, shrugging off the papoose that had, until a few moments ago, contained a baby.

My own bag is still over my shoulder. The weight of it gives me comfort.

'That's better,' Sally says. She hooks the baby carrier onto the door handle, then puts her hands on her lower back and stretches. I'm sure I can hear the cricking of her bones beneath her pale, dried-out skin.

She removes her thin rain jacket and hangs that on the door, too. My eyes are drawn to her bare arms, searching for track marks and bruising in the crooks of her elbows.

I don't find any, but my gaze lingers on the faded scars on the insides of her wrists.

She sees me looking and turns her arms inward, then squeezes past so she can get to the shopping.

'Half this stuff's about to go off. Need to get it in the freezer,' she tells me, and I shuffle out of her way while she unpacks.

I'm standing directly between her and the door. She turns and shoots me a quizzical look as I pull it closed.

'That OK?' I ask her. 'Didn't know if us talking would wake the baby.'

She looks past me to the closed door, then meets my eye again. Finally, she shrugs.

'It'll take more than talking to wake him. Been awake all night. Wee bugger'll be out of it for hours now. He'll just be getting his second wind when I'm getting Katie off to bed.'

She smiles, but there's a sadness to it. She's tired. I get the impression she's sick of all this, sick of them both.

What sort of mother is that? I ask myself.

'Yeah, they can be a handful,' I say, my smile still pinned in place.

'You got kids?'

I hesitate. Does she know? Is this all an act?

'One,' I tell her.

Sally doesn't react, just keeps unpacking shopping from the bags, and finding spaces for it on the crowded counter.

'Boy or girl?'

'Girl.'

'Nice. What age?'

I swallow. Blink. 'Nine.'

The hand reaching into the bag pauses. It lingers there for a moment, then takes out a tin of spaghetti hoops and places it on the worktop with a solemn-sounding *thunk*.

'Oh? What's her name?'

'Hollie.' The word shatters in my mouth, so it's indecipherable. I clear my throat and try again. 'Hollie. Her name's Hollie.'

'That's a beautiful name,' Sally tells me.

She finishes unpacking the bags, folds them up, then tucks them into a drawer. I watch her as she pulls open an undercounter fridge and crams the discount mince into the small freezer compartment at the top.

'What about you?' I ask. My gaze is trained on the back of her head. I'm amazed she can't feel it. 'Just the two?'

'Aye, just two,' she says.

She straightens up, closes the fridge, then leans on the counter, her hands gripping the front edge. Sally stares straight ahead, like she's looking out of a window. There are no windows in the kitchen, though, just woodchip walls stained yellow by nicotine and grease.

'I had another one. She'd, eh, she'd be about the same age as yours.'

There's a weight in my stomach, like a ball of lead. I take my bag from my shoulder and sit it on the draining board beside me.

'Oh? She not with you?'

Sally opens her mouth, like she's about to say something, then she shakes her head. 'No.'

She pulls open a cupboard and starts sliding some tins inside.

'Where is she?' I press. 'If you don't mind me asking.'

'I *do* mind you asking, actually,' she snaps, and in that second, she's the monster I remember, all scowl and savagery.

My hand grabs for my bag. From the living room, muffled by the door, the next episode of *Peppa Pig* starts to play.

'Sorry.' Sally's shoulders sink.

She rubs at her eyes with a finger and thumb, like she's trying to clear the sleep away.

The breath she draws in is long, and slow, and shaky.

'She died,' she says.

The statement is pretty definitive, but there's a suggestion of uncertainty in her eyes.

'When she was a baby. She died.'

'Oh. I'm so sorry.'

Sally sniffs, then runs the back of her hand across the bottom of her nose. Her body language and her build make her look like little more than a child herself.

But her face, her eyes, they're older. Much older. Far too much.

'What happened?' I don't really expect an answer, and so am surprised when she gives me one.

'I was... in a bad place.' She's back to looking out of the non-existent window again. 'She, eh, she... I shouldn't have had her. I was too young.'

I can only nod and smile, too afraid I'll say something that reveals I know some of this story. She *was* young, of course. Seventeen or eighteen. But her age wasn't the problem, the drugs and the neglect were.

'I was fifteen when she was born,' Sally says, which stops me in my tracks.

'Fifteen? Good God. I didn't realise.'

She turns and fixes me with a curious look. I replay the last sentence in my head and try not to visibly wince.

Idiot.

'How old were you when you got pregnant?' I ask, trying to power right through my mistake. 'Again, if you don't mind me asking?'

'Fourteen.'

She holds my eye, like she's daring me to judge her for it.

'That must have been rough,' is all I can think to say.

Sally snorts and shakes her head. 'What do you know about rough?'

'Oh, you'd be surprised,' I tell her, but she doesn't look convinced.

I do some quick calculations based on the funeral notice I read just a few hours ago. Hughie Green was twenty-two when he died in 2019, which would have made him nineteen when Hollie was born.

I hadn't realised the age gap was so large.

'I had no idea,' I tell her.

'Why would you?'

I smile, but it feels gossamer thin. 'Her dad, is he...?' I tip my head vaguely towards the door. I already know the answer, but I'm curious as to what she'll say.

'What? No. No, they're to someone else. He's not on the scene. Neither of them are.'

'I'm sorry to hear that.'

I should stop now. I don't need to know any more. But her pain is a scab I can't stop picking at.

'It must have been very upsetting for you both.'

She looks at me like I've spoken in a foreign language. 'Both?'

'You and your daughter's father. Your first daughter, I mean. Something like that must be hard,' I say. I'm pushing my luck, and I have no idea why. 'Is that what broke you up?'

'We weren't together,' she says, pulling open another cupboard and all but lobbing a packet of pasta inside.

I can't hide my frown of confusion. Fortunately, she's not looking at me, so she doesn't see it.

Her and Hughie were together. They were a couple. A messed-up and dysfunctional couple, but a couple, all the same.

'No? Oh.'

I don't know how to ask any more questions without it giving me away, but I don't have to. Sally volunteers the information as she opens and closes cupboard doors, shoving her shopping away.

'He was older than me.'

I nod but feel the need to check my calculations.

'How much older?'

'Don't know. Never asked him,' she says. A Pot Noodle gets slammed down on the counter. I move aside to let her fill the kettle from the tap behind me. 'Fifteen years, maybe?'

I can feel another frown forming. 'Wait, what?'

There's an itch in my brain, too deep to scratch.

'What do you mean?' I press. 'So, he was, what? Thirty? How is that...? I thought...'

'You thought what?' Sally asks.

I shake my head, playing dumb. 'I mean, I just assumed it would be someone around your age.'

'Nope,' she says, and she folds her arms while she waits for the kettle to boil.

They're as thin as sticks. The angle of a wrist shows a corner of one of her scars.

'What happened?' I ask. I'm no longer just curious for the sake of it. I need to know. I'll make her tell me, if I have to.

Thank God, I don't.

'I was in a care home,' she says. With another sniff, she looks back at the spot where there isn't a window, but somehow stares off into the distance. 'He worked there. Greig something. Did, like, guidance stuff. Next steps stuff. College, work, whatever.'

'Jesus Christ.'

I hear the words coming out of my mouth like it's someone else saying them.

'He seemed nice enough. But, you know' – her eyes meet mine for the briefest of moments – 'he wasn't.'

'What are you saying? Are you saying he raped you?'

She doesn't answer that one, and I don't blame her, given how I've practically squealed the question at her.

'I said no. I did, honest,' she tells me, lowering her voice like she doesn't want her daughter to hear. Like she doesn't want *anyone* to hear. 'But he said no one would believe me. Said they'd take his word over mine, because everyone knew I was a liar and a wee slut.'

Her eyes meet mine again. There are tears there. I have no idea why she's telling me all this, but it seems impossible for her to stop now. I get the feeling that she's turned on a tap and can't shut it off until every last drop has drained out of it.

'But I wasn't. I hadn't done that. Ever. With anyone,' she says, and I can only nod along, letting her know that I believe her.

Despite everything, I believe her.

'And he got you…?' I swallow. 'He got you pregnant?'

The kettle rolls to a boil behind her, spilling steam upwards until it hits the bottom of a wall-mounted cabinet and rolls up the front, glossing the wood with a layer of condensation.

'Did you tell him?' I ask. 'Did he know?'

'Does it matter?' she asks, tightening her arms across her flat, bony chest.

It does. It matters. It might be the most important thing in the world.

'Yes. You need to talk about this, Sally. You need to get it all out.'

She looks up at me, and her eyes widen a fraction. My stomach tightens. Has she recognised me? Does she know who I am?

'I, em, I shouldn't have told you all that,' she says, turning and busying herself with the shopping again. Her cheeks sting red, like she's mortified she's just spilled her life story to a complete stranger.

Then again, I get the impression she's not the type to keep her secrets to herself. It wouldn't surprise me if everyone in the block had already been told the story.

'Please, keep talking. Keep telling me,' I urge.

She turns just long enough to sneer at me. 'Why, so you can put it in the paper? So you can make a story out of it all?'

'I'm not a journalist,' I tell her. I see the worry on her face, and the tension that makes her body go rigid. 'I mean, I'm not a journalist right now. I'm just a mum. I'm just… I'm just someone to talk to.'

She relaxes, but only a little.

'You not going to write about this?'

'Not if you don't want me to,' I tell her.

She shakes her head, her expression adamant. 'No. It's done. I don't want to go over all that again.'

'Of course. I get it,' I assure her. She's not forthcoming with the answer, so I ask the question again. 'Did he know? Holl—' I draw in a tight, narrow breath of panic, before correcting course. 'Your daughter. Did he know about her?'

At first, she doesn't respond. I'm about to ask the question again when she nods, just once.

'He wanted to take her.'

A wave of heat prickles up my neck and face. My hand grasps for the worktop, steadying myself.

'He wanted to take your daughter?'

'Aye. And... and maybe I should've let him,' she says, swallowing back a sob. 'Maybe then, she'd still be here. But I knew what he was like. The stuff he'd done. I thought I could keep her safe, but I couldn't. I didn't!'

For the first time since the night I clapped eyes on Hollie, I experience something unexpected.

Guilt.

I put it behind me. I have to.

'I'm so sorry, Sally. And thank you for sharing this with me.'

She sniffs and wipes her nose on her sleeve again. 'I don't know why I even told you.'

'Maybe the truth just had to come out,' I tell her.

She turns away to slosh hot water into the Pot Noodle. When her back is turned, I reach into my handbag, and quickly rummage around until I find what I'm looking for.

When she turns back, she stops and stares at me, momentarily taken aback by what I'm holding.

With a click, I extend the nib of the pen, and bring it closer to the notebook.

'You said his name was Greig,' I remind her. 'I don't suppose you happen to know where he is now?'

Sally shakes her head. It's fast and mouse-like. I can't tell if she doesn't know, or if she just doesn't want to talk about it.

'Do you remember his last name?'

She turns to me then, her dark eyes becoming thin, narrow

slits. 'What's that got to do with the playgroup? What are you...?'

She blinks, like she's waking from some kind of trance. A moment ago, she'd seemed relaxed in my company. I'd barely asked her anything when she started opening up about her past.

That's all changed now, though. Her defences are up.

'What the hell is this about?' she demands. She might be small and frail-looking, but she's squaring up to me. 'Who even are you?'

'I told you, I'm—'

'Get out,' she tells me.

'Sally, listen, it's important that we talk about this. I can help. I can help bring him to justice.'

'I don't care. I don't want to talk about it. Get out.'

'Just give me the name of the care home. I can find him from—'

'Get out!' She screams it this time, shoving me in the chest for good measure, driving me a step backwards towards the door.

I grab for my bag. I feel the weight of the knife inside it.

Sasha would do it. Sasha would make her talk.

Sasha will.

'Sally, I can't explain why, but it's important you tell me. If she finds out you know something that can help, she'll come here. I don't know what she'll do. I won't be able to stop her.'

'What are you talking about? Who?'

'My sister. My twin sister. She'll come, and she'll make you talk, Sally. I don't know how, I don't know what she'll do, exactly, but she'll—'

'Mummy?'

Sally's daughter is suddenly right there, right behind me, wide eyes peering anxiously through a gap in the door.

Sasha wouldn't care.

Sasha would make this woman tell her everything.

But I'm not my sister.

'It's OK, darling. Everything's fine,' Sally says, all smiles for the little girl's benefit.

I've hated this woman for so long. I've lived in fear of her this whole time. I built her up to be a monster.

Have I had it the wrong way round?

The little girl's gaze is still on me. Still worried for her mum.

'I'm, uh, I'm really sorry to bother you, Sally,' I tell her, gripping the top of the bag to seal it closed. 'I'm so very, very sorry.'

'Get out,' she instructs, her voice more level now.

I open the door and the girl rushes in to clamp onto her mum's leg.

Through the thin partition walls, I hear the rumblings of the baby.

Sasha will come here.

But she wouldn't hurt them.

She wouldn't.

Would she?

I can't take that chance. I won't.

'Is there anywhere you can go?' I ask, as she ushers me along the hallway. 'Anyone you can stay with, just for the night?'

She stops then and looks at me – really looks at me – like she's seen something in my eyes that she's trying to make sense of.

'What is this?' she asks, one hand on the door handle, the other smoothing down the hair of the girl clinging to her in long, slow strokes. 'What is this really about?'

'I can't tell you. I'm sorry. But, please, just in case, if there's anywhere—'

She pulls open the door. 'Please leave,' she spits, 'Before I call the police.'

I want to say more. Despite who she is – or because of who she is – I want to make sure she's safe.

But I can tell from the look on her face that there's nothing I can say to make her trust me now. And why on earth should she?

'I'm so, so sorry, Sally,' I tell her.

With a final smile at the girl, I step out of the flat, and the *bang* of the front door echoes through the stairwell when Sally slams it closed behind me.

FIFTY

ELIZABETH

I can see her watching me when I get back to the car. She's standing on the balcony, hands gripping the rusted railing, staring down.

I stop with one hand on the door handle and look back up at her. Maybe she's had a change of heart. Maybe she'll shout a name to me, or an address. Anything that might help me find my daughter.

Her daughter, a toxic little voice in my head suggests.

She doesn't. All Sally does is watch for a while, then turn around and head back inside.

Back in the car, I fire up the engine and pull out of the car park. No time to lose.

I find a Costa, head inside, and order the strongest, blackest coffee they have. It takes them an age to make it, but then I install myself in a corner table, tucked away from the handful of other punters in the place, my phone open in front of me.

I first encountered Sally Ferguson in Dyce, just outside Aberdeen, up in the north-east. It's a small town, outside a fairly minor city. There can't be too many children's homes.

If I can find the right one, and figure out who this Greig is, maybe that will be enough. Maybe that will give Sasha something else to go on.

Maybe that will keep Sally and her children safe.

A quick search gives me the names of three local authority residential children's homes in Aberdeen, and a bit more digging brings up contact details.

I try googling the names of each home, along with the name 'Greig'. Nothing useful comes up. I switch 'Greig' for 'Sally'.

Again, nothing.

'Damn it,' I whisper. It's too loud, and a couple of older women at the nearest table shoot me matching looks of outrage.

I offer a smile by way of apology, then take a big gulp of my coffee. It's blisteringly hot, and disgustingly strong, and the old women are still watching me as I spit it back into the mug.

They both shake their heads, then go back to their conversation.

I rattle through several new searches in quick succession.

'Greig care home Aberdeen.'

'Sally Ferguson social services.'

'Aberdonian care home worker Greig.'

They all bring up pages of results, but a quick scan through them gives me nothing to go on.

I take the notebook from my bag and scribble down the names and phone numbers of all three homes. Phoning is a last resort, as the chances of me finding anything out by calling are staggeringly slim.

Data protection laws would make it difficult at the best of times to get information on an employee from any company. Throw in the fact that it's a sector as sensitive as social work, and it'll be next to impossible.

Still, if it comes to it, I'll have to try.

I try another search.

'Greig care home Dyce.'

My phone takes a moment to load the results. I force myself to take a tiny sip of the coffee while I wait.

I spit it back out again, though this time it's nothing to do with the temperature or taste.

The top result gives me an address for a care home in Dyce itself. There's no mention of a Greig when I click through to the page, but then I didn't expect there to be. I take note of all the details, back out to the search box, and try rattling off a few combos using the name of this new home.

Each page of results chips away at my momentary surge of hope.

Nothing comes up for a Greig.

Nothing comes up for Sally.

'Damn it,' I hiss again, even louder this time than before.

The old women turn on me again, but I'm already on my feet, pushing my chair back, the awful coffee abandoned, almost untouched.

'Oh, piss off, you judgemental old bastards,' I eject as I pass them.

They cluck out an objection, but I don't hear it. I'm out the door, striding across the car park, a plan already forming in my head.

It's not a great plan. It's almost certainly going to fail. But it's all I have left.

In the car, I stop the phone connecting to Bluetooth. I don't want this conversation to be broadcast over the speakers.

My thumb is shaking so badly that it takes me a few attempts to punch in the number. When I manage, I hesitate, breathing deeply, before hitting the button to place the call.

It rings half a dozen times before it's answered. It's a man. Older, I think.

'Greig?' I ask.

'Uh, no. Sorry, I think you must have the wrong number,' he tells me.

I blurt out the name of the care home before he can hang up. He hesitates, then confirms I'm through to the right place.

'I'm... I'm looking for Greig,' I say.

'There's no Greig here, I'm afraid.'

'Did there used to be? I'm trying to get hold of him.'

'I'm afraid I can't give you that information. I'm sorry.'

'Wait!' I cry, sensing again that he's about to end the call. 'I, uh, I used to stay there. At the home. I, eh... Greig was really kind to me. I never got a chance to say thanks.'

'Like I say, I don't know a Greig. You'd have to put the request in through official channels, and maybe—' He sighs. I can hear him rummaging around, perhaps searching for a pen. 'Listen, I'm fairly new here. Give me your name and number, and I'll get one of the older hands to give you a call back. If you were here, I'm sure they'll remember you.'

It's not the flat-out 'no' I was prepared for. That might still come, of course, but for now, there's still hope.

'OK. Sure. Thank you,' I reply. 'And it's Sally. My name is Sally Ferguson.'

FIFTY-ONE

ELIZABETH

I try my luck with the three homes in Aberdeen on my drive back to Clive's flat, using slight variations of the same approach on each of them. One is profusely apologetic that they can't share any information with me. The other two appear outraged that I'd have the audacity to ask.

None of them gives me any clue who Greig might be. Nobody reacts in any meaningful way when I identify myself as Sally Ferguson.

The first one – the friendly one – directs me towards the official channels I can apply to for information but warns that they might not be able to tell me anything either, and if they can, it'll take weeks.

I thank her, but don't bother making a note of the information. I don't have weeks. I barely have hours. It's already after dinnertime. Just fifteen or sixteen hours from now, I'll either have to prove to the school that Hollie is safe and well, or I'll have to make a public confession about my late husband's death. I'll have to take responsibility, even though it wasn't my fault.

I will. If it means Hollie's safe, I'll say anything.

But not yet. I still have time. I can still save her. Things can still go back to the way they were.

The home in Dyce still hasn't returned my call when I'm pulling onto India Street. There's a light on in the living room window of Clive's flat. Great. Something else for me to have to deal with.

I glance along the street, and up to Weird Alan's flat. I'm not sure if I'm expecting to see him standing at the window, or a squad of uniformed police officers barricading the entrance, but I see neither.

Alan must still be in there, pickling away in the cold, dirty water of his bath.

Poor bastard.

Sitting in the car, I try a few more searches that occurred to me on the drive home. They're mostly variations on 'Greig', 'Aberdeen', and 'social services', but I also try to find any news reports about Greigs being charged with sexual offences in Scotland, given his history with Sally, and assuming she was telling the truth.

There are a few results, but none of them seem like matches for the man I'm looking for.

I can feel myself starting to obsess over this. I know why. It's the only lead I have left. If Sally was being honest, then this Greig character is Hollie's biological father. Based on what she told me, he has already expressed a desire for custody of the child he fathered. Sally's child.

My child.

It's a stretch, but if he knows who Hollie is, and what I did, then he couldn't just go to the police. Telling them that I stole his daughter would mean admitting that he raped a teenage girl in his care.

So he'd need to find another way of getting me out of the picture. A bit of digging into my past would soon bring up Kenny's death, and the circumstances surrounding it. Even if he didn't know the truth of what happened, he'd know there was scope to pressure me into a confession.

It's a theory. I'm too close to it to be able to tell if it hangs together, but I'm completely out of other ideas, and almost out of time, and so this is my number one focus. This is my only hope.

The phone rings. My heart leaps into my throat in case it's the kidnappers changing the timeline, or the terms of their deal, but it's the same number I called earlier. The home in Dyce.

My heart hammers in my throat as I tap the button to answer. It connects automatically to Bluetooth, and the voice that responds to my tentative, 'Hello?' comes booming from the stereo system.

'Hello. Is that Sally?'

It's a woman. Older. Sixties, maybe. She doesn't sound unfriendly, just a little bit impatient, like she's got a list of things to get through, and this call is an unwelcome addition.

'Um, yes. That's right. Hi,' I say. 'Who's this?'

I'm hoping for a name, but I don't get one. 'My colleague says you lived here with us,' she says. 'Can you tell me when?'

I do some quick arithmetic in my head. 'Twenty fourteen,' I say, then I add an 'ish' for safety's sake.

'Hmm.'

It's not the most forthcoming of replies, and certainly not the one I'd been hoping for.

I chance my luck and press on. 'I'm trying to get hold of Greig, who—'

'I'm sorry, I don't remember you,' the woman tells me. 'I've been here since 2009. I remember pretty much all the kids who've come through these doors, but I don't remember you, Sally. Are you sure you've got the right place?'

'What about Greig? Do you remember Greig? He worked there.'

'I don't know a Greig, either. I really think you must have

the wrong place. I'm sorry. I can direct you to the proper channels, if you like, and they might be able to help. I have to tell
you, though, it could take a few weeks to...'

She keeps talking, but I can no longer hear her.

Another dead end. Another failure. Another step further
away from finding Hollie.

Was Sally lying? I don't think so.

But just because I met her near Aberdeen, doesn't mean
that's where she was in care. The home she was in could've
been anywhere. How many children's residential homes are
there in Scotland? Dozens? Hundreds?

I need to narrow it down. I need her to help me, whether
she wants to or not. If I don't convince her to, Sasha will, and
her methods will be far more extreme than mine.

'Sorry to bother you,' I say, cutting short the woman on the
other end of the line. I hang up before she can reply.

With a final glance up at the light burning in the living
room window of the flat, I crunch the car into reverse, speed
away from the kerb, and head back towards the tower blocks of
Muirhouse.

FIFTY-TWO

ELIZABETH

'She's gone.'

The woman in the doorway across the landing is in her seventies, dressed in a pink velour jogging suit, and holding a tiny plastic dumbbell in each hand. The colour of her hair and eyebrows is so dark it can only have come from a bottle, and she's made an attempt to fill in the lines and crags of her face with thick, powdery foundation.

'Sorry?'

'I said, she's gone, hen,' the woman replies, slowing her words and raising her voice, like she's talking to a foreigner, or an imbecile. Her accent isn't local. Glasgow somewhere, I think. Maybe Ayrshire.

'Gone?' I look at the door I've been hammering on for the past few minutes, then back to the woman. 'What do you mean? Gone? Gone where?'

'Oh, you're asking the wrong person there, darlin',' she replies. As she speaks, she begins a series of slow bicep curls with the weights. 'I don't like to pry. I'm not one for sticking my nose in. But her and the weans went rushing out of here twenty minutes ago. She had them bundled up, dragging a suitcase with her and everything. Buggy. Changing bag. The works. Seemed to be in a hurry, if you ask me. Got in a taxi. A black cab. None of my business, of course. Don't ask me more, I wouldn't know.'

She nods and smiles. I can practically hear her bones creaking as she continues to pump the dumbbells, first one arm, then the other. A thin film of sweat is already threatening to undo her make-up efforts.

'You don't know where she's going?' I ask.

'Oh, no. Like I say, I keep myself to myself, hen,' the woman insists. 'They went left out of the car park, though. I didn't get the number plate – the eyes aren't what they used to be – but, like I say, it was a black cab. Council registered.'

She switches from bicep curls to shoulder presses, raising each dumbbell straight up above her head in turn, then bringing it back down so it rests beside her ear.

'I hope she's OK. She's a great wee lassie. Always quick to help out. And the weans are lovely. She dotes on them, so she does.'

I feel a pang of something. Guilt, maybe? But there's no time to dwell on it.

'You a friend of hers?' the woman asks.

I blink, caught off guard by the question. 'Uh, no. Not exactly,' I admit. 'I just... I need her help with something. Do you have her number?'

'Her number? No. What the hell would I need her number for? She lives ten yards away. If I need her, I just knock.'

I feel sick. All of a sudden, the pungent stench of the stairway is too much for me. It clings to the lining of my nostrils, and clags at the back of my throat.

I need outside. I need fresh air.

I swallow it all back as best I can.

'You don't know how to get in touch with her?' I ask.

'Afraid not, hen. But I'm sure she'll be back soon enough.'

She stops pumping iron – or plastic, at least – and shoots me a look of concern. 'You alright there, darlin'? You're looking a bit peaky. You need a wee sit-down?'

'I'm fine,' I manage.

'You sure? You look like your head's about to drop through your arse.'

'I said *I'm fine!*'

I shout the words. Roar them at her. The sound rumbles through the building and forces her back a step. The kindness and concern in her eyes are swept away by a sudden swelling fear.

The stairway spins. It presses in around me, narrowing the walls and condensing the stink.

She was my chance. Sally was my best shot of finding Hollie, and I blew it. I let her slip through my fingers.

The woman stares back at me like I'm a monster. She's not wrong.

'I... I'm sorry,' I manage to blurt, then I rush down the stone steps, out through the front door, and a spray of hot vomit splatters onto the litter-strewn car park.

FIFTY-THREE

ELIZABETH

It's late when I arrive back on India Street, and there are no parking spaces to be had.

In the end, I just abandon the car behind a couple of the neighbours' vehicles. If they complain, or I get a ticket, so be it. I don't have the energy to give a damn.

I try calling the number for the playgroup again, but every time I do, the call is cut off after half a ring. I think she's blocked me. I guess Sally got in touch with Big Ange to warn her about me. I can't really blame her, I suppose.

I wish she'd stayed, but I'm glad she's gone. She's safer that way. Her kids are safe.

I wish I could say the same.

I try calling the kidnapper's number again but am met with the same tones as earlier. They've probably blocked my number, too, so they can call me, but I can't call them.

Another dead end.

Getting out of the car, I slam the door and trudge back to the flat. My legs ache. My whole body, in fact. I don't know if it's the stress, but the last couple of days have taken a real physical toll. Every muscle feels like I've run a marathon.

I'm exhausted, too. Physically, mentally, emotionally – you name it.

The surge of adrenaline that accompanied the rush back to Sally's flat has long since left me. I can barely focus as I slip the key into the front door lock.

They can call me, but I can't call them.

Something about the thought niggles at me as I push on inside and haul myself up the stairs, but my brain is too woolly to latch onto it. And when I enter the flat, the sight of Clive standing waiting for me pushes all other thoughts aside.

'Where the hell have you been?' he demands, all folded arms and tapping foot.

'Getting whipped and ridden like a racehorse by Mabel Walker,' I say, closing the door. 'Wait. No. That's you.'

The comment immediately punctures his air of superiority, and his arms flop down by his sides.

'Elizabeth, come on, I can explain.'

'Clive,' I say, holding up a hand. 'I can't do this right now. I don't care.'

'No, but if you just listen, I can—'

'Clive!' His name is a hiss. A snarl. It shocks him into silence. 'I don't mean that I don't care about the explanation. I mean I don't care that it happened.'

He frowns, clearly confused. 'What?'

I clarify for him, as brutally and as honestly as I can.

'I have no emotional response to you taking it through the back door from Mabel Walker. None. I don't care what you do with her. I will not lose a wink of sleep over it. You have my blessing to do whatever weird, sordid nonsense you want with her. I literally have no opinion on it, because I have no feelings for you, Clive.'

He steps aside as I walk towards him, sensing that it's not in his best interests to block my path. I lean on the wall as I pass him. I'm so exhausted I feel drunk.

'You don't mean that,' he tells me.

I laugh. A sharp, staccato burst that quickly dies in my throat. 'No. No, OK. You're right. I do have some feelings for you,' I admit.

The look of relief in his eyes is short-lived.

'Revulsion, mostly. I find you physically repulsive. You're weak and needy. Every time we have sex, I try and imagine I'm with someone else. Anyone else.'

'What? No. But... That's...'

I spit out a series of spluttering noises, mimicking him. It's childish, bottom of the barrel stuff.

But the bottom of the barrel is where I've reached.

'It was nothing personal, Clive. I thought maybe I could fall in love with you someday, but it didn't work out that way.'

I watch his face fall, and sense something inside him start to crumble. Guilt nips at me. He's not a bad man. Not really. He gave us a home, and loved Hollie like she was his own.

'I'm sorry, I really am. I know it's a cliché, but it's not you, it's me. I was using you, that's all,' I tell him. 'Like I use everyone.'

I turn my back on him and raise a hand in a wave over my shoulder. 'Now, I need to go charge my phone.'

My phone.

They can call me, but I can't call them.

The thought rushes back in but is quickly shunted aside by the next words out of Clive's mouth.

'I called the police.'

I stop.

I turn.

Slowly, I turn.

'What did you say?'

He swallows, like he's afraid of me. 'I was worried. About you. About Hollie. So I, uh, I—'

'You called the police?' I close the gap between us in two big paces. 'And said what, Clive? What did you tell them? What did you say?'

His eyes are wide. He shakes his head. He's seeing something in me that he's never seen before. That I'm not sure I've ever felt before.

And he is afraid.

'No, I just... It was just 101, not 999. I just said I was concerned.'

'About *what*?'

'About, you know, Hollie. And you. Because I hadn't heard from you.'

I feel my fingers stretching out, flexing wide, then tightening into clenched fists.

'What exactly did you say?'

He smiles, like he's trying to laugh it off. I don't join in.

'No, just... I said that you'd said she was at your sister's, but that I wasn't sure if that was... I didn't know if that was the case, or—' He holds his hands up, like he's surrendering. 'But they didn't really take me on. Said they'd pass it on for a welfare check, but that it didn't sound like anyone was in any immediate danger. Someone will... someone will come round to talk to us.'

'When?'

'I don't... They didn't say. Maybe tonight but could be tomorrow. I just... I was worried, that's all. I just wanted to make sure that—'

My turning away silences him. Though it's under his breath, I hear his faint sigh of relief as I march through Hollie's bedroom and rip my phone charger from the wall.

It's all I need. Everything else can be replaced when we move on. It always is.

He's lurking in the living room doorway when I return to the hall. He holds out a hand and opens his mouth to stop me as I go marching past, but I shoot him a look that halts him in his tracks.

I don't even pause long enough at the door to mutter a good-bye. Instead, I step out, throw his keys at him, then I slam the door, head down the stairs, and leave the flat forever.

The chirping of the car unlocking is far too cheerful. I get in and slam the door, like I'm punishing it for sounding so upbeat.

I have no idea where I'm going when I start the engine, or when I pull away from the flat, or when I reach the corner at the end of India Street.

A police car screams past on the main road, blue lights flashing. I watch it for a moment, until I'm sure it's not turning in at the next junction along.

Then, when it has continued down the hill, I hang a right, and drive, headed nowhere, into the city.

PART 4
MONDAY

FIFTY-FOUR

ELIZABETH

Weak, watery sunlight, and the blasting of a horn conspire to wake me.

I sit upright, hands instinctively grabbing for the wheel to right the car on the road.

But I'm not moving. I'm parked up, straddling the line between two spaces, in a car park. The blasting of the horn isn't an irate driver, but a boat passing in the Firth of Forth just ahead of me.

I'm at the docks. Leith. The car park of Ocean Terminal shopping centre.

And I have only the faintest memory of how I got here.

I remember driving around the city, headlights blinding me, cars behind tooting to warn me that my tail lights were out.

I remember phoning... everyone. The kidnapper. The play-group. The care homes I'd spoken to earlier that day.

I even called the school. There was nobody there, of course, but the answering machine invited me to leave a message to inform them if my child was going to be absent that day.

I sat in silence, considering my options, then ended the call.

I called the police, too, on their non-emergency number, but hung up before anyone could answer.

Was I here when I did that? I'm so exhausted I can barely think straight, let alone remember the finer details.

A sharp, stabbing pain in my jaw wakens me all the way. I fold down the sun visor and check my reflection in the mirror. The swelling from the DJ's right hook is worse now, the rainbow of blues and purples really coming into its own. There's a red welt running through it, too. A scratch, or a gouge.

I rub at it, like I can wipe it away, but the pain quickly becomes too much.

Did I do that? Did I lose my temper, lose control, and hurt myself?

I don't remember. The whole night is a haze.

I check my phone. It's just turned eight. I'm out of time.

The battery is down to the last seven per cent, the little icon in the corner warning me with its redness.

There's nothing I can do about it. The charger I took from the house doesn't plug into the car. My phone is going to die.

And, if I don't do something, so is Hollie.

Some part of me still thinks the phone could be the answer to all of this, or at least a clue. They could call me, but I couldn't call them. I thought something in that was important, but at some point during the night I realised that wasn't what my brain was trying to tell me. That wasn't the question I should be asking.

The question I should have been asking was how did they get my number?

Hollie didn't have her phone, so they couldn't get it from that. She doesn't know it off by heart, so she couldn't just tell them.

So, how did they get it?

It doesn't matter now. It's too late to dig into it. There's no more time for chasing leads or following hunches.

All that's left for me to do is battle through the Edinburgh rush hour traffic, from one end of the city to the other, and rock up to the school, ready to make my confession.

The kidnapper wants it to be public. Televised. I have no contacts in the media. There's nobody I can get in touch with to put me on TV.

But I have a school packed with teachers and children.

And, God help me, I have a plan.

FIFTY-FIVE

ELIZABETH

No one is going to get hurt. That's the main thing. They'll be scared, yes. There's no avoiding that. But I'm not going to hurt them. I just need to cause a big enough scene to get everyone's attention.

Nationwide attention.

Then, when I have the eyes of the media on me, I'll confess. I'll tell them whatever they want to hear about Kenny's death. I'll take the blame for it.

And then, when that's done, I'll step outside and face the consequences.

Maybe, if I explain why I did it, they'll go easy on me. I'm a desperate mother, after all, just trying to get her daughter back. I'm just following the orders of the kidnappers who have taken my child.

We'll see.

The morning bell has gone by the time I arrive at the school, and I'm able to get parked out front. It's a drop-off only zone, but to say that a parking infringement is the least of my worries would be something of an understatement.

Even with the adrenaline starting to surge again, I'm so tired that I almost forget to take my handbag with me when I set off for the school and have to double back to collect it.

Stupid. Stupid mistake.

The front gate is still unlocked. It's usually Donnie's job to secure it after the parents have finished dropping off their kids, but, well, I guess that won't be happening today.

I wonder where he ended up, and how Sasha was able to get him into the car and out again right under my nose.

Maybe, if she ever appears again, she'll tell me.

I won't hold my breath.

The front door is closed, but a press of the buzzer brings a response from Claire, the secretary.

'Good morning,' she trills. It's her usual upbeat tone, but there's something a little strained about it today.

'Uh, hi. It's Elizabeth. Hollie's mum. P6.'

I'm braced for an interrogation on whether Hollie is with me, but if Mr Wilkinson has told her about his ultimatum to me, she doesn't mention it. Instead, the buzzer chimes to announce that the door is unlocked, and I push on into the school.

The bag on my arm feels heavy, like it's weighing me down, trying to stop me going any further.

I press on.

Claire sits at her desk near the front door, partitioned away in a cube of glass and plasterboard. Her desk phone is ringing, and she picks it up to answer just as I arrive at her sliding window.

She raises an index finger to me to let me know she'll just be a minute, then takes the call in low, hushed tones. She doesn't say much, just nods a lot, and confirms she understands the caller with a few, *uh-huh*s and *sure*s.

Claire has been the school secretary since before Hollie started. She's in her mid-thirties, but with the bubbly enthusiasm of someone ten years younger. She considers herself the public face of the school, and is always dressed well, with make-up that's both subtle and immaculate.

If she wasn't so likeable, I'd hate her.

While she talks on the phone, I take the opportunity to refine the plan. I'll need to get her away from the button that unlocks the doors. I can't have the police rushing in until the TV cameras are here.

I doubt I'll be allowed to speak to the cameras, of course, but it doesn't matter. By that point, I'll be at the centre of a media whirlwind. I've already got an email queued up to send to all the major channels, with a full confession to Kenny's murder attached.

All I have to do is hit the button to send it. But first, I need to make sure they're going to take me seriously.

I can't believe it's come to this. But what other choice do I have? All that matters now is Hollie and keeping her safe.

'Sorry about that.' The window slides aside, and Claire flashes me a smile that looks frazzled around the edges. 'Mad morning. Got a few staff off. Janny hasn't turned up either, so we were scrabbling around trying to find keys.'

She runs a hand down her face, pats at her bob of brown hair, then rearranges her smile into something more convincing.

'Anyway. Sorry.' Her gaze darts past me, searching for Hollie. The empty space beside me throws her but she rallies quickly. 'How can I help?'

'I, uh, I need to talk to Mr Wilkinson,' I say.

'Ha! Join the queue,' she says. Her laugh isn't unkind, but the sharpness of it takes me aback.

'Is he busy this morning?' I ask. Maybe he'll be too distracted to think about Hollie.

Or maybe he's already busy with the police.

'I wouldn't know,' Claire says, and there's a hint of admonishment in there somewhere. 'He's not here.'

I adjust the grip on my bag. 'Not here?'

'He didn't show up. No message, no call. Nothing.'

He's not here. Mr Wilkinson isn't here. Does that change things?

The next word out of the secretary's mouth starts strong, but then falters into silence. I get the impression she wants to tell me something more but is holding back.

'Bloody hell,' I say, glancing along the corridor and lowering my voice. 'Scandal?'

'Well...' She mimics my body language and leans in closer. 'You didn't hear it from me, but Ann's not here either.'

'Ann?'

'Miss Goodall.'

Her neatly plucked eyebrows shoot up her forehead, and her lips purse together.

'God. Right. And, of course, they're...'

'They are,' she confirms. 'I don't know what to think. Have they eloped? Kathryn is convinced they've eloped. Mrs Ross, I mean.'

'Wow. That's... wow.'

I'm reeling from the news. Not about the possibility that the teachers may have run off together, but the fact that one of my deadlines no longer exists.

Does that help me? Do I now have time? A chance to find Hollie?

Is there still a chance I can salvage things?

'Uh, OK. Right. Well, I'll just...' I look around, not quite sure what I'm doing, or where I'm going. 'I'll go. I'll just... I'll go.'

Claire flashes me another of her rehearsed smiles, then reaches for the handle to slide her little window closed.

'Righty-o. And if Greig turns up, I'll tell him you were looking for him.'

'Thanks,' I say.

I make it three paces. The fact that it takes me that long to process what she's said is a testament to how exhausted I am.

'Wait,' I say, turning back to the desk. 'What did you say?'

'If he turns up. Mr Wilkinson. I'll let him know you were looking for him.'

I'm not aware of moving, but I'm back at the desk. Claire still has one hand on the handle of the window, holding it halfway closed.

'Greig. You said Greig.'

She nods. Her smile is still there, but it's been tainted by a frown of confusion. 'Yes. Mr Wilkinson. Greig. If he comes in I'll—'

'Where does he live?'

She misses a beat. Just one.

'I'm sorry?'

'Mr Wilkinson. Greig. Where does he live?'

'I'm sorry, I can't give out that sort of information.'

I slam my bag down on the counter, making her jump. I thrust my hand inside, fingers wrapping around the handle of the knife I've got stashed there.

I don't want to do this. I don't.

But I have to.

Unless...

Wait.

Maybe I don't.

Maybe I've had everything I needed this whole time.

'Thanks for your help,' I say.

And as I turn and run for the door, I hear Claire pull her window firmly closed behind me.

FIFTY-SIX

ELIZABETH

There's almost no charge left on my phone as I open the email app and find the one from Sasha. On Saturday morning, all I cared about was the video showing Hollie in the hall.

Now, though, I open up the first attachment, containing page after page of confidential information about the school and its staff.

Since he's the acting head teacher, I expect Mr Wilkinson to be the first name on the list. He isn't. I scroll through it quickly, thumb swiping, heart sinking lower and lower when I fail to spot his details.

It's only when I scroll back up, more slowly, that I find him.

Greig Milton Wilkinson. Born 17 December 1979.

I have his name, his date of birth, his National Insurance number, and his bank details for his salary.

But no address.

I remember one of the attachments was a bundle of résumés. My phone lets out a low-battery warning bleep as I open up the CVs and hurriedly swipe through.

Behind me, the driver of a van toots his horn, encouraging me to get the hell out of the way so he can get past. I ignore it.

There.

I scroll straight past his name, but quickly back up when my brain registers it.

I see his past work experience first. One role jumps out at me. A learning support officer in a care home in Dundee.

It's him.

It has to be.

His address is across town, which means there was no way he was randomly running past the flat yesterday morning.

He's a liar.

He's a rapist.

He's the man who has my daughter.

I scribble down the address just before my phone finally gives up the ghost, and then floor it away from the school, earning another drawn-out horn blast from the van that was trying to get past me.

It takes me fifteen minutes to get to the house on Old Kirk Road, just a stone's throw from Edinburgh Zoo. It's a fairly compact detached bungalow in a row of similar buildings, with a small garden and a dormer window in the triangular roof.

I pull the car up just in front of the house, jump out, and hurry along the path, my bag held tightly by the straps.

The door is ajar. A breeze inches it in and out, opening it slightly, then clunking it closed against the frame every few seconds. In, out. Thump, thump, thump, like the rhythm of a slow, steady heartbeat.

Bracing myself, I ease the door open, revealing a short hallway that's in complete disarray. An antique phone table has been tipped over, breaking one of its curved, spindly legs. The phone itself is shattered into pieces, like it's been thrown to the floor and stamped on. Repeatedly.

A mirror has been pulled from the wall and smashed. Jagged shards of its reflective surface lie scattered on the brown and white patterned carpet. They crunch beneath my feet, and when I look down, a fragmented version of myself stares back up at me.

From an open door at the end of the hallway, I can hear music. It's familiar, but it isn't until I step into the room and the chorus kicks in that I recognise it as the theme to *SpongeBob SquarePants*.

Quietly, breath held, I take the knife from my bag and creep into the room.

The SpongeBob cartoon is playing on the TV, but it's not the brightly coloured animation that draws my eye.

It's the blood on the screen.

And on the coffee table.

And on the white leather couch.

The coppery tang of it hits the back of my throat, triggering yet another wave of nausea that I'm forced to swallow back.

I turn away from the spray of crimson, and that's when I see it.

That's when I see the body.

Miss Goodall – Ann – sits with her back to the wall, slumped sideways, so her spine is curved at an impossible angle, and her head hangs down like an overripe fruit that might drop off her shoulders at any moment.

She has been stabbed. The knife sticking out of her chest is the big giveaway, but the wounds on her neck and arms could only have been inflicted by a blade.

She's wearing a big baggy T-shirt that almost comes down to her knees, a picture of Tinkerbell from the Disney movies emblazoned across the front.

At least, I think it's Tinkerbell. The rips and bloodstains in the fabric make it difficult to be certain.

What is certain, though, is that Miss Goodall is dead. Nobody could lose that amount of blood and not be.

And no living person has ever looked quite like that.

My legs feel like they're going to give way beneath me, but I lock my knees and force them into submission. I can't afford to break down. Not here. Not now.

The living room, like the hallway, has been trashed. Everything not covered in blood has been knocked over or broken. The cushions of the couch have been split open, and white wads of stuffing spew out of them and onto the floor.

The curtains are closed, but one end of the rod has been pulled out of its fixing, so it droops at a thirty-degree angle.

And the paperwork.

The whole room is carpeted in printouts and receipts and letters and bills, as if a tornado has ripped through a packed filing cabinet, scattering the contents in all directions.

The sight of all those letters makes me turn back to Miss Goodall's body, alerting me to a detail I missed.

She has a piece of paper in each hand. Her bloody fingers have smeared red across them both, but I can still make out most of the text.

The first is from Vodafone, thanking the recipient for their recent order of a pay-as-you-go SIM card. The number is printed at the top. If there was still charge in my phone, I'd be able to confirm it for sure, but I'm fairly certain it's the same number that sent me the photo of Hollie and called me the next day.

The other letter is harder to read. There's a lot more text, more densely packed, and Ann's blood obscures much of it.

I have to pluck it from her grip to read it properly. Her fingers keep hold of it, refusing to let it go, until I yank it free with a short, sharp tug.

It's from the council, confirming approval of a change of usage for a property in East Lothian from residential to holiday let.

The address has been circled in black pen. A message has been scrawled beneath it in my sister's sharp, angled handwriting.

Meet me here.

It's out in Tranent. Half an hour, if I take the bypass. Less, if I floor it.

I fold up the letter and tuck it into my bag.

I steal another look around the room, spot a phone-charging cable that should fit my car, and snatch it up.

And then, with an evil cartoon plankton cackling away on the TV behind me, I set off to meet my sister.

FIFTY-SEVEN

ELIZABETH

My mobile phone stays dead when I plug it in and doesn't spring into life until I'm hitting the bypass and hanging a left.

The road is busy, both lanes of traffic moving slowly around the junctions for the airport. I type the address into Google Maps, then prop the phone against the dashboard just as the vehicles in front start to move more freely.

There's a screeching of brakes from behind me when I swing out into the right-hand lane and power past the slower-moving cars on the left. The young driver of a hatchback behind me furiously flashes his lights, but I'm already pulling ahead, pulling away, closing the gap on the car in front.

I drive right up behind him, blasting my horn and flashing my lights, until he pulls over into the left-hand lane.

At that, I'm off again, foot to the floor, hands gripping the wheel until the rubber groans and my knuckles turn white.

Twenty minutes. Maybe less.

Twenty minutes until I can end this. Until I can have Hollie back in my arms.

The thought of her wrapped around me, holding me,

sobbing into my shoulder drives my foot even harder against the pedal.

Twenty minutes.

Maybe less.

Spots of rain dot the windscreen. In moments, it's rattling against the roof and slicking the glass, forcing me to ramp the wipers up to high speed. I don't slow down, though. I can't.

By the time I reach the address, just outside Tranent, a full-blown storm is raging overhead.

The farmhouse is laid out in an L-shape and seems to be made up of several separate buildings that have been joined together over time. It's a Frankenstein's monster of architectural styles, ranging from quaint eighteenth-century whitewashed cottage, to modern metal and glass.

A semi-circular driveway curves off the road, before rejoining it again forty feet further along. It reminds me of the layout of India Street, and roughly where Clive's flat would be is an archway with a set of double doors recessed into it.

There are no cars parked here. No sign of life in any of the windows.

I pull up near the entrance, jump out, and run for the door, the storm driving me on. All thoughts of stealth or caution are thrown to the wind at the thought that Hollie might be in there, hurt and scared. Desperate for her mum.

I'm in such a rush to get to her that it isn't until I'm throwing open the doors that it occurs to me I've left my bag and the knife in the car.

There's no going back now, though. No force on earth can stop me.

'Hollie? Hollie, are you here?' I cry. My voice sounds shrill and weak in the half-dark. It bounces shrilly off the bare floorboards, then is lost somewhere up near the high ceiling.

I press on through the entrance hall, pulling open doors and flicking on lights, calling Hollie's name, promising that I'm here, I've got her, she's safe now.

The inside of the building is a work in progress. Piles of wood and plasterboard panels are stacked in empty rooms. Some of the walls have been stripped back, revealing tangles of wiring and old lead plumbing, all bound together with cobwebs.

Floor coverings have been lifted, and furniture huddles together in corners like scared sheep, tarps draped over it to shield it from scratches and sawdust.

It's in one of the three living rooms that I spot the green couch. I bring up the photo the kidnapper sent me and compare them. They're the same. This is the couch in the picture.

But my daughter isn't on it.

'Hollie?'

The shout rolls around the room, before being absorbed by it. The windows rattle in their frames as the storm hammers at them, slicking them with rain and whistling in through the gaps in the ancient frames.

This is the place. Right address. Right couch.

So where is she?

I hear the whimper when I run into the next room. It's not her, though. Not my Hollie.

When I look in the direction of the sound, my gaze falls on Mr Wilkinson.

We're in what I guess either was or is going to be a small dining room. He's tied to a rickety old bar stool, his hands bound together at the wrists beneath the seat, while his ankles are secured halfway up the stool's legs.

Tied like that, his spine is curved and his shoulders are stooped, like he's being pulled down into himself. Folded up.

A bundle of fabric has been jammed in his mouth. A single strip of silver tape holds it in place, wrapped all the way around his head.

It's his eyes, though, that shock me most of all. One of them is bloodshot, a bruise blooming across the socket. That's not the thing I notice about them, though.

It's the fear.

His irises are two islands surrounded on all sides by pools of white. They're fixed on me as I enter, brimming with tears, darting from my hands to my face, and back again, over and over.

I take a step closer. He tries to draw back, but his bonds won't let him. All he can do is choke, and sob, and frantically shake his head at me. Pleading with me. Begging me not to come any closer.

Not to hurt him.

He seems to be secured. If he could have moved, he'd have done it before now. I approach slowly, carefully, hands raised in front of me like I'm soothing some savage beast.

Snot and tears have slicked the front of the tape. It overlaps at the back of his head, and his eyes bulge in their sockets, fixed on my face, as I reach around and peel the strip free.

The fabric is rammed so deep in his mouth that he can't force it out. I'm forced to reach in with finger and thumb and pull it free, which makes him cough and gag, his whole body convulsing as he retches.

'Where is she?' I ask. My voice is a whisper. I don't know why.

'P-please. Please, I'm s-sorry.' He's babbling, his lips trembling, his voice raw and hoarse. 'I'm sorry, I'm s-sorry.'

'Where's Hollie? What have you done with her?'

His eyes are still bulging, like they might pop right out of their sockets at any moment. They flit left, right, up, down, searching my face as it hovers just a foot or so from his.

I'm almost afraid to ask the next question, even though I know what the answer will be.

'Who did this to you?'

His breathing is fast, short, erratic, like he's hyperventilating and suffocating at the same time. His chest and shoulders shake as the air rasps in and out of him. He searches my face again.

'W-what?' he squeaks.

'This. Who did this to you?'

I'm still whispering. I still don't know why.

'I don't... I d-don't understand,' he whimpers, then his face crumples like a snot-filled tissue, and he chokes on a series of deep, desperate sobs.

I should hate him. I *do* hate him.

And yet, he's so very, very scared.

Despite everything, some part of me almost wants to help him. Whatever else he is, he's a human being. And he might be the only person who can tell me where Hollie is.

'It's OK, it's OK,' I assure him. But when I reach a hand out to him, he jerks back, screwing his eyes shut and flinching.

The sudden movement rocks the stool on its legs. His eyes open again, wider than ever. I hear his ejection of panic, and watch as he topples backwards, still tied to the stool.

There is a thud. A crack. I'm not sure if it's the stool, or the sound of his head hitting the bare wooden floorboards. Either way, his scream stops, like the impact has knocked it right out of him.

And silence fills the house.

I kneel beside him. Shake him. Slap at his face.

'Wake up. Wake up,' I whisper. 'Where is she? Tell me where she is!'

He's not responding. Not moving.

Not dead, but out cold.

He can't help me now. No one can. I'm on my own.

Leaving him on the floor, I get to my feet, and set off to find my daughter.

FIFTY-EIGHT

ELIZABETH

The next door leads me into the skeleton of a kitchen. The frames of the cabinets are in place, but the tops and fronts are stacked up against a wall. There's nowhere here for Hollie to hide, so I press on into a narrow hallway with woodchip wallpaper and a ceiling of dated-looking dark wood.

'Hollie?'

I'm whispering her name now, not shouting it. The sound barely carries to the end of the hall.

'Hollie, it's me. It's Mum.'

The next door reveals only an empty cupboard, with a modern gas boiler fixed to the wall, and a few tubs of paint lined up on the floor.

No Hollie.

The bare floorboards creak and groan as I creep along the hall, head lowered, fists clenched, ready for anything.

Almost anything.

I find her in the next room. She stares back at me from the other side of a cracked bathroom sink, smiling like she's been waiting for me.

Not Hollie.

Not my daughter.

Sasha.

'Hey, sis,' she says. 'Long time, no see.'

I freeze.

What is this?

How is this possible?

'What's the matter?' she asks, pulling her face into an exaggerated mock frown. 'You surprised to see me?'

'This isn't... I don't understand,' I say. There are so many questions in my head, spinning around, crashing into one another. I can only voice the vaguest one. 'How?'

Sasha's smile returns. It's a wide, twisted thing that shows too many teeth. Not like my smile. Not remotely.

'How what?' she asks. 'Come on, sis, spit it out.'

'How are you here?'

She shrugs. We step closer.

'Because, for all your talk about being the smart one, I figured it out first,' she tells me. 'I worked it out last night. While you were sleeping. I dealt with it, like I deal with everything.'

I shake my head. She copies.

'No. I mean... how are you *here*? Like this? How are we... how are we talking like this?'

'Ah! Gotcha.' She shrugs. 'Hollie.'

We move closer again. 'Hollie? What do you mean? Where is she?'

'She's safe,' Sasha tells me.

'Where?'

Her smile becomes wider. Crueller.

'We'll get to that,' she says. 'Right now, we've got bigger problems.'

'You mean all the people you killed?'

'No one who didn't deserve it,' she tells me. 'Your weirdo

neighbour did himself in, we don't even need to talk about that DJ, and poor Donnie, the janitor? Well, he was on you, wasn't he?'

'It was an accident,' I blurt.

She sticks out her bottom lip and makes a rubbing motion in front of her eyes, like she's a crying child.

She looks so like me.

She looks nothing like me.

'Poor Lizzie. Messed up again and had to call in her sister to sort it all out. It's Kenny all over again.'

'I didn't... I didn't tell you to do that. You did it. You did it by yourself.'

She raises her voice, but there's a sing-song quality to her reply, like she's a playground bully, taunting me. 'Because you went and told him. You told him the truth. About Hollie. Didn't you?'

'I thought... I thought I could—'

'Trust him?' She laughs. It comes from somewhere deep down and shakes our shoulders. 'How many times have I told you, Lizzie? You can only trust me. He was going to tell the police. You know that. Maybe not right away, but someday. One wrong word to him, one falling out, and we were done for. The truth would be out about what we did to Kenny. To his brakes. I couldn't have that. We couldn't. Could we?'

'I... I didn't want—'

'*Could we?*' She roars the words at me. Flecks of foamy spit dot the glass between us.

'N-no,' I admit. 'No.'

'Exactly. So, you messed up, I fixed it. Like this weekend. Like always.'

She glances past me to the open bathroom door.

'You know who he is?'

I nod. So does she.

'Hollie's father.'

'You let him find you. You let him find Hollie,' she says. 'You let him dig around in our past until he had something to use against you.'

'I didn't know. I didn't know he even existed.'

She snarls at me. Her breath fogs the glass. 'It was your *job* to know. It's the one thing you have to do. The one thing I trusted you to do. Keep Hollie safe. But you can't even do that, Lizzie.'

'I can!' I insist. 'I can!'

I watch, breathlessly, as the smile creeps back across her face. 'Then, where is she, Lizzie?'

We take another step closer. My hands grip the edge of the ancient basin.

'What have you done with her? Where's my daughter?'

'Like I said, she's safe,' Sasha assures me. We lean closer, until we're almost nose to nose. 'You'll never find her without me.'

'Then tell me!' I cry. 'Tell me where she is.'

She looks at me. Properly looks at me, like she's counting up all the similarities and the differences between us.

'No.'

My hands tighten their grip. My heart thrums inside my chest.

'What? What do you mean?'

'I can't trust you with her, Lizzie. You can't keep her safe. You've proved that.'

'I can!'

She shakes her head. There are tears on her cheeks, but they're not hers, they're mine.

Every part of her is me. Every part of me is her.

'No. You can't,' she tells me from the mirror. 'When you were running crying to those teachers on Friday night, they had Hollie in the boot of their car and you had no idea. You can't protect her, but I can. I can keep her safe. I can make sure she's *always* safe.'

'What?' The thought is like a slap to the face. A knife to the chest. 'No. No, you can't. I won't. You're not her mother.'

'I'm as much her mother as you are.'

'*You're not her mum!*'

I scream at her. She screams back.

'*Neither are you!*'

She looks shocked by her outburst. Or maybe that's me. This close up, it's hard to tell.

She recovers quickly, though. Much more quickly than me.

'So, here's the deal, Lizzie. It's my turn.'

There's a ringing in my ears. In my head.

'What?'

'You won't find her. I know where she is. You want her to be safe? You want her to be protected? Then, we swap.'

'Swap?'

'I take your place, you take mine,' she says. 'I come up there, and you take your turn down here. In the dark.'

We shake our head.

'N-no. No. I can't. I won't.'

'You have to. You don't have a choice. You want to save Hollie, don't you? This is how you do it, Lizzie. This is the *only way* you do it. You had your chance, but it's my turn now. It's my turn! It's—'

She stops. Cocks her head. Widens her eyes.

'Wait.'

I see the movement behind her. Hear him rushing up at my back.

His hand grabs me by the hair, shoves me. My head meets Sasha's, shattering the mirror, splintering us into a dozen different pieces that tumble, one by one, into the sink.

Blood cascades down my forehead, filling my eyes. The

hand on my hair pulls me backwards, spinning me across the bathroom and out into the hallway.

I stumble. Fall. Slam against the wall.

The last thing I see before the blood blinds me is Hollie's head teacher – Hollie's father – racing across the bathroom towards me.

With murder in his eyes.

FIFTY-NINE

ELIZABETH

I move. Kicking and scrabbling, I move.

The blood stings my eyes as I stumble along the hallway, feeling my way along the wall, searching for an exit, or a place to hide.

I can hear Greig Wilkinson lumbering along behind me, dragging his feet, whimpers of pain bursting like bubbles on his lips.

I don't know what Sasha did to him, but he's hurt. He's slow. I still have a chance.

The front door appears on my right. I try the handle. Locked. I catch a glimpse of Sasha in the window, but I'm staggering past, hurrying on, trying to get away from him.

And from her.

The end of the hall opens up onto another near-empty room, with holes in the walls and bare wood on the floor. A big glass frontage opens onto the courtyard.

My car is there. Right there. Right outside.

I look around for something to smash the window with, but there's nothing here, and he's coming, he's here, he's right behind me, hissing and muttering as he closes in.

Blinking and wiping away the blood, I press on, throwing myself clear just as his hands swipe at the air where I was. I feel the brush of his fingers, feel the grunt of his effort, and then I'm running again, leaving him behind, charging through a tarpaulin sheet that hangs over an open doorway and into...

A dead end.

It's a bedroom, I think, or it will be. The frame of a built-in wardrobe is in place, and two floor-to-ceiling mirrored doors stand propped against the wall beside it.

Sasha looks back at me from both of them as I stop. She doesn't speak. She doesn't have to. She's waiting. Watching.

And then, from the corner, there's a sound.

A whimper.

A creak of a floorboard.

And the world around me falls away.

I turn, and she's there. Sitting there, on the floor, back against the wall, arms wrapped around her knees. Not blindfolded now. Not tied.

Scared.

But alive.

I should stay quiet, I know. I should hide. But her name is on my lips before I can stop it.

'Hollie?'

It sounds like a question. Like I can't believe she's really here.

But she is. I've found her. I kneel down, and she's on her feet, running to me, choking on her tears, arms open wide.

'Mum? M-mum?' Her voice is a whisper. A croak. But it's her. She's alive, she's here, and she's safe.

The tarp over the door is torn aside, and the rest of the world returns with a *crash*.

Greig Wilkinson charges in, all blood and fury.

Hollie screams and shrinks back. I turn to face her kidnap

per, fists raised, but he drives a shoulder into my stomach, hissing and roaring, as he pulls us to the floor.

The impact, and the weight of him, drives the air out of my body. My lungs go tight, grow small. I try to breathe, but the air won't come.

There's red on his face, and on his shirt. He grabs me by the hair and pulls my head up towards him. I catch a glimpse of his other hand, rolls of bloodied bandages tied at the stumps where three fingers should be.

He screams as he slams my head back down, white foam frothing on his lips, his eyes wide, and wild like an animal's.

'Crazy *bitch*!' he slurs, as he bangs my head back down. Again. Again. 'Crazy fucking *bitch*!'

Hollie screams. The pain and the shock spin my thoughts into a scramble. I hear Sasha's voice but can't tell if it's out loud or inside my head.

He's going to kill you, Lizzie.

I try to turn, try to grab for him, try to pull his hand away, but he's too strong, too angry, and there's nothing I can do.

He's going to kill you, then he's going to take Hollie.

'N-no!' I wheeze.

He drives my head against the wood again. I taste blood. Feel the room becoming a whirlpool around me, dragging me down into the floor.

Into the dark.

What do you think he'll do, Lizzie? Will he be a good dad? You know what he did to Sally. He likes them young, doesn't he?

'Stop! P-please!'

He snarls something, but I can't hear it, can't hear anything but Hollie's desperate cries, and the whooshing of blood through my veins, in my ears. His hand – the good one – wraps around my throat. His weight pins me, pushing me down, choking whatever air is left out of me.

Out of the corner of my eye, I see my sister in one of the mirrors. She's looking back at me. Watching me.

Waiting on me giving the word.

'You *bitch*!'

Greig sobs out the words. Hot spit hits me in the face. My head feels too big, too full. I can't breathe. Can't move. Can't think.

And still, Sasha waits. She's not coming to help me. Not yet. Not until I give her what she wants.

My daughter. My life. Everything.

I can't. I can't do it.

I have to.

I think of this man, and the things he might do.

I think of my sister, and the things she has done.

To protect me. Protect us. All of us.

I see Hollie, standing there, frozen in terror. So small, so helpless. So afraid.

I think of her future. Of all the possible futures that stem from this moment. This choice.

I think of my daughter.

I'd do anything for her. Give anything for her.

I think of my daughter.

From there, the rest is easy.

SIXTY

HOLLIE

What do I do?

I don't know what to do!

He's hurting Mum. Mr Wilkinson is hurting her. He's going to kill her! He's going to kill my mum, and I don't know what to do!

I'm screaming so loudly, but nobody is coming. Nobody can hear me, but I scream, and I scream, and I scream, because I can't stop. I can't help it.

He's hurting her. He's going to kill her.

I don't know how I got here, in this room. I was somewhere else, tied up, blindfolded. And then, I was here, on my own, untied but too scared to move in case he heard me. In case he found me and did something terrible, like hurt me. Or even killed me!

I don't want to get near him. He's so angry. So mad. But I run at him, shouting at him to get off her, to leave her alone, to *stop hurting my mum!*

He takes his hand off her neck. I think he's letting her go, but then he pushes me. Hard. I fall backwards, tripping on my feet, and I hit the floor.

I don't know why, but Mr Wilkinson roars like he's an injured animal. I hear movement, and by the time I sit up, Mum is rising to her feet. Slowly, like Godzilla in the movies when he comes up out of the water. Big. Giant. Stretching all the way to the sky.

And Mr Wilkinson is on the floor, on his back, one hand pressed to his eye like he's got sand in it. Or maybe an eyelash.

'Hollie.' Mum is using her serious voice. More serious than I've ever heard it. She points to the doorway, covered by the plastic stuff that hangs down over it. 'Go and wait out there,' she tells me. She smiles. It's a big, warm, beamer of a smile that doesn't match her voice. 'I'll be out in a minute,' she says.

I look down at Mr Wilkinson, but only for a second, because I don't like the sight of blood, and I can see some on his cheek now.

I hurry through to the other room, through the plastic, shivering as the cold hits me.

I rock from side to side, from one foot to the other, trying to stop myself crying, but it's like there's a tap that someone turned on, and I can't shut it off.

I don't scream, though. Not even when I hear the crash from the room I just left, and the sound of broken glass hitting the floor.

Not even when I hear Mr Wilkinson shout, 'No, please, no!' or the wet tearing sound that comes next. That comes again, and again, and again.

And then, there's nothing.

No sound.

No movement.

No nothing.

'M-mum?' I'm not sure if I manage to say the word out loud, or if it's only in my head. Nobody answers. Nobody speaks back.

I take some deep breaths, the way Mum and Clive always

taught me to when I had a bad dream. That's what this feels like
– the worst nightmare ever – only it's real, and I'm awake, and
nobody is answering from the room next door.

Even the plastic stuff isn't moving. It just hangs there, flat,
like Darth Vader's cape.

I creep towards it. I know she told me to wait, but I need to
know. I need to look.

'Mum?'

The plastic is right in front of me. I still can't see anything. I
still can't hear.

I don't want to be here. I want to go home.

But my hand reaches for the plastic. I can't stop it shaking.

'M-mum?'

There's a sudden burst of movement. The plastic billows up
like it's grabbing for me. I scream and stumble backwards.

No, no, no, no!

And then, she's there. Right there. Looking down at me, all
tears, and smiles.

I run to her. She falls to her knees and holds her arms open,
and I run to her, jumping the last wee bit so she catches me. She
catches me, and she holds me, and she pulls me in close.

And I'm crying so much that I barely even recognise the
shape of Mr Wilkinson on the floor next door, before the plastic
falls back into place, hiding him from me.

I bury my face against her shoulder. Snuggle it right in
against her neck. She feels warm. I feel warm, too.

'Oh, Hollie. Oh, baby.'

She's crying. We both are. Her arms are tight around me.
Tighter, I think, than they've ever been.

'I've got you,' she tells me. 'I've got you. You're mine. And
I'm never going to let anyone take you away from me again.'

PART 5

ONE YEAR LATER

SIXTY-ONE

HOLLIE'S MUM

Mabel Walker does not look happy. The Wolfman has been up at the snack table half a dozen times already, and she's clearly getting sick of him. She won't complain, of course. She daren't. Not to me.

I give her a little wave and a smile, just to remind her that I'm watching. She returns it, but her heart isn't in it.

That just makes it all the sweeter.

It's been six months since her husband left her. Despite her many eye-watering indiscretions, Malcolm agreed to joint custody of Jessica, which means that for one week out of every two, Mabel moves back into her house, while Malcolm heads to a holiday home he bought out in East Lothian.

Then, on Sunday evening, she packs up her stuff and moves into whatever Premier Inn happens to be cheapest that week.

It must be hard for her.

I really, really hope so.

She's no longer seeing Clive, as far as I know. He tried to reach out to me after I left the flat, but I made my feelings very clear, and I haven't heard from him since.

A year. Has it really been that long?

One of the other mums smiles and rolls her eyes at me when 'Monster Mash' starts blasting from the speakers. I return the gesture, and we laugh.

She's nice. Most of them are, if you give them a chance.

Mrs Ferris, the new head teacher, is on the decks this year. She's been a blessing for the school, everyone says so. The kids love her. The teachers, too. After everything that happened, she really brought us all together.

It helps that her husband was able to step into the janitor's role. He's a former high school woodwork teacher, bored rigid by early retirement. Right now, he's wrapped from head to toe in toilet paper, and stomping around the hall as part of the costume parade, holding a broom in the air like it's a wizard's staff.

It's a bit of a mixed bag on the actual costume front, but there's no denying that he's getting into the spirit of it.

I lean against the wall and smile at him and the kids as they pass. Darth Vader is at the front of the line, the dim red glow of his plastic lightsaber leading the rest of them.

We tried to convince him to wear something different this year, but he was having none of it. Say what you like about Conrad, he's certainly a creature of habit.

I don't notice Daniella approaching until I feel her hand on my lower back, then brushing, just briefly, down the curve of my arse.

It took a while to convince her I wasn't a psychopath, and even longer to win her round.

Relationship wise, it's still early days. There's scope for it all to go wrong. But... I don't hate it. Even though so much of it is out of my control, I'm not terrified by that thought.

For the first time in a long time, I'm hopeful.

The parade continues past until the final participant sweeps into view, her curved horns stabbing towards the sky, her long black cloak trailing on the floor, sweeping up scattered Haribo and crisp bags.

No wonder the new janny looks so happy.

Daniella and I both give a big thumbs up to Maleficent as she passes. She spent hours practising her evil sneer in the mirror, but she can't stop herself grinning, or keep her hand from waving at us, as she continues on by.

My girl. My daughter.

Mine.

It's nice to see her smiling again. For a few months back there, I wasn't sure we'd ever get there.

But it all worked out. The police have questions, of course, mainly about why three members of school staff all disappeared without a trace over the space of one weekend.

But I'm not on their radar. I was careful. Everyone in the school already suspected they'd run away together, which also helped.

And besides, it's not like they'll ever find the bodies.

I'll have to keep my ears open and my eyes peeled, of course. There's no saying the police won't come round asking questions someday. But I'll be ready for them, just like I'll be ready for Sally Ferguson, if she ever puts two and two together.

Like I'll be ready for anyone who tries to get between my daughter and me.

All in all, everything has wrapped up pretty nicely. There's just one more thing needed to make it absolutely perfect...

'Ladies and gentlemen, boys and girls, the time has come,' Mrs Ferris says into the microphone, and I see excitement flashing in Hollie's eyes. 'It's time to line up for the judging of the best costume prize!'

* * *

'Aw, hard lines, Jessica. Better luck next time,' I say.

Jessica Walker scowls at me from behind her mask of make-up. 'There isn't a next time. We're in Primary 7,' she spits.

I smile. Something about it makes her shrink back.

'Yes,' I tell her. 'I know.'

I put a hand on Hollie's shoulder and turn my attention to Mabel. I almost ask her if there's something she wants to say to my daughter. I almost belittle her in front of her child.

But I don't. I'm bigger than she is. I'm better.

'Nice to see you, Mabel,' I tell her. 'Thanks for all your hard work tonight.'

And then, I turn Hollie away, before the look of hatred in Mabel's eyes can trigger a flare-up of the PTSD we've been working through for the past twelve months.

The trophy is cheap plastic. It's worthless. But Hollie carries it nestled in her arms like it's a newborn baby.

After six years of trying, she's earned it.

We both have.

We head back to her classroom and gather up her jacket and shoes. I ping Daniella a text, letting her know we're still on for our coffee date tomorrow morning. Then, I listen to Hollie's breathless blow-by-blow account of her victory as we head for the door.

She's talking so quickly, her excitement spitting the words out like a machine gun. She's happy. After everything, she's happy.

The door's closed when we get there. I put my hand on the metal panel to push it open, then pause when I see the reflection in the little square window.

My sister stares back at me from the darkness. Watching. My mirror image, waiting for her chance to rise up and seize control.

She'll be waiting a long time.

I nod at her, acknowledge her with a smile.

And then, my daughter's hand slips into mine, and we head on out into the brisk, bracing air of Halloween.

A LETTER FROM JD KIRK

Dear reader,

I want to say a huge thank you for choosing to read *My Daughter Is Missing*. If you did enjoy it, and want to keep up to date with all my latest releases, just sign up at the following link. Your email address will never be shared and you can unsubscribe at any time.

www.bookouture.com/jd-kirk

I hope you loved *My Daughter Is Missing* and if you did I would be very grateful if you could write a review. I'd love to hear what you think, and it makes such a difference helping new readers to discover one of my books for the first time.

I love hearing from my readers – you can get in touch through social media or my website.

Thanks,

JD Kirk

facebook.com/jdkirkbooks

x.com/JDKirkBooks

instagram.com/jdkirkbooks

PUBLISHING TEAM

Turning a manuscript into a book requires the efforts of many people. The publishing team at Bookouture would like to acknowledge everyone who contributed to this publication.

Audio
Alba Proko
Melissa Tran
Sinead O'Connor

Commercial
Lauren Morrissette
Hannah Richmond
Imogen Allport

Contracts
Peta Nightingale

Cover design
The Brewster Project

Data and analysis
Mark Alder
Mohamed Bussuri